By SARIA BRYANT

ELEMENTAL THRONES
Shadow's Wound

UNDERWORLD MAGES
Mage's Marines

TOUCH OF LEATHER
If You Let Me

Published by DREAMSPINNER PRESS
www.dreamspinnerpress.com

If You LET ME

SARIA BRYANT

Published by
DREAMSPINNER PRESS

8219 Woodville Hwy #1245
Woodville, FL 32362 USA
www.dreamspinnerpress.com

This is a work of fiction. Names, characters, places, and incidents either are the product of author imagination or are used fictitiously, and any resemblance to actual persons, living or dead, business establishments, events, or locales is entirely coincidental.

If You Let Me
© 2025 Saria Bryant

Cover Art
© 2025 Graphicsoulart
https://99designs.com/profiles/2146561
Cover content is for illustrative purposes only and any person depicted on the cover is a model.

Trade Paperback ISBN: 9781641088244
Digital ISBN: 9781641088237
Trade Paperback published July 2025
v. 1.0

To noobdestroyer.
Without your enthusiasm this book may never have made it this far.

CHAPTER ONE

SPRING BREAKS had never been more than a week of Jasper locking himself in his room and keeping quiet. How enjoyable the week was always inversely correlated to the number of times he saw his father, which meant spring breaks were usually shit.

This year was different. Now that he'd moved in with his cousin Amber, her fiancé Terrance, and their three housemates, he no longer had to sneak around his own home to avoid verbal or physical blows. This year Jasper intended to enjoy himself, especially while he had a small break from both college and his part-time job. Which was how he ended up standing inside a kink club on Saturday night.

He scrubbed his palms against his slacks—a bit too small since they were borrowed from Matt, one of his housemates—for the fifth time since getting out of the car. Touch of Leather was far classier than other clubs he'd been to, but then, none of them had catered to anything more than dancing and drinking. The bar was well stocked with every kind of nonalcoholic drink imaginable, and there was a sitting area with posh leather sofas and dark-wood, live-edge coffee tables. Black-and-white photos were interspersed along the walls, but he was too far away to make out anything more than the shapes of bodies.

Amber and the others—Terrance, Keith, Matt, and Reiko—had already vanished into the play area, and while he was curious what was in there, he wasn't ready to cross that threshold yet. Despite the fetish videos he'd watched and his growing curiosity about bondage, seeing all this up close and personal was something else entirely. Especially when Amber had invited him along only a few hours ago.

Instead he went to the bar and ordered a soda, wishing he was a few months older and could have downed some liquid courage before they left the house. Then again, Amber would probably kill him if he got drunk just to try something new with a stranger. He wasn't *that* stupid, thanks.

He took his drink to a comfy armchair and settled in to people-watch, ignoring the little voice in his head piping up with a *You're stalling.* Maybe he'd get lucky enough to catch someone's eye while lingering in the sitting area. He sipped his drink with a soft snort. *Yeah, right.*

People weren't wearing as much leather as he'd expected. Most were in casual clothes, but there were a few who dressed the part: leather pants, corsets, fishnet. He caught sight of a man wearing a collar with a leash attached. A shiny silver collar that glinted against his dark skin.

Jasper watched him as his partner led him into the dungeon, absently touching his own throat as he slumped further into his chair. No way was he going to get anyone's attention sitting in the corner like this, but the thought of going in there alone made him feel like puking. He wasn't entirely sure if that was the excitement or the nerves or both. With a sigh he pulled his phone out and found a game to keep himself occupied until his cousin was done.

At least he'd gotten out of the house for a bit. He could even call it experiencing something new… if he ignored the heat of self-loathing in his gut for getting all the way here and chickening out.

He'd only finished half his soda when someone sat in the chair next to him. From the corner of his eye, he caught the dark fabric of an expensive suit. Someone way out of his league. Probably waiting on someone. Probably *straight*. Such a travesty.

"Seeking pain or pleasure?" a quiet voice asked, and it took Jasper a moment to realize Mr. Suit was talking to *him*.

Jasper glanced up, choking on his soda and nearly shooting it out his nose. Dark hair, hazel eyes, and a face that belonged on a *Forbes* issue about the hottest entrepreneurs of the decade. "Uh, what?" he asked, pinching his stinging nose, his eyes watering. *Real smooth, dumbass.*

Mr. Suit raised an eyebrow, and Jasper kissed his chances of making a good impression goodbye. "Are you here to play?" he asked, glancing at the white band on Jasper's wrist. The band had a red line through the center that marked him as a guest, new to the scene, and "vanilla." Because Amber was a bitch.

Jasper sat up, nerves fluttering in his stomach. "Maybe? Are—" He cut himself off, taking in the rest of Mr. Suit's appearance: mussed but effortlessly styled hair, expensive watch, shoes so polished he could nearly see his reflection. Definitely out of his league. "Are you offering?"

"Depends." Mr. Suit tilted his head and offered his hand. "I'm Vincent."

"Jasper," he replied, shaking Vincent's hand. "And pleasure. Definitely pleasure."

Vincent smiled briefly and let go. "In that case, why don't we talk?" He stood and motioned to a set of doors near the bar.

"Sure," Jasper said, hating how he was suddenly breathless. No way was he this lucky. "Holy shit, he's hot," he whispered as he stood and followed Vincent into another lounge, this one empty aside from chairs and tables.

This was fine. Have a talk with the gorgeous guy who hopefully wanted to play with him.

He totally had this.

Chapter Two

Vincent motioned to a chair at one of the smaller tables, then sat across from Jasper. Once they were settled, he leaned back and crossed his legs. "What kind of pleasure are you seeking?"

Jasper wrapped both hands around his glass and bit his lip, shifting once in his seat and then stilling like he was trying hard not to fidget. "What do you mean?"

Well, that partly answered the question of how new to the scene Jasper was. The white band had caught his eye on his way out, and the way Jasper had been absorbed in his phone was not an image he liked to see in his club. He wasn't sure who'd brought Jasper in—few of the members even had guest access—but maybe he should rescind that completely if this was the result. He didn't mind members bringing in their friends, but abandoning them was a dick move.

"Some people enjoy being tickled," Vincent said. "Or having hot wax dripped over their bodies. Others are more interested in sexual release." He tilted his head when Jasper shifted in his chair again. "What is it that brought you to my club rather than a seedy strip joint?"

Jasper cleared his throat. "I-I kinda want to know what being tied up is like."

"Kinda? Is that a 'I like thinking about it but don't really want to experience it' kinda, or a 'please tie me up and torment me' kinda?" Vincent asked, holding back a chuckle when Jasper's breath caught.

"I've never done any of this before." Jasper glanced up, his blue eyes bright in the low light. "But I want to. I'd like to try. With you."

Vincent couldn't exactly say no in the face of that eagerness. Especially since he didn't like the idea of someone so inexperienced getting in over their head. He did everything he could to keep his club a safe space, though there were more than a few hard players among the members.

"All right." He clasped his hands in his lap, tapping his thumbs together. "Do you have a safeword?" he asked. When Jasper shook his head, he continued, "Are you familiar with the stoplight system?"

"Yes…. Sir."

Vincent smiled. "Good," he said, glad when Jasper smiled back and finally seemed to relax. "So tell me how you'd like tonight to go."

"Besides being tied up?"

"Once you're tied up. Do you want to be naked? Touched, kissed, fingered?"

Jasper licked his lips. "Y-yeah. All that."

"Anywhere you don't want to be touched? Anything you don't want done?"

"Tickled."

Vincent chuckled. "No tickling. How about aftercare?"

Jasper shrugged. "I don't think I really need it?"

"Is that a question?"

"No. I think I'm good without it." He glanced towards the door with a grimace. "Do we have to use the dungeon?"

Vincent followed Jasper's gaze as he considered. The rooms upstairs were for select members, but there were no rules about guests not being allowed, though maybe that had been an oversight. Not that he had any reason not to trust those he'd screened, but then, few as green as Jasper ever made it to his club. At least not alone. "No," he said. "If you'd prefer a private room, we can go upstairs."

"Yeah." Jasper drained the last of his soda. "That sounds good."

"This way, then."

Vincent stopped by the security room on the second floor. Ian was on duty as part of the night's security team, and he eyed Vincent in surprise when he poked his head in. Vincent had said he was going home an hour ago, and technically this was supposed to have been his day off to begin with. "I'll be in room two."

Ian saluted and didn't bother to hide his grin when he caught sight of Jasper. "Yessirrr," he drawled.

Vincent stifled a sigh and counted himself lucky when Ian didn't wink. He turned and continued down the hall.

Room two was one of their tamer rooms by far. There was a bed near the far corner, a sofa, a low table long and wide enough to tie someone down on, and a large wingback chair with a cushion in front of it. Next to the bed was a small chest with basic necessities and toys and a mini fridge stocked with water. A door in the adjacent corner led to a bathroom.

Vincent closed the door behind Jasper and shrugged out of his jacket. He draped it over the end of the bed, then turned to face him. "So. To reiterate, you'll be tied up. Naked. I can touch you, kiss you, and finger you. No tickling. And at the end, you'd prefer to get off, yes or no?"

"Yes. Definitely yes." Jasper let out an unsteady breath where he still lingered by the door. He took a step forward and stopped. "What is it you want in return?"

Vincent raised an eyebrow. "Tonight is about you. I'll show you a good time and hopefully bring your fantasy to life."

"That's it?"

"Were you expecting me to only do this if you gave me a blowjob?" he asked, frowning when Jasper shrugged. "That's not how this works, Jasper. I'll only do what you've given me permission to do, and if you decide you don't like it, you give me the word. No sex or sexual favors in return. Understood?"

When Jasper nodded, Vincent turned the chair and sat facing him. "Let's get started, then. When you're ready, strip."

CHAPTER THREE

JASPER FLEXED his fingers and stared as Vincent sat with an expectant expression. "Strip," he repeated.

Vincent really expected him to strip in front of a stranger? Just like that? Even if he'd agreed to it, he'd expected *something* to happen first. Like making out, maybe. Or at least being naked *together*. Not to be watched like he was a stripper, though that could be kinda hot too.

"You do know how to undress yourself, don't you?" Vincent asked, sounding amused.

Jasper glared, a brief flare of indignation stamping out his nerves. "Fucker," he grumbled, swallowing hard when Vincent raised an eyebrow. That might have been all he did, but somehow that conveyed a warning all on its own.

He cleared his throat and muttered under his breath as he accepted that he was really about to do this. Then he toed off his shoes and socks and stepped closer to the chair. He was hyperaware of Vincent's eyes on him as he toyed with the bottom button of his shirt.

"Changing your mind?"

Jasper took a breath and shook his head. "No."

"No, what?"

"No, Sir."

"Good boy," Vincent purred, and *damn* if that didn't do pleasant things to Jasper's stomach. "When you're ready, then."

Jasper resisted the urge to roll his eyes and shrugged his shirt off, then tossed it in Vincent's face and kicked his pants aside. His boxers followed his shirt, and he smirked as Vincent dropped them to the floor with narrowed eyes.

Now that he'd committed to this, he sure as hell was going to have fun. It was either that or let the nerves paralyze him.

He let out a slow breath as he was left standing there. Naked. While Vincent sat and studied him, like he was some kind of statue to be admired.

He refused to fidget. This was some kind of test, he knew. He'd been around his cousin and her housemates long enough to at least know that much. He may not understand all the finer subtleties of the whole kink thing, but hopefully he knew enough not to make a fool of himself.

Vincent finally let out a soft hum that sounded like approval and stood. He moved across the room to the chest and pulled out a long strip of black silk. "Hands behind your back."

Jasper clasped his hands behind him. He glanced over his shoulder as Vincent adjusted his arms until they were bent at the elbows, his hands clasping his forearms instead. The feel of the cloth winding around his arms set off a spike of panic in his chest, but he breathed through it. When Vincent finished, Jasper found he couldn't budge his arms an inch, and the panic intensified enough that he squeezed his eyes shut.

Shit. This was such a bad idea. He didn't even know this guy!

Vincent gripped Jasper's biceps and pulled until Vincent was pressed flush against Jasper's back. "If you say Red, I untie you, you get dressed, and you can go back downstairs," he murmured into Jasper's ear. "Understand?"

Jasper licked his lips and forced in a deep breath. And then another. He could do this. He could get free whenever he wanted, right? That was how this was supposed to work, at least according to Amber. "Yes," he whispered.

"Good. Then give me a color."

Jasper swallowed, surprised when Vincent didn't move at all until he said, "Green." He shivered as Vincent hummed again and finally moved his hands, sliding them down Jasper's arms and over his chest.

That felt nice. For some reason, he'd expected a rougher touch. To be manhandled and pushed around, and he couldn't stop the hitch in his breath when Vincent merely skimmed his palms over Jasper's skin.

"You said you didn't want pain," Vincent said. "Does that mean you don't like things rough either?"

"I don't mind rough," Jasper murmured, cracking his eyes open to watch Vincent's hands. "But I don't see how pain can be pleasurable."

Vincent chuckled. "I see." He moved a hand up to Jasper's nipple, circling a finger around it. "Maybe I'll show you sometime," he said, rubbing the nipple between his fingers and then squeezing it.

Jasper bit back a groan as his head dropped to Vincent's shoulder, sure he'd fall over if Vincent weren't standing there. Why was it so hard to keep his balance with his arms trapped behind him? "You assume there'll be a next time." He tried to sound taunting, but the words came out breathless.

"Not enjoying this?"

Jasper valiantly tried to think of a smartass response, but then Vincent found both his nipples and tugged, and coherent thought abandoned him. He whimpered, his knees threatening to give out on him too. The low, rich sound of Vincent's laugh in his ear didn't help in the least. "Fucker," he moaned.

Vincent *tsk*ed and pulled his hands away. He tangled his fingers in Jasper's hair instead and gave a sharp tug. "You have a strange way of showing your appreciation. Don't tell me you don't know at least basic etiquette."

Jasper shivered, surprised at the intensity of the arousal that shot through him and pooled in his gut from the tug. "Yes," he said, moaning at the pointed jerk Vincent gave his hair. "Yes, Sir."

"Good boy," Vincent said, releasing him. He dragged blunt nails down Jasper's back and stepped around him, glancing down with a smirk. "You sure seem to be enjoying yourself."

"Fuck you, Sir," Jasper replied lightly, because he could.

Vincent snorted, then grasped Jasper's chin and tipped his head back. "I should have known you'd need a gag," he said, pressing two fingers past Jasper's lips. "For now this will do."

Jasper's eyes widened, and he let out a muffled curse around Vincent's fingers. What the hell? He tried to pull away, but Vincent held his chin in a firm grip, moving his fingers in and out in quick thrusts. When he finally pulled them away, they were slick with saliva. Jasper hardly had time to tell Vincent off for putting his *fingers* in Jasper's *mouth* before those same fingers were rubbing against his entrance.

"Oh fuck," he gasped. He arched into Vincent with a strangled whimper as a single finger pressed into him.

"I would have enjoyed playing with you more, but you obviously have no desire for foreplay," Vincent said, as if he were commenting on the weather. "I might have even sucked you off, but if all you want is a quickie, I'll give you what you want."

Jasper moaned when Vincent nudged his finger deeper, his hips jerking forward at the thought of Vincent's mouth on him. No way would

Vincent really do that. Would he? "No. Wait," he said, trying to get away from the finger and only managing to rub against Vincent. "Please."

Vincent stilled with a soft hum. "Please what?"

Jasper squirmed as embarrassment crawled through his veins, dropping his forehead to Vincent's shoulder. Bastard. Of course he was the perfect few inches taller. "Please…. Foreplay."

Vincent hummed again as if considering it, then pulled his hand away. "I don't think you've earned it."

Jasper swallowed, a strange warmth spreading through him. He wanted Vincent to tell him he'd earned it. He wanted—he very much wanted—to earn it.

He turned his head, carefully nuzzling against Vincent's neck. "How can I?" he asked, momentarily distracted by how good Vincent smelled. Sandalwood and citrus. "Sir."

Vincent slid his fingers into Jasper's hair again and pulled. Not hard, disappointingly, but tight enough that Jasper swallowed a groan. Vincent studied him with his intense hazel eyes for a moment before loosening his grip. "Ask nicely for what you want."

Heat crept into Jasper's face as he imagined all the things he could ask for. He never thought he'd ever be in this kind of situation in real life. Standing in a private room in a fetish club. With an actual Dom. If there was anyone on the planet he could actually ask to indulge any of his fantasies—

But he was already tied up. Kinda. He wasn't sure he could handle adding blindfolds or gags tonight.

His attention flicked to Vincent's lips, and he tipped his head back. "Will you kiss me?"

"With pleasure." Vincent's fingers caught Jasper's chin, holding him steady as he closed the distance between them.

And *fuck*, Vincent could kiss. He kissed Jasper with intention. Like kissing was his sole purpose of existence. Maybe it was all part of being a Dom, but Jasper could get used to it *far* too easily. No one had ever kissed him like it was a luxury rather than a means to an end. By the time Vincent's lips ghosted across Jasper's jaw and moved to his neck, his apprehension at being bound and helpless faded. Forming in its place was something else he was all too familiar with.

Infatuation.

He stared at the ceiling and fought the sudden urge to laugh. Fuck, what was *wrong* with him? He'd sworn off anything close to relationships after the last one ended in a dumpster fire. Like hell he was going to even *think* about getting involved with Vincent. As if it were even possible. This was a one-time deal. A bit of fun before the next semester started.

"Planning on kissing me all night?" he asked, his voice hitching as Vincent's teeth grazed his neck. "Thought you were going to make my fantasy come to life?" Taunting the guy who had him tied up was probably a worse idea than letting a stranger tie him up in the first place, but at least it helped him keep his feet under him, instead of throwing himself at said stranger like a dumbass.

Vincent chuckled and lifted his head from Jasper's neck. "Your mouth ever get you into trouble?"

Jasper grinned, his smartass response cut off by Vincent claiming his lips again. At least Vincent seemed to have a good sense of humor. And *gods*, he was such a good kisser. To the point that Jasper chased after Vincent when he pulled away.

"In the chair," Vincent said, his voice a bit rougher.

Goose bumps broke out on Jasper's arms; Vincent sounded as wrecked as Jasper felt. He barely even considered protesting as he took a seat.

Vincent stood in front of him and let out a slow breath. "Good boy."

Jasper shivered at the warmth that traveled through him from the praise. He tipped his head up as Vincent touched his cheek and leaned into Vincent's palm, still surprised by the gentle touches.

Vincent guided Jasper back against the chair with his fingertips against Jasper's chest, then traced his thumb along Jasper's lower lip. "Relax," he said. He hooked a hand under Jasper's knee and lifted it up and over the arm of the chair before leaning down.

Jasper shifted against the awkward position, his eyes widening as Vincent secured something around his leg, above his knee. He let out a strangled sound as he tried to pull his knees back together, only to have his leg kept in place by the restraint.

"Shh," Vincent soothed, running his fingers through Jasper's hair. "I thought you wanted foreplay?" He pinched Jasper's nipple, then secured his other leg to the opposite arm.

Jasper whimpered as Vincent stepped back, his skin tingling as Vincent's intense gaze took in every inch of him. He was utterly exposed and helpless and… fuck. He liked it. Something not quite panic and more intense than excitement coursed through him, settling in his gut. Whatever it was, he relaxed into it as easily as a warm bath.

It was liberating. This…. This was what he'd been wanting without really knowing how to get it.

Vincent ran his fingers through Jasper's hair again with an approving murmur. "That's it. Now the real fun can start."

Jasper shivered and had a momentary thought that maybe he should be worried but decided to hell with it.

He had a safeword for a reason.

Chapter Four

Vincent returned to the chest for lube and a condom, eyeing the numerous clamps and gags. The clamps were tempting, but he decided not to risk overwhelming Jasper his first time in a scene.

He closed the chest, grabbed a latex-free glove from the wall dispenser, and deposited everything on the table. Then he stepped behind Jasper's chair and tipped it back, biting back a laugh as Jasper gave an undignified yelp. He gripped both sides of the chair and dragged it towards the table and sofa, turning it to set it on all fours again.

He sat on the edge of the table, raising an eyebrow at Jasper's glare. "Problem, brat?"

Jasper raised an eyebrow in return, then rolled his eyes and shifted against his restraints. "No," he replied. "Sir."

"Good." Vincent pulled the glove on and popped the lube open to coat his fingers, aware of Jasper's eager stare. He tilted his head, waiting to see if Jasper had anything more to say. When he remained silent, Vincent leaned forward. He braced his ungloved hand on the chair and sealed his lips around Jasper's nipple without preamble.

Jasper arched with a groan. It turned into a hissed curse when Vincent bit into the sensitive flesh, and he regretted not grabbing the clamps.

Vincent tugged at the nipple with his teeth, rubbing his fingers against Jasper's entrance at the same time.

The sound Jasper made was somewhere between a whimper and a sob, and he alternated between fighting against his restraints and slumping in defeat. Vincent moved his lips to the other nipple, circling it with his tongue until it hardened. When he sucked it into his mouth, he pressed a finger into Jasper, enjoying the drawn-out groan as it rumbled through his chest. He sank his teeth into Jasper's nipple again, hard enough to make Jasper's entire body jerk, and then he let go and sat back.

Vincent moved his hand from the chair to Jasper's thigh, taking in the delectable sight of him—flushed, exposed, and panting. "How's it feel?" he asked, pushing his finger in until his knuckles settled against Jasper's ass.

Jasper struggled against the restraints again briefly before slumping and turning his face away. As if he still had some misconception that he could hide. "Get on with it," he muttered, his ears pink.

Vincent *tsk*ed and curled his finger a bit. "That wasn't an answer."

Jasper whined and managed a weak glare, though it failed to cover his pout. "Would feel better if you got on with it."

"I know it would." Vincent pulled his finger out and absently fondled Jasper's balls instead. "But I can do this all night without breaking a sweat. Keep being a brat and I will."

Jasper grumbled something that sounded like "Fucker" as he stared at Vincent's chest. He licked his lips and let out a slow breath. "Feels good."

Vincent hummed in approval. He added more lube and a second finger when he pressed in again. "How long's it been since you were taken care of?" he asked. Surely Jasper had a boyfriend or girlfriend somewhere. He'd been almost infuriatingly responsive so far—in the way that made Vincent want to seek out every single one of Jasper's buttons and push them until he begged for mercy.

"None of your business," Jasper said through clenched teeth. "Sir."

"Fair enough," Vincent replied, flexing his fingers.

Jasper turned his head with a soft choked-off whimper, trying and failing to press his face against the chair.

Vincent contented himself with working his fingers into Jasper. Stretching him. Avoiding his prostate and the pleasure it would bring. With his other hand, he explored Jasper's body, sliding over a straining thigh and the taut muscles of his stomach.

He brushed his palm over the swollen leaking head of Jasper's arousal, his touch light enough to draw a shuddering gasp out of Jasper, then moved his hand away. Up Jasper's chest to rest against his throat and feel the quick pulse beneath.

"Are you enjoying this?" he asked, tracing his thumb over Jasper's lip.

"You call this foreplay?" Jasper asked, his voice coming out remarkably steady, considering. "Sir?"

Vincent snorted softly at the pointed delays in the "Sirs." Jasper's future Dom was going to have their hands full breaking him in. "You're tied up, naked, and completely at my mercy. What would you call it?" he asked. "Pet?"

He noticed Jasper's expression shift, but didn't give the brat time to figure out if he liked the pet name or not. He pressed his fingers deeper, finding the spot he'd been avoiding.

The response was instant and glorious: Jasper's eyes widened as his body arched as much as the restraints allowed, his mouth open on a gasp that didn't quite escape his throat. Ignoring the way his pants felt tighter, Vincent drew his fingers out, let Jasper take a single shuddering breath, then pushed them back in to hit the same spot.

This time Jasper choked on a groan, shifting his hips to try and drive Vincent's fingers in deeper. His eyes squeezed shut as Vincent continued moving his fingers. Drawing out slowly, then shoving back in with a quick thrust, ensuring he pressed nice and hard, and repeating.

Over. And over. And over.

Vincent didn't stop until Jasper let out a choked sob, tears of frustration in the corners of his eyes.

"Please," Jasper gasped.

Vincent let his fingers go still inside Jasper. "Please what, pet?" he asked, cupping Jasper's cheek with his other hand. He pressed his thumb against Jasper's lower lip, swollen from where Jasper had bitten down on it.

"Please let me."

"Let you what?" Vincent asked. "I'm not stopping you from doing anything." He raked his eyes over Jasper, thoroughly enjoying the sight: a warm, healthy flush in his limbs, neglected erection hard and steadily leaking, precum smeared against his stomach.

Jasper whimpered again, breaths hot and quick against Vincent's thumb. "You can fuck me. Please, just—"

Vincent pressed his thumb against Jasper's lips to stop him. "I didn't ask to fuck you, so that's off the table," he said firmly. Christ, this brat was worse than any overeager sub he'd ever met. He refused to think how much trouble Jasper could end up in by playing with the wrong people.

He pulled both his hands away from Jasper and sat back, ignoring the frustrated whimper. "Now that you're sufficiently aroused," he said dryly, chuckling at the lovely flush that spread across Jasper's nose, "why don't you tell me what you want? And I suggest you be specific."

Jasper remained silent for a moment, finally licking his lips and glancing up at Vincent. "You said you would suck me off."

Vincent raised an eyebrow, keeping his expression neutral. "Did I?"

Jasper pressed his lips together in a frown. "You said you might."

"I did say that," Vincent agreed, enjoying the way Jasper squirmed when the silence stretched between them.

"Will you?"

"Will I what?"

"You know what," Jasper snapped.

"Do I?" Vincent couldn't help but rile Jasper up, especially since he was such a brat. He was quite a sight when flustered and aroused. And completely helpless to do anything about it.

Jasper glared at him, his throat working and muscles shifting as he strained against the straps holding his legs apart.

Vincent chuckled. "Is that what you want? For me to untie you? Let you go back to your friends like… that?" he asked, motioning between Jasper's legs. "Flushed and hard and in desperate need of release?"

Jasper stilled and turned his head away. "No," he whispered.

"Then you want to sit here while I admire every inch of you?" Vincent asked. "Not that I mind. I'm a voyeur, and you're quite the sight. All hot and bothered. Hole twitching, in need of something to grab on to."

Jasper made a strangled sound and turned scarlet, though his dick certainly enjoyed the visual.

Vincent hummed and lowered his voice. "You like hearing how good you look? I'd frame a picture of you right now and hang it near the entrance. Let everyone see the amazing little pet I found."

"You wouldn't," Jasper said, breathless.

"I would. If you'd let me," Vincent replied. "You don't know half the things I would do to you given the chance," he purred.

Jasper licked his lips and tilted his head enough to eye Vincent from the beneath his lashes. "Like sucking me off?"

"Is that what you want?"

Jasper nodded.

Vincent raised an eyebrow as he waited a moment. When Jasper didn't take the hint, he *tsk*ed softly. "Then say it. I want to hear you say exactly what you want."

Jasper swallowed, closing his eyes as he took a breath. "I want you to suck me off. Sir."

Vincent nodded in approval and leaned forward. He grasped Jasper's chin, holding him in place and pressing their lips together. He took his time deepening the kiss, exploring Jasper's mouth for a few leisurely moments before pulling back.

"And is that all you want, pet?" he asked, trailing a line of wet kisses down Jasper's throat. He took pity on him when all Jasper could do was make a strangled sound in reply. "What am I supposed to do with my hands?"

Jasper shivered, arching into Vincent's lips. "In me," he murmured. "I-I want your fingers inside me, Sir. Please."

Vincent smiled against Jasper's throat and pulled back. There was the sub he'd been catching glimpses of. Apparently it merely needed the proper coaxing. "All right, then." He picked up the condom, opened it, and worked it onto Jasper with his ungloved hand. That done, he glanced up long enough to find Jasper watching him with wide eyes, then bent forward. With a soft hum, he dragged his tongue up the underside of Jasper's erection.

"Oh fuck," Jasper breathed, valiantly trying to buck his hips forward.

Vincent chuckled, sliding his hand up Jasper's chest to rest it loosely around Jasper's throat. His pulse was rabbit-quick beneath Vincent's fingertips. When he was about to properly take Jasper into his mouth, a phone went off. It wasn't his own cell, and it wasn't the security line. He straightened and glanced towards Jasper's pants. "Do you need to get that?"

Jasper blinked, squinting at Vincent in confusion. Then his eyes widened. "Fuck. Yeah, probably."

Vincent got up and retrieved Jasper's pants. He dug the phone out and hit the Answer button before it could go to voicemail. He stepped in front of Jasper, holding the phone to his ear.

"Heeeeyyyyy," Jasper said, clearing his throat as he tried and failed to move his legs. "I'm upstairs," he said, rolling his eyes as the faint sound of laughter echoed from the phone. He glanced up at Vincent, then quickly looked away again. "His name's Vincent," he murmured. "Uh, yeah." A frown formed between his eyebrows as he pulled his ear away. "She wants to talk to you."

Vincent raised an eyebrow, bringing the phone to his own ear. "This is Vincent."

"Vincent. It's Amber."

Well, that answered the question of who'd brought Jasper to the club. "Been a while." Only a few months since they'd last seen each other, but over a year since they'd had an actual conversation.

"No shit," she replied dryly, and Vincent turned a bit to keep Jasper from seeing his wry smile. "So here's the deal. You have my cousin in whatever contraption you have up there. Today is Keith's birthday, and we've finished here. How long are you going to be?"

"That depends on the brat," Vincent said, turning back to Jasper in time to see his huff of indignation. He pressed the phone against his shoulder. "Your friends are finished. Should they wait, or should I arrange a ride for when we're done?"

Jasper eyed the phone and seemed to be weighing the pros and cons of ditching his cousin and friends, though to be fair, they seemed to have ditched him first. "You don't mind?"

"No." Even if he didn't know Amber, Vincent had a standing rule that anyone in the club had a way to get home safe. "Your night, your choice."

"Then I still want what I said I wanted."

Vincent snorted softly, giving Jasper a pass on being vague since his cousin was in hearing range. He lifted the phone back to his ear. "I'll see that he gets home."

There was a beat of silence, and then Amber sighed. "Fine. Be nice."

"No promises," he replied, ending the call and tossing the phone onto the couch. "Where were we?" he asked. He turned back to Jasper, pleased he'd chosen to stay. It wouldn't do to have his first taste cut short.

Jasper flicked his tongue against his lips. "You were going to suck me off, Sir."

Vincent hummed to hide his laugh; at least the brat recovered quickly. He retrieved the small cushion from the middle of the room. He dropped it beside the table, turned Jasper's chair to face it, then picked up the lube and coated his gloved fingers again. "Was I?" he asked, sinking to his knees on the pillow. It'd certainly been a while since he'd found himself in this position, and he ignored the mild ache in his knee, focusing on Jasper instead.

"Uh-huh." Jasper let out a shuddering breath as Vincent ran a palm over the inside of his thigh. "Definitely."

"You want my mouth on you?" Vincent asked against Jasper's neck. He breathed in the scent of soap and the hint of mango on his skin as he kissed his way down Jasper's neck, chest, and stomach until he could pick up where he'd left off. He pressed his fingers into Jasper, gripping the arm of the chair with his other hand before finally taking Jasper into his mouth.

How he loved the taste of rubber in the evening.

"Oh *fuck*, yes." Jasper groaned each time Vincent's fingers pushed into him with enough force to nudge the chair.

He heard the skips in Jasper's breaths every time the chair rocked back and would have smirked if his mouth weren't otherwise occupied. He made sure to keep a steady pace with his hand as he worked Jasper's cock deeper into his mouth.

Jasper gasped, limbs pulling against the restraints as he tried to push deeper into Vincent's mouth, his body tightening around Vincent's fingers. "Yes," he breathed. "Fuck, yes, please. Please!"

Vincent hummed around Jasper again and curled his fingers, enjoying Jasper's shout. Not quite a scream, but close. He pressed his thumb against Jasper's balls, shifting his hand to rub against them as he added a third inside.

"F-fuck!"

Vincent sucked harder, taking Jasper into his throat and swallowing around him. He found and rubbed against Jasper's prostate. And then he held there, nudging his fingers in, in, in, enough to bump the chair back each time, and growled around the twitching dick in his mouth.

Jasper screamed, bucking in the chair as he came. He shuddered, his yell turning into a loud moan until his voice choked off with a strangled gasp.

Vincent pulled away and replaced his mouth with his hand, another soft growl echoing in his chest as he coaxed every last drop out of Jasper. Once Jasper was spent, Vincent slid his fingers free, tossed the condom and glove to the floor, and unfastened the restraints.

Jasper was a panting, shivering, borderline incoherent mess as Vincent freed his arms. Once completely free, he sagged forward, clutching at Vincent's shirt.

"Breathe," Vincent murmured, running his fingers through Jasper's hair. He helped Jasper to his feet and guided him over to the bed, then allowed Jasper to tug him down beside him.

So much for not needing aftercare. He hesitated, torn between watching over Jasper and holding to what they'd agreed to.

But Jasper curled into Vincent before he could pull away, latching on like an octopus and nuzzling at his throat. One hand wandered across Vincent's chest, inching its way down to his pants.

Vincent caught Jasper's wrist and pressed it into the pillow. He ignored the soft pleading whine and silenced Jasper with a quick kiss. "That's not necessary," he murmured.

Jasper sighed, going limp and pliant beneath Vincent.

And that was infuriating on a completely different level. Vincent suspected he could pin Jasper on his stomach and fuck him raw, and Jasper wouldn't even protest. Vincent ran his fingers through Jasper's damp hair and pressed his lips against Jasper's neck, lingering against his pulse point. When he pulled back, Jasper was watching him with a satisfied smile.

"Hey," Vincent said.

Jasper blinked, his smile faltering and turning almost shy. "Hey," he said, his voice hoarse.

Vincent squeezed Jasper's wrist before pulling back, sliding off the bed, and retrieving two bottles of water from the fridge. He opened one and passed it to Jasper, then sat next to him again. "How do you feel?" he asked, opening his own water.

"Good." Jasper flipped the bottle lid in his fingers, watching it with a brief grin. "Great. That was fun," he said, glancing up at Vincent.

"Good. Drink your water."

Jasper rolled his eyes, but he lifted the bottle and sipped. "So that's it?"

"That's it. When you're ready, I'll call someone to take you wherever you need to go." Vincent looked Jasper over for any signs of distress, but they hadn't done anything too intense. "Take your time," he added. He didn't want Jasper to think Vincent was kicking him out. He shifted back to sit against the headboard, suspecting from Jasper's initial clinginess that he was a tactile person and needed aftercare more than he thought he did.

It only took a few moments for Jasper to lean into Vincent's side. He pulled his legs up as he continued drinking. "Sooo if, theoretically, I didn't want to go yet…."

Vincent chuckled. "You want to be tied up again?"

Jasper groaned and buried his face in Vincent's shoulder. "I mean, I wouldn't complain if it happened."

Christ, this kid. Amber's cousin or not, Jasper was practically *begging* to be taken advantage of.

"My night, my choice. Right, Sir?"

A soft chuckle escaped before he could help himself. "Utterly shameless," Vincent muttered. Jasper might have been new to kink, but at least he seemed to know what he wanted. And wasn't too afraid to ask for things. "I assume that means you have all night?" he asked dryly. He set his water aside and got up, opened the chest, and pulled out a pair of leather cuffs.

Jasper's water bottle crinkled loudly as he squeezed it, spewing water all over the bed and himself, his eyes fixed on the cuffs. "Yeah," he breathed. "Yup. All night."

Vincent took Jasper's bottle and set it aside. "All right." Who needed sleep when they had an eager new sub to play with? "Lie back."

Chapter Five

Thanks to Vincent's patience and expertise, Jasper managed to get off a total of three times, then immediately passed out. There was a vague sense of a warm body next to his as he slept, but when he woke up sprawled across most of the bed, he was alone.

He sat up with a groan, foggy and sore in all the right places, and grimaced at the lingering stickiness. But it was worth it. Even the mild ache on his left asscheek where he vividly recalled Vincent biting him.

He hadn't realized how badly he'd needed that until he was an incoherent mess and more relaxed than he'd been in months. There was a bottle of water on Vincent's vacated pillow, and he drained most of it as he glanced around the room.

A door he hadn't noticed before was ajar with a light on, and he dragged himself out of the bed to investigate. Of course it was a modern luxury-style bathroom, because this club was high-end as shit. He shouldn't have been surprised Amber could afford the membership here, considering he was living in her six-bed, four-bath house. Even with all that space, living with five other people felt crowded most of the time.

He found a cloth and cleaned himself up, splashed water on his face, and then grinned at his reflection. He'd been tied up all night by the hottest guy in this place. He'd been *picked* by the hottest guy in this place. And Vincent actually made him feel wanted.

His ex could shove a ghost pepper up his ass.

He turned to hunt down his clothes and found them in a messily folded pile on the chair he'd been restrained in. His phone was sitting on top with a few texts from Amber, which he ignored in favor of dressing. He was pulling his shoes on when the door opened and Vincent returned, pushing a cart.

Of course this place had room service. There was probably even a basement with a kinky gym and swimming pool. "Do you treat all your one-night stands this well?"

Vincent gave him an amused smile and closed the door. "Only the ones who scream loud enough to wake the dead."

Jasper bit his tongue as his face heated. He hadn't been *that* loud.

"Oh?" Vincent raised an eyebrow as he stopped the cart near the sofa. "I was expecting an eloquent 'fuck off' or 'ass' response."

"Goest and fucketh thyself, good Sir," Jasper replied brightly, grinning when Vincent chuckled.

Vincent pulled covers off the dishes, revealing waffles, blueberries, maple syrup, and whipped cream. Along with a pot of coffee with cream and sugar beside it.

Jasper accepted a plate and covered a waffle in a bit of everything. He watched Vincent settle into the chair, like Jasper hadn't been sitting there, bound and completely naked, a few hours ago. He focused on his breakfast and ignored the weird flip his stomach did at the memory.

The waffles were light and the perfect amount of crunchy, the fruit was sweet and juicy, and the whipped cream tasted fresh. The coffee wasn't bitter in the least, and he went through two cups as he ate.

Vincent watched Jasper over his own waffle covered in blueberries and whipped cream. "Did you enjoy yourself?"

"Yeah," Jasper replied around his last large bite. He licked syrup off his lips and added, "Yes, Sir." He didn't miss the faint smile that earned, or the brief tingles he felt because of it. "If, hypothetically, I wanted to come back, will you be here next week?"

"I'm told I'm a workaholic, so yes." Vincent set his plate aside when he'd finished eating. "You can ask for me at the bar if you'd like. For now there's a car downstairs to take you wherever you need to go."

There was a dismissal if he'd ever heard one. He was disappointed he didn't get Vincent's number, but that was probably for the best. He finished his coffee and snagged a few more blueberries as he stood. "So long, and thanks for all the orgasms," he said, heading for the door.

"Jasper."

He stopped with one foot out of the room and glanced over his shoulder.

"If you do choose to come back, I'd like to show you how sensual a spanking can be."

Jasper made a strangled sound, nearly choking on his blueberries, and bolted. Thankfully, the club was pretty much empty, and he made it outside without anyone seeing him.

The waiting car was sleek, black, and expensive enough to have leather seats, and he was absolutely certain it wasn't an Uber. He gave the driver the address to Amber's place and prayed everyone was still asleep. The last thing he needed was anyone witnessing his walk of shame.

What little luck had been at work last night had run its course, because everyone was *not* still asleep. Jasper almost suspected Vincent had alerted them somehow, considering all five of them were waiting in the living room. Amber was enough of a morning person that Jasper wasn't surprised she was awake and fully dressed. Her fiancé, Terrance, and his best friend, Keith, were both bright-eyed and bushy-tailed, still sweaty from their gods-forsaken sunrise jog. Matt and Reiko, Keith's partners, were still half asleep, slumped against each other on the sofa.

At least they were all dressed. If Jasper never saw proof that Amber or Reiko shaved their vaginas again, it would be far too soon.

Amber picked up a cup of coffee and held it out to Jasper. "Finally popped your kink cherry?" she asked, grinning behind her own cup.

Jasper made a face and took the coffee, sinking into a recliner. "Shut up."

Terrance snickered. "Didn't enjoy it?"

He grumbled and slumped lower in his seat, wishing a sinkhole would open up and swallow him. "It was fine," he muttered, wrinkling his nose as he sipped the coffee. It was a little bitter and nowhere near as good as Vincent's. "Better than fine," he added under his breath.

"Oh?" Amber asked, and Jasper didn't miss the glance she shared with Keith. "You were with Vincent, right?"

"Yeah. You know him?"

"We went to college together," Keith said.

Matt piped up from the sofa. "He's a dick."

Jasper narrowed his eyes at Matt, holding back the urge to say Vincent hadn't been a dick to him. Not that they'd really had much of a chance to get to know each other, but he wouldn't mind getting that chance. He should give it a couple days before he decided whether to go back, but he already knew where he'd be next week.

Matt squinted blearily at Jasper over the top of Reiko's head. "You're not going back to see him." It sounded like an accusation.

Jasper shrugged, setting his coffee on the table. "What if I am?"

Matt snorted. "He'll string you along until he's bored and then toss you aside."

"Oh, you mean like Shayne did?" Jasper asked with a sneer. At least Vincent wasn't teasing him with something he wasn't willing to give.

"Matt—" Keith said, but Matt talked over him.

"He goes through play partners like you go through games. He doesn't even stay with them long enough to form a relationship."

Who the hell was asking for a relationship? "Great. Then I'll have maybe a few months of great sex before I go back to being miserable." He shoved to his feet, about to ask Amber how he could use her guest access next week when he noticed the way Matt was staring at him. "What?" he snapped.

"He had sex with you?"

"How the fuck is that any of your business?" He wasn't sure what the hell Matt's problem was, but he was done with this conversation. "I'm going back to bed," he said, escaping up the stairs to his room.

He locked the door behind him and collapsed on his bed with a groan. He knew they meant well, but having so many people prying into his life after so many years of being ignored was too much to deal with sometimes. He tried not to be a dick about it, since he was living here rent-free, with the promise to help with chores, but *fuck*. Did they have to be so overbearing?

He needed to finish registering for his classes since they filled up fast. He couldn't risk losing his scholarship because he missed a required course, but he couldn't muster the strength to get up and deal with that scheduling nightmare yet.

He buried his face in his pillow with another groan. All he could think about was Vincent's hands on him. The memory of Vincent sinking to his knees in front of the chair, with all that refined grace and authority, was the single hottest thing he'd ever seen. He didn't know why Matt was so shocked by the idea of Vincent having sex with him, but he couldn't help but assume it was because they both knew Vincent was way out of his league.

Chapter Six

Vincent wasn't too surprised when he woke to a text from Amber on Sunday afternoon. It was a simple: *WTF did you do to my cousin???*

He ignored it and rolled over to doze another half hour, already cursing himself for not sending Jasper back downstairs when Amber called. The moment those five applied for membership to his club, he'd sworn not to get involved with them again. Which hadn't been too hard, considering how he fell out of touch with them after his mother's death, but Amber was as vigilant as she was strict. There was no way to avoid her, especially if Jasper returned to the club next week.

When he finally got out of bed, a mild buzz of irritation under his skin made his reply a bit harsher than he intended. *Nothing so bad as abandoning him in a fetish club.* When he hadn't received a response a few minutes later, he tried softening it a bit with *Why?* Not that he was worried. At least not beyond his obligation to ensure someone he'd played with didn't have a breakdown because of him.

Amber didn't respond until after he'd eaten lunch and showered. *He's asking about club membership*

Vincent chuckled, glad he hadn't scared the brat off. Despite his reservations about Amber and the others, Jasper was fun to play with. And his bratty, snarky wit might have been exactly Vincent's preference. He sent a *You know how to apply* and took the lack of any further response as a good sign.

He headed to Touch of Leather and busied himself with work, ignoring the few of his staff who knew him well enough to tell him to take an actual day off. Tuesdays were his usual day off. The club was closed Monday and Tuesday, and closed early Sunday night, but he had a few other businesses to check in on when he wasn't at the club, and a standing appointment on Monday.

The club's grand opening had been less than a year ago, and while it was doing well, he couldn't quite bring himself to leave its day-to-day operations to his staff yet.

Especially when someone as wet behind the ears as Jasper had managed to find his way in without a proper safety net.

By the time the weekend came around again, he found himself in his office, glancing at the security feeds while he finished checking over the finance reports. Amber hadn't contacted him again, and there'd been no application for a Jasper, but he was willing to wait and see. He might have even been hopeful.

As a Dom without his own sub, he was requested by club members for the occasional scene, but few of them compared to Jasper. The ones who did were already attached to a partner or two in some way and were merely looking for a specific bit of play they couldn't get at home. Some only needed the kink, others wanted release, but Vincent never got off with any of them. He didn't have sex unless it was with his own sub, with a contract in place.

Around ten, Jasper finally arrived and propped himself against the bar. Vincent caught a brief glimpse of Amber before she headed for the dungeon with Terrance.

Vincent waited a moment, then picked up the phone, keeping an eye on the screen as the bartender picked up on the other end. "Blond with blue eyes—his name is Jasper. If he asks for me, give him the key to room three."

"Right-o, boss," she sang and hung up. She spoke briefly to Jasper, laughed at something he said, and flashed a grin at the camera as she turned to find the keycard. She handed it over with a flourish and a wink.

Jasper took the card, lingering at the bar a few moments before turning. He passed from camera to camera as he headed upstairs, finally stopping in front of the third door.

Vincent waited until Jasper stepped inside, then left his office. He'd already let security and the floor monitors know he might have an appointment for the night, so he headed to the room. Room three was similar to two on the inside—bed, fridge, chest, chair—but instead of a sofa, it contained a spanking horse. The wall across from the bed was lined with paddles and floggers, which currently held Jasper's attention.

"See one you like?"

"Huh-uh," Jasper replied, glancing at Vincent and tilting his head. "Do you always wear suits?"

"Usually." He slipped his jacket off and draped it over the back of the chair. He sat, pointed to the cushion in front of him, and waited.

Jasper eyed the cushion a moment, tugging at the hem of his shirt. Finally he sank to his knees on top of it.

"Good boy." The praise at least eased some of the tension in Jasper's shoulders, but he still shifted where he sat with nervous energy. "I'll ask the same questions as last week. Are touching, kissing, and fingering still on the table?"

Jasper huffed and glanced around the room, his gaze landing anywhere but on Vincent. "Yes. You can do whatever you want."

"Is that so," he said flatly. Apparently he should have called Amber out on sending Jasper into the proverbial lion's den without so much as a basic understanding of setting limits.

"So you're fine with me cutting on you with a scalpel?"

Jasper's eyes widened, and he paled considerably. "What? *No!*"

"So you're *not* okay with me doing whatever I want?"

Jasper glared. "That's not what I meant, and you know it."

Vincent raised an eyebrow. "How do I know what you meant? You assume anyone who gets you tied up is going to have your best interest in mind? If you tell someone 'anything you want' and they decide to be stupid or brutal enough to take you at your word, you'll end up with scars you don't want," he said, managing not to yell. Barely.

Jasper paled and swallowed like he was going to be sick. "That's not… what I meant."

"I figured as much. So tell me what you meant."

Jasper glanced towards the door, his fingers twisting his shirt hem even further. "You said you'd ask the same questions," he finally said, staring at Vincent's knees. "Everything I said yes to last time is still a yes."

"Fair enough. Then I'll ask a new question. How do you feel about anal plugs?"

Jasper made a soft sound and gripped his shirt until his knuckles turned white. "I don't know." His tongue darted out to wet his lips. "But you can use one."

"And what about spanking?"

Jasper's breathing sped up as he eyed the horse. "I don't… want to not be able to sit after."

Vincent chuckled. "I think I can manage that," he said dryly. "Is that a yes?"

Jasper swallowed and turned his attention back to Vincent. "Yes…. Sir. You can spank me."

Vincent watched Jasper a moment to see if he'd take it back. When he didn't, Vincent propped his elbow on the arm of the chair. "Then strip," he said, resting his cheek against his fist. "And make it sexy."

Jasper narrowed his eyes at Vincent, and a hesitant smirk touched his lips. "I'm always sexy, Sir." He stood and wiggled his shirt up his chest and over his head, then tossed it at Vincent.

"Are you," Vincent said, fighting a laugh. He dropped the shirt to the floor. "How sexy do you think you'll be, bent over with a red ass?"

Jasper fumbled the button on his jeans. "Very."

"Oh?"

"Uh-huh." Jasper stuck his tongue out and began moving his hips in what he apparently thought was a sexy gyration. He pushed his jeans and boxers off at the same time, cursing under his breath when he had to stop to get his shoes off. His socks followed in a decidedly unsexy manner until he was finally standing naked in front of Vincent once again.

Vincent snorted. "Well, that was unsatisfying," he said dryly. He raked his eyes over the bare flesh in front of him, a bit disappointed the few marks he'd left were long gone. "Turn around." Once Jasper turned his back, Vincent stood. He settled his hands on Jasper's hips and pressed against him. "Do you want to pick the paddle I use on you?" he asked, pleased by the sound Jasper made in response.

"No," Jasper said, his voice weak. "Something that won't hurt too much?"

"Well, if you don't want to choose…." He stepped around Jasper and picked a wide faux-leather, somewhat flexible paddle. He pushed the chair closer to the bench, set the paddle on the seat, and turned to Jasper. "Up you go," he said, patting the leather cushion on the bench.

Jasper swallowed and moved forward with jerky motions before climbing up.

Vincent guided Jasper's hands and legs where they needed to be, letting his fingers linger on warm skin as he strapped Jasper down. "Did you come up with your own safeword?" he asked, adjusting the bench to lift Jasper's ass a bit higher. It was custom-made and far more adaptable than most, nearly to the point of being extraneous, but this was also one of his most requested rooms because of it.

"Physics."

Vincent paused in locking the leg pieces into place. "Are you a student?"

"Yes," Jasper said, his voice strained. "Studying biology. Want to be a paramedic."

That was an interesting choice. He hadn't pegged Jasper as the type to run towards the disaster. With a hum, Vincent stepped back to look him over.

Jasper's thighs were spread as far as they could go without straining, his hips lifted up at the perfect angle for the paddle. He groped Jasper's ass, squeezing the firm flesh and checking the rest of him. As he adjusted the face cradle down a notch, Jasper wriggled and let out a slow breath.

"Comfortable?" he asked, walking around Jasper while trailing his fingers behind him—down one side, across Jasper's ass, and up the other side.

"Yes."

"Good." Vincent pulled his hand away as he moved to the chest and opened it. "If you start feeling any tingling, pinching, or uncomfortable sensations in your limbs, I expect you to safeword." He grabbed the lube and a slender glass plug, then let the chest's lid drop into place with a bang when Jasper failed to respond. "That should have been met with a 'Yes, Sir,'" he said dryly.

"Yes, Sir," Jasper said, and Vincent could hear the eye roll in it.

He dropped the lube and plug onto Jasper's back and landed a sharp smack on Jasper's ass, thoroughly pleased with the startled yelp he got in return. "Brat," he said, picking up the paddle. He dragged it over Jasper's hip and down his leg, then landed it in a solid thwack against his thigh.

Jasper jumped, his breath catching, but Vincent didn't miss the goose bumps that rippled over his back. With a soft sound of approval, Vincent moved up an inch and did it again. And again. Until he reached the center of Jasper's ass. Then he moved around the bench to do the same up the other leg, eyeing Jasper when he kept quiet despite his unsteady breathing. "Jasper."

He answered with a soft whine. "Yes, Sir?"

Vincent rubbed the paddle against Jasper's inner thigh. "Are you being quiet on purpose?"

Jasper let out an explosive breath and shifted. "Maybe."

"I suggest you stop."

Jasper stilled, tilting his head a bit as if he were trying to look back at Vincent. "Make me."

Vincent laughed. Christ, this brat. He set the paddle across Jasper's shoulders and picked up the lube. He snagged a glove and pulled it on, then coated his finger to press into Jasper's hole, taking his time as he worked the digit in deep. Next he picked up the glass plug, coated it, and spread Jasper's cheeks to watch as it disappeared into his ass with a single smooth push.

"Hnngh!" Jasper squirmed on the bench, fighting against his restraints.

Vincent enjoyed the sight, wiggling the plug a bit and applying pressure to make Jasper keen. Then he picked up the paddle again, while Jasper was still making those exquisite sounds, and brought it down across the center of Jasper's ass.

Jasper let out a sharp cry, his back arching enough Vincent's own spine protested. Jasper's entire body shuddered as he slumped against the bench, panting.

"That was better," Vincent said, surprised by the intense reaction. "Feel good?"

"Only a little," Jasper said, the bratty act ruined by his moan.

Vincent smirked, rubbing his palm over pinkening flesh. "Good. Then politely ask me for another."

Jasper jerked against the restraints, craning his neck to glare at Vincent. "Make me."

"I don't have to," Vincent said with a soft laugh. "You're not going anywhere. And you're sure as hell not getting off until I'm satisfied. So," he said, lightly tapping the paddle against Jasper's thigh, "ask me or lie there, naked and untouched, until I decide we're done."

Jasper's growl turned to a moan as he dropped his head back down. He shifted his hips in an admittedly enticing manner. "Please."

"Please, what? I won't ask you to be specific again," Vincent said, landing a reprimanding swat to Jasper's ankle.

Jasper yelped and muttered under his breath, earning himself another swat. "Fuck! Fine! Please. Please spank me again. Sir."

Vincent whacked the paddle against Jasper's ass, making sure it nudged the plug.

Jasper arched with a frustrated whine. "Again, Sir. Please."

Vincent obliged, satisfied when that seemed to be enough for Jasper to accept the rules. With barely a breath between each of his pleas, Jasper rocked back to meet the paddle every time it landed. At least until he was lost in the pleasure enough he couldn't do more than grip the bench and sob out a "please" every few ragged breaths.

Vincent slowed his rhythm, ignoring Jasper's whine as he dragged his fingers over the reddened flesh. It was warm but shouldn't be anywhere near bad enough to keep Jasper from sitting. So long as he didn't mind some mild discomfort. He tossed the paddle onto the chair as he rubbed his other hand over Jasper's arms and unstrapped them.

"Up," he said quietly, helping Jasper push up off the bench. An extra set of longer straps were attached to the other end, and Vincent used them to secure Jasper's wrists between his ankles. "All right?" he asked, running his fingers through Jasper's hair.

"Uh-huh." Jasper leaned into Vincent's fingers, tipping his head back. His eyes were nearly black from his blown pupils. "Please, Sir."

"Please what?" Vincent asked, readjusting the bench so it was level. That done, he stepped back to admire the sight Jasper made.

Jasper swallowed with a frustrated groan. "Touch me. Please. Want you to make me come."

"Good boy," Vincent purred, straddling the bench and leaning in to brush his lips against Jasper's. He tangled one hand in blond hair, sliding his other over the heated skin of Jasper's chest. When he found a nipple, he pinched it, chuckling when Jasper gasped and jerked against his restraints.

He trailed his fingernails down Jasper's chest and stomach to his arousal, tightening his other hand in Jasper's hair and watching his face. "Enjoying the plug?" he asked.

Jasper whimpered and tried to nod, but Vincent held his head immobile. "Yes, Sir," Jasper breathed.

"Good." Vincent wrapped his hand around Jasper's dick and stroked, squeezing and watching Jasper's lips part on a moan. "So responsive," he murmured, still surprised by that. Jasper was like a perfectly tuned violin that didn't know what music he was best suited for.

He kissed up the side of Jasper's neck, nipping at his ear. "Have you ever come on command?" he asked, keeping his stroking to an almost torturously slow rhythm.

"N-no, Sir."

Vincent dragged his teeth against the flesh of Jasper's throat. "Do you think you can manage not to come until I tell you to?"

Jasper shivered. "I can try."

Vincent sat back, releasing Jasper's hair. "Do and I'll let you ask for a reward." He chuckled when Jasper nodded eagerly. "Good boy." He tightened his grip and stroked faster, his other hand pinching and twisting a nipple.

"Fuck!" Jasper shouted, bucking his hips and jerking against his restraints again.

Vincent groped Jasper's ass with one hand when he devolved into pleading, nudging the plug in deeper and turning it. He didn't expect Jasper to last long; he was already making those desperate little noises Vincent had gotten familiar with last week.

Either Jasper could control himself or use his words, or he couldn't.

It might not have been fair. Vincent suspected Jasper didn't quite understand all the nuances of the scene yet, but that was part of the fun too. With the right sub.

He gripped the plug and gave it a firm thrust, enjoying the resulting strangled groan.

"Oh fuck!" Jasper gasped. "I can't, I can't… please, please." He thrashed on the bench as Vincent continued moving the plug, enough he would have managed to topple it if Vincent hadn't been sitting in front of him. "No, no, no—physics!"

Vincent pulled away completely and stood, quickly releasing Jasper's wrists and then his legs. He rested a hand on Jasper's back when he slumped onto his forearms, his breathing ragged.

"I didn't…. I didn't come," Jasper gasped, ending with a soft whine.

"You didn't," Vincent agreed, inching his fingers into Jasper's hair. He moved around to sit on the edge of the bench. "Maybe if you'd said yellow instead of physics, I would have let you."

Jasper lifted his head with a frown. "What?"

"You ended the scene."

Jasper's frown deepened. "Then start it back up." He shifted closer, frustration and something desperate in his eyes as he grabbed the front of Vincent's shirt. "Please. I don't even care if you let me get off, just don't…. Don't end it like this. Please," he whispered, his expression crumbling.

Vincent silently cursed and touched Jasper's cheek. "You did nothing wrong," he said quietly, tipping Jasper's head back. "Look at me," he ordered, waiting for Jasper's eyes to focus on him. "Say it."

Jasper swallowed and flicked his tongue against his lips. "I… did nothing wrong."

"You did what I told you to do, and you used your word to do it. You did well. Understand?"

Jasper nodded but still appeared hesitant.

"Good boy." Vincent pressed his lips against Jasper's forehead. "Now get on the bed so I can get you off."

Chapter Seven

Jasper let Vincent help him to the bed, the plug in his ass a wholly unusual and strange sensation as he walked. He stretched out on his stomach, immediately grinding his hips against the bed. Fuck, he needed friction.

Vincent chuckled and smacked Jasper's ass before forcing him onto his knees.

Vincent's pants were rough against Jasper's thighs, and his breath caught at the press of Vincent's cock against him. He wanted that. He wanted Vincent to pin him down and fuck him. He bit his lip with a groan, keeping himself from begging for exactly that.

No matter how many times he'd offered last time, Vincent hadn't taken him up on any of them.

Jasper shivered as warm lips trailed kisses up his spine, closing his eyes with a sigh. That was nice. At least until Vincent bit his shoulder. Fucker. He couldn't be too upset about any marks, though, considering how much he'd enjoyed finding them last time. He'd relished the phantom aches when he dug a finger into them. At least until they'd faded.

He tilted his head enough to glance back at Vincent, gripping the covers as he wiggled his ass. "I thought you were going to get me off, Sir?" he asked, yelping when Vincent answered by slapping his ass again.

"You mean like this?" Vincent gripped Jasper's hips and tugged, using his thigh to grind against the plug.

Oh fuck. "Yes," Jasper gasped. It wasn't the same as having Vincent inside him, but he could pretend. When Vincent wrapped a hand around his erection, he thrust into it. He was already near his limit again, and despite what he'd said, he really wanted to get off. Now. He shoved his hips back, grinding against Vincent with a whine. "Please let me come, Sir."

Vincent sat back, pulling Jasper with him so he was leaning against Vincent's chest. He wrapped one hand loosely around Jasper's throat while his other hand began stroking again. "You want to come, pet?" he asked, voice low and rough.

Jasper whimpered at the sound of it, at the way it turned his insides hot and squirmy. Made him want to do whatever it took to make sure

Vincent kept touching him. "Yes. Please, I'm—" He cut off with a groan when Vincent's fingers tightened around his dick. His hands flailed at his sides until he latched on to Vincent's arms for leverage, alternating between grinding the plug against Vincent's thigh and thrusting into Vincent's hand. "So close, I'm gonna—"

And then Vincent's hand disappeared, and Jasper wasn't sure if begging or strangling Vincent would be the better choice.

Vincent tilted Jasper's head back, bringing his other hand up to Jasper's lips and smearing precum against them.

Oh fuck no. Jasper turned his head with a strangled sound, but Vincent didn't let him get away. Part of Jasper wanted to safeword again, and to hell if the scene ended for good, but the way Vincent murmured, "Open up, pet," into his ear overrode his common sense.

Heat spread through his limbs as he hesitantly opened his mouth, unable to stop the muffled sound of protest as Vincent pressed two fingers past his lips.

He'd never tasted himself before. It wasn't an entirely pleasant experience, but the quiet hum he felt vibrate through Vincent's chest made it worth it.

"Good boy," Vincent purred, rubbing his fingers over Jasper's tongue. "Suck them clean and I'll let you come."

Gods. He'd never imagined anything close to *this* in any of his fantasies. Being tied up was one thing. Everyone recognized that as an acceptable kink, right? But this? It was gross and humiliating.

Jasper squeezed his eyes shut and somehow found the ability to swallow. His dick twitched in approval despite what his brain thought, and he sucked Vincent's fingers until all that was left was the taste of Vincent's skin.

Vincent pulled his hand free, leaving a wet trail down Jasper's chest. He slid his palm over Jasper's erection and then farther, grabbing the plug and giving it a solid nudge.

"Fuck!"

Vincent pushed Jasper onto his hands and knees again, pinned him with a hand to the back of his neck, and fucked him with the plug.

Jasper clutched at the covers and gave himself over to the pleasure. He wasn't even sure what he was saying anymore as he begged to come, for Vincent to use him, to fuck him, to make him scream. Every time he got close, the plug disappeared and Vincent's fingers tightened against his neck. Once he got his breath back, Vincent would start from the beginning. Slowly pressing the plug back in and working up to a hard-and-fast rhythm.

How Vincent could keep him at the edge of pleasure so easily was beyond him, but he hoped it would never end, even as he desperately wished for release.

And then Vincent pressed against him, pinning him to the bed with his weight and growling into Jasper's ear, "Come."

Jasper came, screaming as his body shuddered through a release so intense he missed a few breaths.

"Good boy," Vincent purred, tugging the plug free and tossing it aside. He stretched out next to Jasper, running fingers through his hair.

"Mmm," Jasper went limp with a sigh. His eyes drifted closed until he found the strength to roll over and curl into Vincent's chest. "Ass is warm."

Vincent chuckled, tightening his fingers in Jasper's hair. "Will be for a day or two at least."

Great. He wouldn't be able to sit without popping a boner for a week. Jasper sighed as he relaxed beneath Vincent's fingers, enjoying the way his entire body felt heavy.

"What do you want for your reward?"

Oh yeah. He'd managed not to come until Vincent told him to. With a drawn-out hum, he considered his options. He was tempted to ask Vincent to fuck him, but he had a feeling that was not within the rules. "Can I see you again? Outside the club?" he asked, toying with a button on Vincent's shirt.

"Like a date?" Vincent asked with a soft laugh.

Jasper tilted his head back to look at him. "Do you date?"

Vincent hesitated, wrapping his fingers around Jasper's and tugging them away from the buttons. "Not in the traditional sense."

That sounded intriguing. Jasper wriggled closer, toying with Vincent's fingers instead. "What would a date with you be like?"

"That depends."

"On?"

Vincent curled his fingers through Jasper's hair again. "On what it is you're actually asking for."

Jasper swallowed and stared at the exposed skin beneath Vincent's throat. What *was* he asking for? He might have told the others he was only interested in some decent sex for a few weeks, but that was definitely turning into a lie. He wanted more, even though he knew it was a horrible idea. So much more.

He always wanted more than what anyone else was willing to give. That was the problem. If even Shayne had dumped him, there was no way he stood a chance with Vincent. There was nothing between them. This was probably just a job for him.

He wasn't willing to give up these weekends by asking for too much. Not yet.

"Never mind," he said, releasing Vincent's fingers. "I should get going." *Way to make things awkward, dumbass.*

"All right," Vincent replied, standing to retrieve Jasper's clothes. He stopped beside the bed and straightened the clothes out without handing them over. "Jasper," he said, clearing his throat. "Are you interested in something more than me getting you off once a week?"

Jasper froze, his heart skipping a few beats while he tried to remember how to breathe properly. "More?" he whispered, not quite believing Vincent's "more" and his "more" were the same. He sure as hell didn't think Vincent meant a relationship.

"Like you becoming my pet. Outside of the club."

Jasper swallowed, finally looking up to meet Vincent's eyes. "What exactly would that mean?"

"That depends on you and your needs," Vincent replied, sitting on the edge of the bed and setting Jasper's clothes between them. He raised an eyebrow when Jasper squinted at him. "As a sub. Being tied up, for one. Orgasms, obviously. I assume you enjoy sex by how many times you begged me to fuck you last time," he added dryly.

"Obviously," Jasper replied, making a face when Vincent flicked his thigh.

Vincent slid his palm up Jasper's chest, resting it against his throat. "Being my pet would be like it is here, only more intense. I'm told I have particular tastes."

Jasper shivered and leaned into Vincent's hand. He couldn't help the soft groan at the sudden need that burned through him. He'd be fucking stupid to say no to this. "Yes," he whispered, hating how it sounded like a plea.

Vincent pulled his hand away with a soft snort. "Think about it for longer than five seconds," he said, sliding off the bed.

"You're leaving?" Jasper asked, hating the flutter of panic and barely resisting the urge to grab on to Vincent's wrist. "Did—did I do something wrong?"

"No," Vincent said, turning back to Jasper after draping his jacket over his arm. "But if I stay, I'll be tempted to have my way with you again."

The sound of that made Jasper's dick valiantly attempt to return to life. "I'm already yours," he murmured. "At least for the night." He didn't miss the way Vincent's gaze raked over him, shivering beneath the scrutiny. "Please, Sir," he whispered, spreading his knees for balance and clasping his hands behind his back. It was a position he'd caught Matt in a few times, and he'd liked the feel of it when he tried it out in the privacy of his bedroom.

Vincent let out a soft hum of approval, tossing his jacket aside again. "That's a good look on you." He tangled his fingers in Jasper's hair and forced his head back to capture his lips in a kiss.

Jasper opened up eagerly beneath Vincent's tongue, clasping his hands tighter to keep from latching on to Vincent and making sure he didn't try to leave again. When Vincent squeezed the oversensitive flesh of his ass, he moaned. He'd definitely be popping a boner in the middle of classes like this. The sad thing was, he wasn't sure he cared.

Vincent pulled back and studied Jasper a moment before he let go and moved to the chest. "Lie back."

"Yessir," Jasper said, breathless as he stretched out on his back, propping up on his elbows to watch. His eyes widened when Vincent pulled out a purple dildo and proceeded to cover it in lube.

Vincent caught his expression. "Never used one of these either?" he asked, settling between Jasper's legs. He set the dildo on Jasper's stomach, then pushed his knees up and apart.

Jasper groaned, not about to admit to at least having one of those. He dropped the rest of the way to the bed with a shuddery breath as Vincent pressed the thick, blunt head of the dildo into him. His fingers twisted in the covers as it slid inside, filling him more than the plug had. "Feels good," he moaned, cracking his eyes open to watch Vincent.

Vincent caught Jasper's eye with a brief smirk, turning on the dildo and giving it a firm nudge.

Jasper arched with a sharp cry, his eyes widening as the dildo vibrated against his prostate. "Oh gods." He bit his lip when Vincent started moving the toy, squeezing his eyes shut again with a groan. Damn. How the hell did Vincent get him going again so easily when he'd already come? "Please touch me, Sir."

"I think I'd rather watch you touch yourself," Vincent replied, driving the dildo in deeper.

What the hell? He couldn't do that. That was way too embarrassing. "No way."

"Yes," Vincent ordered, his voice as unyielding as the toy grinding into Jasper. "Hand on your cock, pet."

Heat spread across Jasper's cheeks as his hand moved without his permission. His safeword was on the tip of his tongue, but honestly, Vincent ordering him around was hot as shit.

"Good boy," Vincent purred. "Now show me how you like to be touched."

Jasper licked his lips, squeezing his eyes shut as he moved his hand. He could practically feel Vincent staring at him, and it was both mortifying and arousing as hell. He did as he was told, pretending he was in his own bed and touching himself to the memories of last week. It was easy enough, considering he'd gotten off to nothing else since leaving the club.

The memory of Vincent sucking him off. Of finger-fucking him. Of tying him down and making him submit, and how he'd loved every moment of it. And now of spanking him, leaving his ass warm and a touch uncomfortable against the covers.

Fucking him with a dildo.

His hand was quickly covered with precum, sliding noisily over his erection as Vincent matched his pace with the dildo. Or was he matching Vincent's pace? Either way it managed to be more than enough to push him to the edge without ever being enough to send him over.

It was exquisite torment and left him moaning and shifting in frustration. "Please," he whined. He *really* didn't want to safeword in case he fucked up again.

"Stop," Vincent ordered. "Lick your hand."

Fuck. Jasper whimpered even as he lifted his hand to his mouth and licked it clean. "Please let me come."

"Patience," Vincent said, resting his hand on Jasper's hip. "Eyes on me, pet," he said, his voice lower and rougher, sending shivers down Jasper's spine.

Jasper forced his eyes open, watching Vincent lean over him. He tipped his head back, his lips parting as Vincent pushed two fingers past them.

Vincent moved the dildo faster, fucking Jasper's mouth with his fingers at the same pace. Then he turned the toy on to a setting that made Jasper arch off the bed, tipping his head back with a sharp moan and struggling not to bite down on Vincent's fingers.

"Close?" Vincent asked, his warm breath gusting over Jasper's throat in a soft laugh.

"Uh-huh." Jasper dug his fingers into Vincent's shirt, heat and pleasure coursing through him. "Fuck," he whined, bucking his hips. "I can't—" He couldn't hold back much longer.

Vincent removed his fingers and found Jasper's nipple with them instead, then moved his lips to the other nipple and circled it with his tongue. "Come," he growled as he sank his teeth into it.

"Fuck!" Jasper shouted, coming hard over his own stomach. "Oh fuck," he gasped a few moments later, slowly melting into the bed as orgasm gave way to lethargic satiation. He watched with half-lidded eyes as Vincent cleaned him up and tossed the dildo where the plug had gone. "Do you do this for your pets, too?" he asked, utterly unwilling to move and fighting the strong desire to sleep.

"Sometimes. It depends," Vincent replied, stretching out next to Jasper.

"Onnn?" Jasper managed to roll onto his side and snuggle into Vincent's chest.

"Lots of things." Vincent scratched his fingers through Jasper's hair. "The scene. How I feel after. How you feel after. Whether or not you're about to pass out," he said dryly.

Jasper grumbled and nuzzled into Vincent's shoulder. "Not gonna pass out."

"No?"

Jasper shook his head, the rumble of Vincent's laugh a soothing vibration against his cheek, and promptly fell asleep.

CHAPTER EIGHT

TWO DAYS later, Jasper knocked on the door to Keith's room, poking his head in when Keith called that it was open. He bit his lip, making sure Keith was alone as he stepped inside. "Can I talk to you?"

Keith turned his chair away from his computer, motioning to the bed. "What's wrong?"

"Nothing's *wrong* exactly." He sat on the edge of the bed, resting his notebook in his lap. "It's just…." He picked at the metal spirals. "Vincent…." He wasn't sure how to broach the subject, even though he knew Keith wouldn't mind. Probably.

Keith pushed his chair closer. "Did something happen?"

Jasper frowned, fighting his indignation. Keith might not have spoken badly about Vincent, but Matt had made a point to warn him, again, that Vincent was a dick and not worth Jasper's time. "No. He agreed to a date, but only if I bring a list of limits to discuss. So we can see if I wanttobehispet," he said in a rush, risking a peek at Keith when he didn't immediately say that was a stupid idea.

Keith didn't seem as surprised as Jasper had expected. "Do you want to be his pet?"

Jasper let out a breath and resumed toying with his notebook. "I haven't hated any of what we've done so far." He could have done without tasting himself, but even that…. "And you and Matt are happy with Reiko, and Terrance with Amber. I want to give it a try. I just—" He shrugged. "—don't know how this is really supposed to work."

"Which part?"

Jasper flicked his fingers, a bit desperately. "All of it?"

Keith coughed in a way Jasper was sure hid a laugh. "Okay. So Vincent is definitely a Dom. You've been submitting to him?"

"I guess so, yeah. He made me kneel and answer questions, and then ordered me to… do stuff." Like that wasn't an understatement *at all*.

"Stuff you liked?"

"Mostly. I mean, yeah, pretty much," Jasper replied. His ass was still warm enough to get him aroused if he wasn't careful. But he wouldn't mind doing that again. Not in the least.

"And you like submitting? Handing over control?" Keith asked.

"Is that weird?" It seemed weird if he thought about it too much, but that first night, tied up and completely helpless in the chair, he'd finally found a missing piece of himself. And each time after, when he was at Vincent's mercy, he understood that piece a little more. Except that part of him seemed to get a lot bigger at the same time. "I liked taunting him? Not because I didn't want to do what he said, but.... It was fun to make him work for it?"

Keith did laugh then, the one Jasper usually only heard when Reiko or Matt were around. "Of course you're a brat." He shook his head. "All right. So what is it you need from me?"

"He asked for my limits. I don't even know what I don't know about limits." Jasper hesitated as he gnawed on his lower lip, "I told him he could do anything he wanted to me, and he didn't like that. He asked if that meant he could cut on me. Who would even want to do that?"

Keith tilted his head with a raised eyebrow, then shrugged. "Lots of people, actually. But I can list some common kinks for you, and some limits you should probably have until you get more experience."

Jasper sagged in relief. "Thank you," he said, flipping his notebook open.

By the time they were done, Jasper had two pages of kinks listed, with details or definitions Keith had given for the ones he'd never heard of.

Keith had also pointedly gone over basic safety precautions, general expectations, and guidelines on top of everything else.

Jasper suspected most of what Keith told him was prompted by the mention of cutting, which irked him about as much as he was grateful. He'd been tempted to ask what Matt's problem was with Vincent, but he didn't want a biased explanation. Not yet anyway. If the reason was really bad enough that Jasper wasn't safe with Vincent, he was sure Amber would have said something the first night.

He flopped onto his bed with a sigh. His head was swimming as he tried to process all the information, staring at the notebook pages without seeing them. He was supposed to figure out his limits from this? What if he said no to something he would have enjoyed? Like spanking. As much as he wanted to do the whole sub thing, he'd never really gotten past the "being tied up" fantasy.

He didn't want to miss out on something because he didn't know any better. But at the same time, the thought of trying even half of these things made him uneasy.

With another sigh, he grabbed his highlighters and stretched out on his stomach to start marking. Pink for no, yellow for maybe, and green for yes.

No to cutting, knives and needles, and all the different toilet plays, choking, suspension, branding, CBT, and guns.

Yes to restraints, spanking, blowjobs, anal sex, biting, aftercare—Vincent had been doing that already, hadn't he?—plugs and toys, and edging.

Maybe to blindfolds, whips, orgasm denial, gags, piercings, permanent marking, nipple clamps, cock rings, and collars.

He chewed on the end of his highlighter, looked everything over, and then listed them out in neat columns on a separate sheet. Some of his tension eased at having it done and ready to go, and he turned to his homework instead.

WHEN FRIDAY came around, Jasper was antsy again, but excited. He knew Matt disapproved, but Amber seemed happy for him. He could tell she was wary, but at least she didn't keep telling him he was making a mistake.

A car honked from outside and Terrance whistled when he opened the door to see the same sleek black car that had dropped Jasper off the past two weekends. "Who knew what you were really looking for was a sugar daddy?" he teased.

Jasper flushed and elbowed Terrance on his way past. "Very funny."

Terrance laughed. "Call if you're not coming home tonight!"

Jasper waved over his shoulder and climbed into the back seat. He tugged at the button-up collared shirt he'd dug out from the back of his closet. He didn't have many clothes that weren't old and faded or didn't have holes, but he did at least have one nice black shirt he hardly ever wore. Most of his wardrobe consisted of things he'd picked up from Goodwill or discount racks.

When the car stopped in front of a fancy restaurant, the driver opened his door. Jasper swallowed his nerves and climbed out, hoping he wasn't too underdressed in his khakis.

Once inside, he followed a host to the back of the restaurant, where Vincent had apparently reserved a private little room for them. "How rich *are* you?" he asked when the partition slid shut behind him.

Vincent looked up from his phone. "Does it matter?" he asked, pointing to the chair across from him.

Jasper shrugged and pulled his list from his pocket. He sat and handed it to Vincent. As Vincent read it, he struggled not to fidget.

"Which one of them helped you put this together?"

"Keith," Jasper answered, picking up the menu to give his hands something to do. He stared at it a moment in confusion. Nothing had prices listed. And the menu was broken down into courses, with only a few options on each one.

"Good. He's usually the most sensible one," Vincent said, setting the list aside. "Have you thought more about what you want?"

Jasper glanced at him over the top of his menu. "With being your pet?" He shifted in his seat when Vincent nodded, still not quite believing this was really happening. "Keith said you'd probably want a contract?"

Vincent nodded again, pulling an envelope out of his suit jacket. He set it beside his own plate when there was a light knock on the door.

A server came in to take their orders, and Jasper swallowed his impatience at the interruption. Once they were gone, Vincent handed the envelope over.

Jasper pulled out the folded paper, glad Keith had shown him an example contract or he'd have no idea what he was looking at.

As far as he could tell, it was a basic setup for a two-month agreement. Vincent agreed to provide anything necessary for their time together and to adhere to Jasper's limits. In return he expected Jasper to use his safewords as needed and to never lie.

"Does this mean *you* can lie?" Jasper asked with a frown.

Vincent snorted softly. "Lying wouldn't get me what I want."

"What is it you want?"

"For now, you."

Warmth spread through Jasper's limbs, but he forced himself not to be distracted by it. "That's not really an answer."

Vincent chuckled. "Maybe not. I won't know what else I want until I've had a chance to play with you more."

Jasper carefully folded the contract and slipped it into the envelope. "Can I have a couple days to think about it?"

"You don't trust me?" Vincent asked, though Jasper suspected that was another test.

"No, I do," Jasper murmured. "But I still want to talk to Keith and Amber and make sure I'm making the right decision."

"You're more pragmatic than I thought."

Jasper straightened in his seat with a glare. "I'm not stupid."

"I didn't say you were. And I didn't say it was a bad thing either," Vincent replied. "The more mindful you are, the easier my job is."

Jasper snorted. "Like it's so hard to get someone off?"

Vincent raised an eyebrow, his expression shifting in a way Jasper swore cooled the room a few degrees. "You think it's easy?" he asked, propping his chin on his fist and absently turning his glass with his other hand. "If I'd refused to continue the scene when you safeworded, would you have come back?"

Jasper blinked, remembering the mix of panic, shame, and frustration when he'd reached his limit. He'd only wanted to make Vincent stop because he would have come, regardless of trying to hold back. If Vincent had ended the scene there….

"No," he whispered. He would have gone home and locked himself in his bedroom in mortification. Buried himself in coursework to try and forget. And he doubted he would have shown his face in the club again.

Vincent nodded, then straightened when there was another knock, falling silent as their first course was set out for them. He continued once they were alone again. "Begging to continue afterwards isn't all that uncommon. Especially if someone feels they disappointed their Dom, temporary or not. I took the chance you were begging for your own sake rather than mine."

Jasper poked at his salad, which contained pears, goat cheese, and honey drizzle. Was this really how rich people ate? There was silence for a bit as he ate his salad and Vincent his lobster bisque. The salad was, surprisingly, really good. "Sorry," he finally said. "I still don't really know how all this works."

"Another reason I didn't end it. I was glad you remembered you could safeword."

Jasper peered at Vincent, watching him as their plates were switched out for the next course. Once the server was gone, he said, "You're really not as big of a dick as some people make you out to be, are you?"

Vincent raised an eyebrow. "Try saying that again in two months."

Jasper grinned, unbothered by the implication he was going to sign the contract. "Okay."

Vincent nodded towards the envelope. "Take it and think it over. I'll have a new one waiting with your limits included."

"Okay," Jasper said again and took a bite of spaghetti—the only thing on the menu he knew he'd like—and bit back a soft moan. Damn. That was amazing. No wonder Vincent liked this place. He buttered a piece of crusty bread and glanced at Vincent's plate—some kind of fancy dish with duck. He resisted wrinkling his nose, though he had to wonder if Vincent's tastes in kink were as particular as his taste in food.

"So," he said, then realized he didn't have anything to say. What kind of conversation were you supposed to have with a guy who'd fucked your brains out twice before you had an actual date?

Vincent raised an eyebrow expectantly, his lips twitching with what Jasper hoped was amusement. "Yes?"

Jasper shoved another forkful of spaghetti in his mouth to buy some time. "You own the club, right?" Amber mentioned it when he'd asked about club membership.

"Yes," Vincent said, and Jasper was sure it was amusement this time.

"How'd you get into it? The kink thing."

Vincent didn't respond immediately, dipping his own piece of bread in his duck sauce. "It's been a need ever since I was a kid and played doctor with my babysitter."

Jasper blinked and sat up, beyond curious. "How?" He almost imagined a young Vincent pinning his babysitter down and kissing them, but his brain shied away from it.

"When she was on her back for me to operate, I felt this rush of power and control. It wasn't until I was older and experimented with sex that I was able to put a name to it."

"That's… like it was when you had me in the chair," Jasper admitted quietly, poking at the last bit of his spaghetti. "I was finally experiencing something I'd only been able to imagine until then." And his imagination had fallen short.

"You've never been held down?"

Jasper shrugged, hating the hint of surprise he heard in Vincent's voice. "Not like that. Nothing even close to that." He'd never known how to ask.

The server returned to refill their drinks and bring their desserts, and Jasper dug into his chocolate gelato, unable to stifle his moan this time. He glanced up briefly, shifting in his seat when he caught Vincent watching him.

"I'm glad I could make your first brush with kink enjoyable," Vincent said, and despite the genuine warmth, there was definitely amusement in his voice.

The evening ended far too quickly after that, and Vincent rode next to him in the back seat to take him home. He'd hoped to end up in Vincent's bed, or at least at the club, but apparently that wasn't going to happen until he decided to sign or not.

The fact Vincent finally gave Jasper his number at least made up for the lack of sex. Almost.

The car stopped out front, and Jasper started to get out, freezing when Vincent caught his arm.

Vincent tugged him close, pressing his lips to Jasper's ear. "If you do decide to sign, can you handle not getting off until I see you next?"

Jasper shivered, glancing back at Vincent. There went his plans of at least getting himself off as soon as he was in bed, but he found he didn't mind. The idea of holding back because Vincent wanted him to made his stomach do weird and pleasant things.

"Maybe," he finally answered. He closed the distance between them, Vincent's kiss sending shocks of pleasure through his body. He melted beneath the onslaught of Vincent's tongue, blinking when the kiss ended and Vincent pulled away.

"Good night, Jasper."

Jasper swallowed a whine. The way Vincent said his name sent a burst of heat through his gut. "Night, *Vincent*," he replied with a wink.

When he reached the front door, he glanced back to wave, and the car pulled away.

Despite the movie playing on the TV, it was obvious Keith and Terrance were waiting for him. Jasper might have been annoyed if he wasn't intimately familiar with the alternative: A dark house, either empty or with a drunken father passed out on the couch to sneak past.

Terrance immediately muted the sound when Jasper stepped into the room. "How'd it go?"

"Okay, I think," Jasper replied, pulling out the contract and handing it over. He sank into the recliner and watched both of them read it.

After a couple of minutes, Keith handed it back. "Well, it's a good start for a test run, if that's what you want. Anything else that needs to go in it will make itself known with experience."

Jasper breathed a sigh of relief and took it back, then read it again himself. "You think I should sign?"

"Only one who can answer that is you," Terrance replied. "You definitely seem to like him, though God knows why," he added, wincing as Keith smacked him in the chest.

"Two months isn't that long to test the waters," Keith said.

"But what if after the first couple weeks I realize it's not what I want?"

"Then if Vincent is as good as you think he is, he'll realize it too, and you'll figure something out," Keith replied, as if that should have been obvious. "It's not like it's legally binding. It's between the two of you."

Jasper bit his lower lip and stared at the contract another minute, finally putting it back in the envelope. He told himself he needed to think about it, and he did, but he couldn't come up with a single reason not to do this. He liked Vincent. He liked what Vincent did to him, how Vincent made him feel. They may not have had much interaction outside of the two nights in the club and dinner, but they seemed to get along well enough.

TWO DAYS later, he texted Vincent.

I'll sign

The response came a few minutes later.

Car will pick you up Friday night at 6. If you sign when you get here, you'll stay until Sunday morning.

Two days.
Two days for Vincent to do whatever he wanted with him.
Jasper couldn't wait.

WHEN THE car pulled up in front of Vincent's home on Friday evening, all Jasper could do was stare. It was a large two-story house in a nice neighborhood with a well-kept lawn. Flowers and bushes lined the walkway leading to the door. It wasn't as monstrous as Amber's house, but it was obviously meant for someone wealthy and classy.

If the club ownership, personal driver, and restaurant hadn't screamed *insanely rich*, this place certainly did. All except for the large horrendously bright pink plastic flamingo near the porch.

The driver opened the door, and Jasper took a steadying breath as he climbed out and hooked his small duffel bag over his shoulder. Vincent had sent a text saying he wouldn't need anything, but he'd brought a change of clothes and his toothbrush just in case.

He rang the doorbell, eyeing the pink flamingo near the tall fluffy bushes to the left of the door. He fidgeted with his shirt until the door opened. Then he blinked.

Vincent had an apron on. That was so… so… *hot*.

Jasper couldn't help but stare, ignoring the frown Vincent gave his bag. "Hi," he said, stepping inside.

"Shoes off. You can put your bag on a chair," Vincent said, turning and heading into the kitchen.

Jasper closed the door behind him, toed his shoes off next to Vincent's, and trailed after him. He dropped his bag onto a chair in the living room, noting the wood floors and elaborate entertainment center. There was a nice collection of movies and games neatly lined up on the shelves beneath the TV, along with at least two of the latest gaming consoles.

He turned and continued through the living room, dragging his fingertips over the back of a dark gray sofa. This entire part of the house was the living room, dining room, and kitchen. Instead of walls, the only thing separating them was a large island between the kitchen and living room. "You're cooking?" he asked when he reached the kitchen. He leaned against the island counter to keep out of the way.

Vincent wasn't wearing his usual suit. He had on black jeans and a mid-sleeve Henley, his feet socked. "You sound surprised."

Jasper shrugged at Vincent's back. "I never thought of you as the cooking type."

"Your mistake."

Jasper snorted and rolled his eyes. "Need some help?"

"So you can blow up my kitchen?"

"I know how to cook," Jasper replied, only mildly offended. Well, at least enough to know not to put soup on High and wander away for an hour. He raised an eyebrow when Vincent glanced at him with a dubious expression. "I'm not supposed to lie, remember?"

That seemed to convince Vincent. At least a little. "There's cheese bread in the freezer. The oven is ready."

Jasper found the bread and set the slices out on the pan to pop them into the oven. Then he actually saw what Vincent was making. "Spaghetti?" he asked, unable to stop the grin. "You mean you haven't taken expensive cooking classes and know how to make a seven-course meal?"

"I wouldn't waste the effort on someone who orders spaghetti at a Michelin star restaurant."

Jasper blinked, thrown off guard more by the casual tone than the words. "There's the dick I was warned about," he murmured, moving back to the island. He knew he was so far below Vincent's status it was laughable, but for some reason he hadn't thought Vincent cared about that. Then again, once the clothes came off, who could even tell the trash from the elite?

"Is that why you always keep your suit on?" Jasper asked, crossing his arms on the granite countertop. "To remind your pets of their place?"

Vincent didn't respond, but his shoulders tensed as he continued cooking.

For the first time, Jasper almost wondered if Matt was right. Maybe he was making a mistake. But maybe Vincent hadn't meant that to sound as scathing as he had.

Jasper didn't like the silence. It almost felt like Vincent was trying to avoid saying anything else in case it was as abrasive as the last. Or maybe he was as nervous to have someone in his home as Jasper was to be there.

He snorted softly at the thought. *Yeah, right.*

When the timer went off, he snagged the dish towel off the oven handle to grab the tray and transferred the bread to a plate, then decided that if Vincent was going to be a shit host, Jasper would fend for himself. He opened the fridge to find a drink and paused. Not only was it neatly organized, most of the fruits and vegetables were arranged in stackable glass dishes.

"There's tea in the pitcher."

"Oh, so you can still speak," Jasper muttered under his breath. He pulled the pitcher out and poured two glasses.

Vincent filled two plates with spaghetti and set them on the table, glancing at Jasper as he sat. "What's in your bag?"

"A change of clothes. Toothbrush and toothpaste. Deodorant." He'd almost brought his schoolwork, but he'd managed to finish what little homework was due next week before the car picked him up. He settled across from Vincent, stirred his spaghetti a bit, and took a bite. It was good. Almost as good as the restaurant's. He could taste the fresh garlic and basil. "You made the sauce yourself, didn't you?"

"Is that a guess?"

"No," Jasper replied with a grin. "But I thought you weren't going to waste the effort on me?"

"Spaghetti sauce is a far cry from a seven-course meal."

Jasper laughed, relieved when the tension between them finally disappeared. "It's good." The silence that fell as they ate was comfortable at least. He resisted getting seconds in case Vincent tied him upside down tonight, instead sitting back in his chair and sipping his tea.

Vincent stood and cleared the table. He returned a minute later with a fresh contract and pen and placed them in front of Jasper. "Any questions?"

Jasper set his glass aside, taking a slow breath as he leaned forward. "All this includes sex, right?"

"Do you want it to?"

"Yes." Gods, yes.

"Then yes."

Jasper shivered and nodded as he picked up the paper. Vincent put away the leftovers while Jasper read the contract. It was exactly like the one he'd left at home, except this one had his limits listed.

He took another breath and signed.

Chapter Nine

THE CLICK of the pen shot an admittedly nervous thrill through Vincent. Considering how roughly the evening had started, Vincent was sure Jasper seeing him in his own home would ruin whatever fantasy the brat had. Or that Vincent would ruin it by being, well, himself. Christ, how long had it been since he'd had a sub in his home? A year? Not since before he'd gotten the club up and running.

Longer since he'd had a sub he could truly call his own.

He finished putting everything away, then picked up the contract and stared at Jasper's name scrawled across the bottom.

Jasper Saris.

He grabbed the pen to add his name below Jasper's—*Vincent Thornwell*—and set the pen and contract on the island.

Thankfully the not-so-insignificant act of signing a contract, no matter how short-term, eased a tension he hadn't been aware of until he'd had dinner with Jasper last week. But there was also the lingering flicker of nerves. There was a marked difference between playing a temporary role for someone in the club and taking on a sub.

Taking full responsibility for someone for any prolonged period of time was a major undertaking, especially with someone as green as Jasper.

He turned back to Jasper, enjoying the way he was trying not to fidget in his seat. "Come here, pet," he ordered, pitching his voice lower.

Jasper scrambled to his feet, stopping in front of Vincent and even putting his hands behind his back. Another Dom might have found the upturned gaze annoying, or played at being insulted, but Vincent saw no point in posturing. This had never been anything less than a core need for him, and Jasper was new enough to both kink in general and being Vincent's sub specifically that disciplining him for anything would be no different from disciplining him for ignorance.

Which was pointless, and a level of cruel Vincent had no interest in.

"Strip," Vincent said, holding his hand out for Jasper's clothes. He folded and set them beside the contract as Jasper complied. Then he stepped behind Jasper, resting his hands on Jasper's shoulders and slowly sliding them down his back to his hips. "You're to stay naked unless I tell you to dress. Do you understand?"

Jasper made a noise close to a squeak and shivered, but his voice was steady when he replied, "Yes, Sir."

"Good boy." He tilted his head, pressing light kisses to Jasper's neck and along his shoulder. Jasper smelled clean, like soap and a hint of the mango he'd caught in the club. Vincent's hands wandered, tracing the curves of Jasper's hips, following the dip of Jasper's spine and around to his chest.

His fingers found Jasper's nipples and absently circled them, earning hitched breaths. "We're going to go up to my playroom, and I'm going to redden your ass, pet. Then I'm going to play with your body. And if you're good, I may fuck you like you begged me to that first night."

Jasper leaned into Vincent with a moan. "Yes, Sir. I'll be good."

Vincent chuckled and smacked Jasper's ass. "Good. Then get upstairs."

He led Jasper into his playroom and closed the door. Inside wasn't unlike some of the rooms in the club. Two chests for his toys and paraphernalia, a spanking horse only a tad simpler than the one they'd used at the club, a small fridge, sofa, and a low table. One wall had a floor-to-ceiling mirror, and a suspension system lined the ceiling near it.

He pulled the spanking bench out and chuckled as Jasper eagerly settled himself over it. "You said maybe to cock rings. You're not getting off tonight unless I do. Do you need one?"

Jasper's whimper was desperate.

Vincent hoped that meant Jasper understood that how things went from here determined if he got off tonight. Not that Vincent had any intention of them going to bed less than utterly sated.

"Probably, Sir."

"Good answer." Jasper may have managed to hold off an orgasm when ordered, but he didn't want to push him into safewording tonight. He picked out a wide lightweight paddle and a leather ring and reached under Jasper to fasten it in place. "When's the last time you came, pet?" Once he'd secured Jasper's limbs, he slid a hand over his ass, taking his time warming the skin.

"Last Thursday," Jasper said, a pleading whine in his voice.

"Poor boy," he said with a soft laugh, relishing the pleasure that came with Jasper's obedience. He rested his hand on the small of Jasper's back, sliding along his spine to ease his shallow breathing. "Relax. You've done this before."

"Yeah, but—" Jasper squirmed, his breath stuttering as goose bumps rippled across his back.

"But?"

"It wasn't as real then."

"Because in the club I was a stranger who tied you up for a night?"

"Yeah," Jasper replied, arching beneath the fingertips ghosting down his spine.

Vincent curled his fingers, lightly dragging his nails against Jasper's skin, enjoying how responsive he was. And they hadn't even gotten started. "And now?" he asked, shifting to run the edge of the paddle over Jasper's thigh.

Jasper let out a shuddery groan. "Now I'm yours."

"Good boy." Vincent trailed his fingertips back to Jasper's ass and squeezed. "You're mine now, pet. You can trust me to take care of you. All I ask for in return is your honesty. Can you give me that?"

"Yes, Sir."

When Jasper exhaled and relaxed, Vincent pulled his hand away. He pressed the paddle against Jasper's thigh for a moment, then brought it down on his ass.

Jasper arched beautifully with a sharp moan.

He should make it a standing rule that Jasper wasn't allowed to come without permission if this was the result of a few days without release. The paddle landed again on the other cheek, and Vincent slipped into the peace of the steady rhythm, the sharp echo of leather on flesh, and the sweet sounds each swat coaxed from Jasper's throat.

Jasper's cries grew steadily louder as the paddle landed over and over again, his breathing turning ragged.

"That's it, pet," Vincent purred, using a bit more force as Jasper's ass flushed a nice red. "Your ass looks good like this. Pink and rosy and begging to be fucked." He enjoyed the sounds Jasper made and could only imagine how much better they'd be with Vincent buried inside him.

Jasper eventually let out a soft whimper, bordering on pained, before slumping on top of the bench. He let out a long sigh, soft, half-aborted whines following.

Vincent slowed the paddle, sliding his other hand up Jasper's back to run through his hair. "Good boy," he murmured. "Stay just like that for me."

He wasn't sure how close to subspace Jasper was, but he wasn't really pushing for it tonight. Walking Jasper through that recovery might be a bit too intense their first weekend together.

He helped Jasper to his feet and closer to the mirror. He checked the cock ring, palming Jasper's arousal and muffling the resulting moan with his lips. "Hands up," he ordered, fastening the cuffs at the end of the dangling chains around Jasper's wrists. They were high enough to keep Jasper's arms above his head without straining them.

Vincent stepped back, taking in the sight of his pet. All his. For this weekend and the next two months at the very least. "How do you feel?" he asked, walking around Jasper and admiring the red ass. He poked a cheek, the flesh turning white and then reddening again when he pulled away.

"Hot, Sir," Jasper murmured. "Hard and… good. I feel good."

Vincent hummed and turned Jasper around so he was facing the mirror. He stood behind Jasper and rested a hand against Jasper's throat. "You look good, pet." He rocked his hips forward, letting Jasper feel how hard he was, and relished the needy moan that earned.

"I want to make you feel good, Sir. Please."

"You are." Vincent slid his palms over Jasper's chest and down to his hips. He dragged Jasper back, forcing him onto his toes as he rocked forward again, grinding into Jasper's ass. "You're helpless to stop me from doing exactly what I want, pet," he added, digging his fingers into Jasper's hips before letting go.

Jasper stumbled a step as he regained his balance, a flush creeping up his neck when he finally saw himself in the mirror.

Vincent pinched Jasper's nipples, tormenting them until Jasper was panting and fighting to keep his legs under him. Then he slid his hands down Jasper's chest, chasing the tremors to his thighs and coaxing soft, pleading sounds from his throat.

Jasper's ribs were ticklish. As soon as Vincent's fingertips ghosted across them, he tried to twist down and away. Their first night in the club, Vincent had found a spot above Jasper's left hip; every time he pressed his thumb into it, Jasper moaned and relaxed. His nipples and ears proved to be the most sensitive—to everything from caressing to biting.

Everywhere Vincent touched seemed to earn its own reaction. It wasn't long until Jasper was struggling against the restraints and groaning in frustration. Vincent could get spoiled with a sub like this.

Once he was convinced he'd sought out every sensitive spot he'd find tonight, he slowly drew his hands away. "Breathe," he said, leaving Jasper to catch his breath as he grabbed a condom and the lube. As he prepped, he watched Jasper regain his senses and rest more of his weight against the restraints. He thumbed the button of his jeans open as he squeezed a generous amount of lube on his fingers and warmed it between them. By the time he'd gotten the condom on with his other hand, Jasper's breathing was more or less steady and his eyes were closed.

The first press of Vincent's fingers was enough to get him going again.

Jasper's eyes flew open, and he rocked into the pressure with a throaty moan. "Please."

Vincent hid a smile against the back of Jasper's neck, glancing at the mirror to watch him. "Please what?" he asked, continuing to work his finger in. He gripped Jasper's hip to keep him steady and grazed his teeth over warm flesh.

"Fuck," Jasper groaned, all but collapsing into Vincent's support. "Please fuck me, Sir?"

"Is that what you want?"

"*Yes*," Jasper said, somehow sounding offended despite the finger up his ass.

Vincent hummed, pretending to consider it as he worked another finger in. He reached up with his other hand and tweaked a nipple. "All right, then," he murmured, pulling his fingers out and sliding both hands to grip Jasper's hips instead, holding him steady as he slowly pressed inside.

Jasper's head tipped back, and he rocked his body against Vincent's with a long drawn-out moan. "Fuck," he breathed. "Fucking finally." He let out another needy moan as Vincent pushed in another inch. "So good, Sir. Been—*nnngh!*—getting off on imagining this."

Vincent pressed his lips against Jasper's neck, grazed his teeth along Jasper's shoulder, and left a mark on the back of his neck before slowly rocking his hips back and pressing in deeper. "Is this better than your imagination?"

"So, so much better," he groaned.

Vincent tugged Jasper's hips against his body as he sank in completely, letting out a soft sigh of bliss as he relished the tight heat. He slid his hands up Jasper's sides and teased his nipples to draw out a helpless whine. "You feel good, pet," he growled, grinding his hips forward as Jasper clenched around him.

"Way better than fingers," Jasper murmured, his expression dazed, his eyes dark in the mirror.

Vincent's chuckle came out as more of a groan. He snapped his hips forward, Jasper's fingers white around the chains as he arched the full length of his body. Christ, he was so responsive.

Now that Vincent had the time, he intended to take Jasper apart. Learn every inch of him. See what all made him tick and what could make him scream.

He shifted enough to hook a hand against Jasper's thigh and pull his leg up for a better angle. He dragged out his pleasure as long as he could, slowly fucking Jasper for several long minutes, watching the way Jasper twitched or arched or trembled in the mirror. Simply enjoying the experience of having Jasper at his mercy, with no rush to finish the scene and let the brat be on his way.

But then Jasper made the most exquisite, desperate sound with a quiet, "Please," and Vincent reached his limit.

"Please what, pet?" he demanded, gripping Jasper's hip and thigh tight enough to leave bruises.

"Please I-I want to watch you come."

Vincent would have accused Jasper of spouting pretty words he thought Vincent wanted to hear if it weren't for the eager expression on his face.

He growled as he bit Jasper's shoulder and slammed his hips forward. He meant to stop there and get himself back under control, but Jasper's shout urged him on, harder and faster, until he was burying himself deep with each thrust. He came with a harsh grunt, biting at Jasper's shoulder again, gentler this time, though not by much. He took several shuddering breaths, grinding his hips into Jasper as he rode out the last of his orgasm.

He rested his forehead against Jasper's neck, closing his eyes and steadying his breathing. Fuck. He'd expected Jasper to beg him for release. Had intended to let Jasper come with Vincent still inside him. Not to come first like an inexperienced, overeager teen.

Once he got his breath back, he pulled out and away. He tossed the condom in the trash and cleaned himself up, fixing his pants as he turned back to Jasper.

Jasper smiled at him, somehow appearing utterly content despite the painful-looking arousal between his legs.

Vincent definitely filed away that little detail as he tipped Jasper's head back and kissed him. He licked his way into Jasper's mouth, lazily exploring it while he idly circled a nipple with his thumb. He felt the tiny tremors that went through Jasper, coaxing more from him, until Jasper was over-sensitized and whimpering continuously against Vincent's lips.

He pulled back and reached up to free Jasper's wrists. "Couch," he murmured, supporting Jasper as he guided him to said couch. He got them settled, with Jasper lying down, his head in Vincent's lap. "You're not begging to come," he said, surprised.

Jasper nuzzled into Vincent's stomach, clutching at his shirt. "I'm being good."

Vincent laughed, dangerously close to relaxed. He buried a hand in Jasper's hair and tugged his head back so he could see Jasper's face. "You can always beg, pet."

Jasper licked his lips, shifting enough to put more pressure on Vincent's grip in his hair. "Please, Sir, can I come?"

"That does seem painful."

Jasper whined, curling on his side like it would ease his discomfort. "It almost hurts, but… it's good?" he replied, face scrunching like he wasn't sure he was saying the right thing. "I can almost still feel you inside me, and that makes it worth it. You make me feel good. I want to do that for you," he continued, rambling as he nuzzled into Vincent's stomach again.

Pleasure shivered down his spine as he flexed his fingers in Jasper's hair. "On your back, pet," he ordered, waiting until Jasper was sprawled face up over Vincent's lap to slide his hand over every inch of Jasper's chest. "You did well tonight," he added with a soft approving hum.

Jasper sighed and arched into the touches. He would have likely preened from the praise had he not been so far gone. "Thank you, Sir," he breathed, continuing to surprise Vincent at the oddest moments. He licked his lips, letting out a shaky breath as Vincent slid a hand down and removed the cock ring. "Oh fuck, please Sir, please touch m-aah!" He bucked his hips into Vincent's fingers, one hand clutching Vincent's wrist and the other gripping the edge of the couch.

Vincent palmed Jasper's dick in a featherlight touch before curling in a loose grip. With his other hand, he brushed against Jasper's cheek and traced over his lips. Jasper opened his mouth, eagerly sucking at Vincent's fingers. "Such a good boy."

Jasper might have been new to the scene, but he seemed to be taking to submission far more easily than most people Vincent had played with. The lack of a bratty attitude was a bit surprising, but this wasn't neutral ground like the club. This was Vincent's home, and he could understand Jasper wanting to make a good impression the first night of their contract.

He slowly thrust his fingers in and out of Jasper's mouth, muffling his moans and pleas. He tightened his other hand around Jasper's cock and stroked faster. "That's it. Getting close, aren't you, pet?" His own arousal valiantly attempted to return, though he wasn't interested in tormenting Jasper enough to make him wait.

At least not tonight.

He pulled his fingers out of Jasper's mouth and growled, "Come," as he gave a few quick, tight strokes.

Jasper screamed as expected, body taut as he shot all the way to his chin.

Vincent continued stroking until he'd milked every last bit of cum out of Jasper. Then he swiped up some of the mess and pressed his fingers into Jasper's mouth while he was still trembling with the last of his orgasm.

Jasper obediently licked them clean, nuzzling into Vincent's palm with a deep sigh.

When Jasper closed his eyes a moment later, his body slowly going lax, Vincent wasn't surprised in the least. Jasper might be able to get it up a few times in one night, but his stamina vanished after an orgasm. He shook his head, contentment settling in his limbs as he ran his fingers through Jasper's sweat-damp hair.

He waited a few minutes for Jasper to drift off completely before maneuvering him enough so that he could get up. Once he wiped Jasper down, he draped a light blanket over him and headed downstairs to finish cleaning up the kitchen. He locked the doors and flipped off the lights, grabbed Jasper's bag, and headed back upstairs. Vincent grabbed a water from the fridge and set the items on the table, letting Jasper rest while he showered. When he'd changed into a pair of sweats and an old shirt, he returned to the playroom to find Jasper sitting up with an empty bottle.

Vincent propped his shoulder against the doorframe. "All right?"

Jasper licked his lips, twisting the bottle cap on and off and looking anywhere but at Vincent. "Yes."

"Come here," Vincent said, raising an eyebrow when Jasper stood with the blanket wrapped around him. "Leave the blanket."

Jasper made a soft sound of protest, but he dropped it to the couch. The excited eagerness from earlier was gone. Now he seemed shy and uncertain as he stopped in front of Vincent.

"The bedroom is behind me on your right. The bathroom is down the hall on your left," Vincent said, tipping Jasper's chin up to meet his eyes. He liked this hesitant version of him too. "Shower and come join me in bed."

Jasper shivered and nodded. "Yes, Sir."

Vincent tugged Jasper closer and kissed him soundly. "You have ten minutes," he added as he pulled away and moved to the bedroom. He smirked as he heard Jasper scramble down the hall, the shower coming on seconds later.

The next two months were certainly going to be interesting.

Chapter Ten

Ten minutes. That was more than enough time for a shower, though the moment the water hit Jasper's ass, the shock of the sting was almost paralyzing. And that was a novelty he hoped never wore off.

He couldn't believe he'd finally been spanked and fucked like he'd wanted so badly the past few weeks. And Vincent was as good at sex as he was everything else. And the sounds he made when his composure finally slipped a little…. The memory alone was almost enough to get Jasper going again.

And now he was actually going to sleep with Vincent. In his bed. In his *home*. And wake up next to him, and maybe do it all again tomorrow. Instead of slinking home in a not-quite walk of shame.

If his brain hadn't been so blissfully hazy right then, he was sure he'd be having a panic attack.

This was all so unbelievable he pinched himself to make sure he wasn't dreaming. Which was pointless, considering his ass hurt worse than a pinch.

Then he remembered he was on a time limit and quickly finished up. He had to dash back to the playroom to get his toothbrush. Then he barely had time to get the toothpaste on all his teeth before he had to rinse and hurry down the hall, following the only light to the bedroom.

The door was open, and a lamp beside the bed was on. Vincent was sitting up reading a book. With glasses.

Jasper was struck frozen by the sight. First the apron and now glasses…. For some reason that made him question everything. Vincent was always so refined and in control; it was shocking to see him *domestic*.

"You're staring," Vincent said, glancing up as he closed his book.

Jasper grinned and stepped inside. "Am I not allowed to stare, Sir?" he asked, stopping beside the bed. He climbed in when Vincent pulled the covers back and pointed to the spot beside him. "Of course you have silk sheets," he muttered, stretching out and wiggling against them with a soft sigh.

He rolled onto his side, watching Vincent set his glasses on the nightstand. "Terrance said I should call you my sugar daddy," he said, blinking as he heard the book clatter to the floor.

"Don't you dare," Vincent said, leaning over to pick up the book.

"Sorry," Jasper murmured, though he couldn't quite help the grin tugging at his lips. He tried to hide his amusement but apparently not well enough since Vincent paused when he glanced over.

"What?"

Jasper shrugged and decided to hell with it. "Would you prefer glucose guardian?"

Vincent stared at him a moment, then rolled his eyes, though Jasper was sure he didn't imagine the twitch of Vincent's lips. "Absolutely not," he said and turned off the light.

Jasper rolled his eyes right back in the safety of the dark, making a face with a sigh. He was pretty sure Vincent wasn't annoyed, but still. The first few minutes alone with Vincent that didn't involve kink or sex, and he was already fucking this up.

He kept to his side of the bed, unsure what was allowed here. At the club he'd managed to cuddle into Vincent, but this was different. This was Vincent's *home*, and Jasper was glad he'd even been allowed in.

"Is there…." He cursed himself for not just going to sleep. Surely he couldn't fuck anything up while unconscious. "Keith said you might make me sleep on the floor. With a chain."

Vincent snorted, rolling onto his side, his face barely visible in the dark. "If you want to sleep on a mat while chained to my bed, I won't stop you, but it's not my personal preference."

"Okay," Jasper said, relieved. He might be enjoying things so far, but he much preferred being able to sleep in an actual bed.

Something close to a purr escaped him as Vincent's fingers ran through his hair. He took that as an invitation and shifted closer, twisting his fingers together so he wouldn't reach for Vincent's shirt. Even if the lack of a suit made Vincent seem more approachable, he wasn't about to push his luck. "Thank you," he said softly, closing his eyes. "For dinner and everything. I'm glad you found me at the club. And put up with me. And let me come here."

He was babbling, and he knew it, but he'd been fighting a twist of unease since waking up alone on the couch. It wasn't like tonight was much different from what they'd done in the club, but it sure as hell had been more intense.

It wasn't the sex either; he wasn't a virgin. But the spanking had pushed him somewhere. Someplace where it didn't matter what was going on so long as he felt safe and whatever Vincent did to him felt good. Keith had mentioned subspace briefly, but Jasper hadn't expected it to feel like this.

Everything was still a little hazy. Like there was a warm, fuzzy blanket wrapped around all his senses. He didn't exactly mind, but it left him feeling unbalanced. And clingy.

He wondered if this was how Matt felt when Jasper saw him with a dazed, contented, almost vacant expression some weekends when the others came back from the club.

And there was also the creeping doubt that Vincent might decide he wasn't interested anymore, now that they'd had sex. The thought was an incessant scratchiness against the pleasure-numbed cocoon of his brain.

He blinked as Vincent gave a light tug on his hair.

"Something wrong, pet?" Vincent asked, his soft voice doing wonders to soothe Jasper's nerves.

Jasper shook his head. Even sated and blissed out of his mind, he knew better than to voice any of those thoughts. "Can… would you mind holding me?" he asked instead.

"Come here." Vincent shifted and slipped both his arms around Jasper. He tucked the blanket in, then pressed a kiss to the top of Jasper's head. "Like this?"

Jasper nodded against Vincent's shoulder, releasing a shuddering breath as his body relaxed. That felt nice. Really nice. Even if it did come with a flood of *overwhelmed*. Like every tension and fear he'd been keeping bottled up suddenly evaporated and was trying to escape all at once.

He was fine. He wasn't going to cry. He could handle it. It would pass. He wasn't going to cry. It wasn't anything more than an emotional release. He wasn't—fuck.

Somehow he managed to keep his breathing steady as warm wetness slipped across his nose. Thankfully either Vincent didn't notice or didn't mind, though his palm did trace a slow path up and down Jasper's back.

He wasn't sure how long it took for everything to run its course, but it left him exhausted and even more hazy. In a pleasantly dull sort of way.

Vincent ran his fingers lightly through Jasper's hair with a soft, "Good night, pet."

Jasper tried to respond, but it came out a garbled mess. He was already mostly unconscious.

WHEN JASPER woke, the sun was already coming up and he was still tucked against Vincent's chest.

Vincent was asleep, and Jasper wasn't about to move and disturb him. Especially when lying half on top of Vincent was a thrill in itself. The fact he didn't have to get up and leave was even better.

He carefully snuggled closer, rubbing his cheek against Vincent's soft shirt. How could anyone think Vincent was anything other than a surly teddy bear? Who liked to smack people, maybe, but everyone had their vices.

He closed his eyes with a soft hum, resting his hand on Vincent's stomach. When he couldn't fall back asleep, he let his hand inch down and settle against Vincent's thigh. He ignored the nervous lurch in his stomach—what if Vincent didn't want to be touched like he hadn't in the club?—but considering Vincent had chained him up and fucked him last night, he was at least 30 percent certain it was okay.

Vincent let out a sigh as Jasper slid his palm over Vincent's morning wood. It turned into a soft moan when Jasper gently rubbed against it through the thin sweats.

Jasper shivered, surprised how much he wanted to touch Vincent and make him feel good. With Shayne it had always been quick and rough, and if Shayne got off first, Jasper usually had to take care of himself. Vincent hadn't neglected his pleasure once. Even when Jasper had refrained from touching himself, there'd been a sense of contentment in it.

Which made it easy to laze against Vincent's chest and gently coax him into full hardness while trying not to wake him.

"Are you trying to earn brownie points?" Vincent asked, his voice rough with sleep.

Oops.

"Does that work on you?" Jasper asked without lifting his head. Or stopping his fingers.

"No."

Jasper grinned, giving Vincent's balls a firm squeeze. Somehow, he didn't believe that answer.

Vincent sighed into Jasper's hair, sliding his hand over Jasper's back and down to rub the sensitized flesh of his ass.

Jasper bit back a moan, the sharp reminder of his spanking pulsing through his blood. His fingers tightened around Vincent's cock in return. It was definitely harder, and he wondered if he could handle being taken again so soon.

As if reading his mind, Vincent slid a finger between Jasper's cheeks and rubbed against his entrance. "How sore are you?"

Jasper couldn't hold back the soft moan even as he winced. "Sore. Your toys in the club didn't exactly prepare me for you," he murmured, squeezing Vincent through his sweats again.

Vincent's chuckle was half moan. "How do you feel about wearing a plug through the week? To prepare you."

"To class?" Jasper's dick twitched at the thought, but he seriously doubted he could handle that.

Vincent laughed. "I was going to suggest a few hours each night, but by all means."

Jasper grumbled and pressed his face into Vincent's chest. "You really are a dick," he grumbled. "Sir." He yelped as Vincent answered with a quick smack to his ass.

"I'm going to have to do something about that mouth."

Jasper lifted his head with a smirk. "You like my mouth."

"I wouldn't know, I haven't used it yet," Vincent replied, moving his hand from Jasper's ass to his face and pushing him away. "Make me breakfast."

Jasper spluttered as he stared at Vincent in shock. "What am I, your maid?"

"For the next two months," Vincent said, rolling onto his side with his back to Jasper. "Now, pet. And don't burn down my kitchen."

Jasper stared a moment longer in disbelief before crawling out of bed. He headed to the bathroom, still grumbling under his breath as he made his way down to the kitchen. He had half a mind to call Keith and ask if this was really part of the deal, but now that he thought about it, it wasn't like they could do nothing but have sex the entire time he was here.

Not that he was against trying.

The kitchen was well stocked, and when he found a container of blueberries, he settled on blueberry pancakes. They were half gone and were about to start wrinkling, so he picked out the bad ones and dumped the rest in the batter.

If this was really going to be how his next several weekends went, he'd have to learn how to cook better. He could at least make simple things, but he was nowhere near "making spaghetti sauce from scratch" good. Though considering how well Vincent was at cooking, why the hell was *he* stuck making breakfast?

Lazyass rich people.

Vincent joined him when Jasper was sliding the last deformed pancake onto a plate, and he paused at the sight of them with a soft laugh.

Jasper glared. "I said I could cook. Not cook well," he grumbled. He took a plate and a glass of milk to the table, wincing as he sat, but it wasn't as bad as he'd expected. "What do you plan on doing to me today?"

"Why would I tell you?" Vincent asked, settling next to him.

"Because I asked?"

Vincent raised an eyebrow, then turned back to his pancakes and took an almost hesitant bite. "Surprisingly edible."

"Ass," Jasper muttered. He glared as he shoved a forkful into his mouth.

"For someone at my mercy, you seem determined to test my patience," Vincent replied, though he sounded more amused than anything.

Jasper smirked. "What are you going to do, spank me?"

Vincent chuckled, and it had far more dark amusement than it had previously. "You said maybe to orgasm denial."

Jasper swallowed a whimper. Fuck. He had said maybe to that. But to be fair, he was sure everything seemed better in the controlled environment of his imagination.

He licked syrup off his lips and let out a slow breath. "How long?"

Vincent took another bite. "It's not about the duration. But for your mouth so far, I'll say tonight."

An entire day of Vincent likely tormenting him and not letting him get off? It sounded like torture. Wonderful torture. He really hoped the "wonderful" outweighed the "torture" part.

"Okay." He was going to regret that, but he'd gotten through the last week without touching himself. This couldn't be too much harder, right?

IT WAS so, *so* much harder. In every way.

Jasper had been half hard since breakfast, and the cock ring Vincent put on him made everything more surreal. And intimate. And arousing.

Vincent set up on the sofa with his laptop, doing Rich People Things, and Jasper didn't exactly have anything of his own to do. He didn't have any coursework due on Monday, so he took the chance to relax. Sprawled out on the sofa. Found a movie on Vincent's hundreds of cable channels. Even managed to rest his head in Vincent's lap without being pushed away.

By that afternoon, he was used to the way Vincent would casually touch him while he worked. The idle stroke of fingers through Jasper's hair or the not-so-idle toying with his nipples. But even getting used to the touches didn't make it any easier to control his body's reaction to them.

He'd gotten fully hard after lunch when Vincent pinned him against the fridge and kissed him for several long minutes. Several glorious minutes that could have lasted forever for all Jasper cared. He couldn't remember ever being kissed like that.

Like Vincent was interested in kissing him for the sake of kissing him, rather than it leading directly to sex.

And then Vincent pulled away, his hazel eyes a golden ring around his large pupils. Then he smirked, groped Jasper's still-pink ass, and walked away.

Jasper stood in the kitchen for minutes after, still pinned to the fridge by the ghost of Vincent's touch. Damn. He swallowed a whine as he watched Vincent settle in his place on the sofa and get back to work.

His body refused to cool down, but he didn't mind. He liked the slow curl of heat winding its way through his limbs. His lips still tingled from the press of Vincent's teeth.

He finally pushed off the fridge and ran his fingers over his lips, slowly making his way back to the sofa. He gave up trying to get his "problem" to go away, especially since he was mostly naked and hyperaware of every time Vincent so much as glanced at him. Which only served to heighten his arousal.

So far the "wonderful" part of this whole adventure was about even with the "torture."

Not long after that, Vincent finally put his laptop aside and turned his full attention on Jasper. "Have you learned your lesson?"

Jasper tilted his head away from the action movie he'd found. "Was I supposed to learn a lesson, Sir?"

Vincent snorted. "Not if you're enjoying your situation that much. If that's the case, I'll have to find something else to torment you with."

Jasper licked his lips, enjoying the subdued warmth that spread through him at the non-threat. "Promise?"

"How have you avoided the scene this long?" Vincent asked dryly.

Jasper shrugged. "I didn't think it really existed outside of porn or the web until I moved in with Amber." He crawled across the cushion between them and settled into Vincent's side, nuzzling at his shoulder.

"Do you know what cockwarming is?"

Oh fuck. "Basically?" He blinked when Vincent didn't continue, realizing he was actually waiting for Jasper to agree. That was as surprising as it was a relief, but there was still a teeny tiny part of him that wanted to be ordered. Maybe even forced. That's how this was supposed to work, after all. "Do—I mean, I'll cockwarm you. Sir." He didn't even squeak.

Vincent's eyes darkened as he spread his knees. "Get a towel."

Jasper hopped up, taking the stairs two at a time and retrieving his towel from last night from the bathroom. He paused with his hands braced on the sink, nerves and excitement making him momentarily queasy. Gods, what was he doing? Really? He'd known this wouldn't all be restraints and spanking, but it was still exciting to branch into other things. Even something that was basically a prolonged blowjob.

He could do this. Especially since Vincent wanted it. Wanted *him.* Or at least Jasper's mouth.

He took a deep breath and headed downstairs to hand over the towel.

Vincent pointed to the throw pillow between his feet. "On your knees."

Once Jasper was settled, Vincent pushed his sweats down and draped the towel over his lap. He reached over to the end table and pulled a condom out of the drawer, deftly opened it and rolled it on. Then he motioned Jasper closer, guiding Jasper's arms around his waist. "You're going to sit like this, with my cock in your mouth. Don't suck or swallow or try to get me hard. Understand?"

Jasper shivered, his own cock hardening again. Not that it had waned much. "Yes, Sir."

"Good. When you're ready."

Jasper licked his lips, glad Vincent wasn't ordering him to get right to it no matter how much he expected otherwise. He shifted his legs to sit sideways instead of kneeling, getting as comfortable as he could. Then he leaned in and opened his mouth. He wrapped his lips around Vincent's cock, wrinkling his nose at the taste of rubber. He took a breath and slowly inched his way down. It took every ounce of control not to start sucking Vincent off, but he managed to keep still.

Vincent sighed, burying a hand in Jasper's hair. "Good boy," he purred, scratching at Jasper's scalp. "Relax, pet. You're going to be there a while."

Jasper moaned and closed his eyes, taking slow breaths through his nose and forcing his tongue to stay still. Gods, this was weird. And hot. And a little humiliating. At least they were alone and no one could walk in on them.

After a few minutes, he was finally able to relax, sinking into Vincent's lap with a low moan.

In none of his fantasies had he ever imagined he'd be on the floor with some guy's cock sitting in his mouth. This was certainly not what he'd expected for the weekend, but he was happy he was finally able to touch Vincent. He dared to wiggle his fingers until his fingertips settled against the warm skin of Vincent's hips.

Vincent sighed again and seemed to relax into the couch, his fingers continuing to stroke through Jasper's hair as he turned the TV up a bit.

It was strangely intimate. Even more intimate than Vincent fucking him last night. He could practically feel Vincent's heartbeat through his cock, beating a steady rhythm against Jasper's tongue.

"If you need to stop, tug my shirt," Vincent murmured.

Jasper couldn't help the soft hum as warmth spread through him. He hadn't even thought about how he was supposed to safeword it he needed to. He carefully took Vincent a little deeper into his mouth and went still.

The towel soaked up the drool that leaked past his lips, and he tried not to be grossed out by it. He could only imagine how good it felt for Vincent, having his dick resting in a hot, wet mouth. He wanted to ask if he was doing it right, if Vincent was enjoying it, but if he wasn't, Vincent surely would have said something by now.

Minutes ticked by as he slowly gave himself over to whatever this was. Being a sub? He was a bona fide sub now, wasn't he? With a proper contract and everything. It might not have been what he'd expected, but somehow this felt like what he'd been wanting ever since he saw those first kinky pornos.

At some point he heard the movie ending, which seemed to be what Vincent was waiting for. His fingers tightened in Jasper's hair, tugging lightly to get his attention.

"Suck me off, pet," Vincent growled, his cock thickening in Jasper's mouth.

Jasper moaned as he came back to the present, wiggling his tongue as he forced his throat to swallow. It took an effort not to gag at the taste of the condom, but he managed. He gripped Vincent's hips and bobbed his head, sucking and working his tongue as best he could. Shayne said he gave shit blowjobs, but he hoped he could do better now.

Vincent grunted and gripped Jasper's hair tight as he let out a soft moan, his hips lifting a bit to push deeper, hitting the back of Jasper's throat.

Jasper gagged, his breath hitching as he instinctively tried to pull away, only for Vincent to stop him. His stomach shuddered with a strange mix of fear and excitement, and he didn't realize he was digging his fingernails into Vincent's hips until Vincent hissed.

"Jasper." He didn't sound angry, so Jasper risked a quick glance up at him. "If it's too much, pull my shirt."

That alone made him willing to do anything but stop. Shayne would have mocked him. He swallowed around Vincent's cock, moaning when he felt it twitch and thicken further inside his mouth. He gave a slight nod of his head, sliding one hand under the towel and against Vincent's thigh on the way to fondle his balls.

Vincent shivered with a sharp moan. His fingers tightened in Jasper's hair, and he almost gently pushed into Jasper's throat again.

Jasper squeezed his eyes shut as he fought his gag reflex, getting his knees under him, tilting his head to pull against Vincent's grip, and moaning in encouragement. Vincent let out a hoarse curse and settled his other hand on the back of Jasper's neck, his thumb pressing against Jasper's jaw to hold him steady as he lifted his hips again. This time, Jasper did gag as Vincent's cock hit the back of his throat.

Even if he'd wanted to pull away, Vincent's hands were unrelenting, forcing him down as his hips pushed up. Over and over again, until Jasper's eyes stung and his throat started to feel raw. Despite that, his own arousal was almost painful with how hard he was.

"That's it, pet," Vincent groaned, his voice rough and his breathing ragged. Because of Jasper. Because Jasper was giving Vincent exactly what he wanted.

Jasper shivered and flexed his tongue, sucking and swallowing around Vincent as he continued thrusting in deep. He gave a squeeze to Vincent's balls and tugged, moaning as Vincent cursed, burying both hands in Jasper's hair and gripping tight.

His hips jerked twice, and then Vincent was coming, his cock pulsing as he filled the condom.

Jasper moaned, part relief and part satisfaction, and held Vincent in his mouth until he'd stopped twitching. Once Vincent's fingers went slack, he pulled his mouth away, resting his cheek on Vincent's thigh.

"Good boy," Vincent said, voice softer than Jasper had ever heard it. It sent tremors of warmth through his entire body.

Jasper closed his eyes, content to sit there while Vincent stroked his hair for the next hour.

WHEN THEY finally headed to bed, Jasper was starting to realize he didn't mind not getting off all day. Even without the contentment that blanketed him after giving Vincent his first cockwarming-turned-blowjob, this had been the most relaxed and aroused and at ease he'd felt since…. He couldn't remember.

They hadn't talked much, but he had a feeling it was more because he hadn't dared speak first than from Vincent ignoring him. On the contrary, Vincent had been far more attentive than he'd been expecting.

Which really shouldn't have surprised him, considering everything else, but apparently he still had a ways to go until he stopped being surprised.

He stopped beside the bed as Vincent pulled out black straps from the top corners, shivering as he recognized the cuffs on the ends. Even without Vincent's smirk, he knew what he was likely in for.

He stretched out in the center of the bed and lifted his wrists to let Vincent secure them beside his head.

Vincent took his time, running his palms along Jasper's arms as he secured the cuffs and pressing Jasper's wrists into the mattress. Once he'd put a condom on Jasper, he straddled Jasper's hips, his thumbs rubbing small circles into Jasper's palms. When he leaned down, he claimed Jasper's lips and kissed him breathless, then moved to Jasper's neck. "I want to mark you," Vincent growled, biting Jasper's throat and making him jump. "Right here."

"Okay," Jasper moaned. "Yes." That didn't seem so bad. Actually it was pretty hot that Vincent wanted to mark him up. Lay a claim that others could see. Maybe he should have been worried that he got off on the idea, but it was nice to be wanted.

Jasper gasped as Vincent bit harder and moved his lips and tongue until there was surely a bright red mark standing out on his throat.

"Here?" Vincent asked, moving barely an inch.

"Yes," he said, shifting restlessly as Vincent went through the process again.

"Here?"

"An-anywhere," Jasper gasped, whimpering when he tried to move his arms to wrap around Vincent and was held in place. He jumped as Vincent bit his nipple and then did the same to the other before marking up his chest and stomach. "Fuck," he said when he glanced down at himself. He could feel the bright aches blossoming across his torso, but he knew he wouldn't regret them.

He dropped his head to the pillow and stared at the ceiling as Vincent continued, arching with a gasp when Vincent reached his dick. "Please, Sir!"

Vincent hummed and bit the inside of Jasper's thigh. "Patience."

Fuck patience. Jasper wasn't even aware he'd actually said that until Vincent chuckled and nipped him in warning.

"Poor boy," Vincent soothed, and Jasper almost hated how much Vincent seemed to be getting off on his desperation. That didn't bode well for him. Or maybe it did. What did Jasper know?

Vincent dug his fingers into Jasper's thighs and finally, *finally*, licked along the length of Jasper's dick.

Jasper groaned, thrashing as Vincent's tongue mercilessly teased the head. Fuck, fuck, fuck. So good. And dancing on the border of *too much* after being on edge all freaking day. If not for the condom, he would have come instantly.

Vincent held Jasper's hips down when he started to thrust, growling around his dick in an undeniable warning until Jasper stilled with a whimper.

"Please, please, please, Sir, please. Let me come, please," Jasper begged. Fuck. His cheeks were wet. It wasn't fair that Vincent pushed him to the emotional edge as easily as the physical one. Fucking bastard. He yelped as the cock ring vanished, Vincent's fingers squeezing tight in its place.

"Nooo," he groaned, gasping as Vincent took him all the way to the back of his throat. "Fuck, Sir, please! Please, I'll be good—I'll—fuck!"

Vincent pulled his mouth away with a dark laugh. "Why don't I believe you, pet?"

Jasper whined. "'Cause you're a dick, Sir," he muttered, yelping as Vincent pinched his thigh. Right where he'd bit.

"That mouth again. I must be losing my touch."

Jasper lifted his head to pout at Vincent. "You like my mouth."

"Do I?" Vincent replied dryly, pressing a finger of his free hand against Jasper's entrance.

Jasper gasped and rocked into it, his head dropping to the pillow. "Oh fuck. Yes."

"Not so sore anymore?"

"No, Sir," Jasper breathed. He let out a long pleading moan. "Please let me come, Sir. I'll do better to please you, I promise."

Vincent chuckled. "That one I can believe. You can come whenever you want, pet."

Jasper snarled and almost asked how the fuck he was supposed to do that when Vincent *wasn't letting him*, but then Vincent's mouth was on him again, and there was a finger in him, and the tight grip holding back his orgasm was gone, and then he was coming. His vision went white and spotty. Orgasm ripped through him fast enough that he hardly even realized it was finally happening until he was already coming in Vincent's mouth.

He slumped against the bed, fingers twitching with the after-tremors, gasping as he tried to catch his breath. Damn. That was…. Intense was an understatement. Best orgasm of his life was better. He glanced up with a tired smile as Vincent crawled up his body, blinking when he grasped Jasper's chin and kissed him.

"Good boy," Vincent purred once he pulled away. He released Jasper's wrists and disposed of the condom. Then he turned off the light and settled beside Jasper, resting a hand on Jasper's hip with tiny soothing circles.

Jasper continued staring at the ceiling in the dark, waiting for his limbs to cooperate again.

He finally found the strength to roll over and grope around until he got an arm over Vincent's stomach and curled into his side. "Night, Sir," he murmured. "Thank you."

Chapter Eleven

Sleep was a long time coming for Vincent, but he didn't mind. Especially not when Jasper was a warm, relaxed, softly snoring mound of flesh beside him. The brat was actually cute when he wasn't running at the mouth. The way sleep softened the edges of his sharp angles, and the closed eyes that hid the wary uncertainty that lived inside them.

Vincent may have suspected Jasper had deeper depths, but he still wasn't prepared for how easily Jasper surrendered and submitted himself.

Or the intensity of his own reactions.

It didn't help that Jasper responded as well to a spanking as he did to a kiss or a caress. As if he instinctively sought any and all attention, like a plant seeking sunlight. And the way he gave himself over to the scene, like he didn't know how to hold part of himself back. Completely unafraid to experience what Vincent had to offer in full.

Vincent had been like that, once upon a time. Now he tried to hold parts of himself back, even when the oxytocin flooding his system was screaming at him to collar Jasper and keep him forever.

He rubbed his eyes with a harsh sigh.

This was all such a bad, bad idea, but it was far too late now. He'd had a taste, and he wanted more. Much more. He wanted to find the edges of Jasper's limits. Wanted to see his expression when he was lost in both excruciating pleasure and sweet pain. Wanted Jasper's body as a canvas for the flogger of Vincent's dominion.

Fuck.

Fuck.

He wasn't young enough to wax poetic. And too old to be imagining an impossible future with a young man who hadn't even learned to kink-swim yet. Given a couple of years, Jasper would be able to hook any Dom he wanted. And Vincent was petty enough to enjoy knowing not even half of them would be able to satisfy the damn brat.

"Jasper," he whispered.

Jasper made a soft sound in his sleep and nuzzled closer, cutting Vincent off from continuing. Not that he knew what he would have said anyway.

He breathed a sigh into Jasper's hair instead and closed his eyes.

VINCENT WOKE while it was still dark, with a raging hard-on and a lingering dream involving Jasper and tentacles. He scrubbed both hands against his face with a groan. Christ. Jasper was affecting him in all the wrong ways.

His only consolation was that Jasper affected him in all the right ways too.

The cause of his torment was stretched out on his stomach, an arm thrown over Vincent's chest. The covers had ridden down enough that Vincent could make out the curve of Jasper's ass in the dark.

He groaned again at the sight, reaching into the drawer of his nightstand for lube and a condom, thankful he could at least take care of one of his problems. The rest he'd deal with later. He smeared lube on his fingers, rolled over, and pinned Jasper beneath him, grazing his teeth against Jasper's sleep-warm shoulder.

Jasper stirred with a soft "Nnngh?" and pushed into Vincent's probing finger, his eyes fluttering open. "Vinc't?"

Vincent chuckled, adding a second finger as he nibbled at Jasper's ear. "I'm going to fuck you, pet," he growled.

Jasper shuddered and woke a bit more. "Oh. Yes, Sir," he gasped, gripping the sheets by his pillow. He spread his legs and hiked up a knee.

Vincent took it as the eager acceptance it was. He pulled away long enough to get the condom on and lubed up, then stretched out against Jasper's back. The tentacle dream still clung to him, and he couldn't help but indulge the fantasy. Jasper would look good with tendrils of color coiled around his arms and legs. Held open and at Vincent's mercy, like when he'd been tied to the chair.

He pressed his face into blond hair, breathing in the lingering scent of his own shampoo as he rubbed himself between Jasper's asscheeks.

Apparently finally having sex told Vincent's body to make up for lost time, rather than simply scratching the itch. Another thing to deal with later.

He nudged his knee in behind Jasper's and reached down to guide himself in.

Jasper moaned and rocked to meet him, his body pliant with sleep. "So good," he breathed, his eyes closing again.

Vincent buried himself balls-deep and held there, lying on top of Jasper and slowly grinding into him. His hands slid to Jasper's wrists, pinning them and relishing the helpless sound it earned. "Good boy," he murmured, then kissed across the back of Jasper's neck. He didn't need much to get off with the heat of the dream still coursing through him. His imagination and Jasper's eagerness did the rest. He muffled his grunt in Jasper's hair as he came, still doing little more than grinding into him.

Jasper sighed and slumped into his pillow, already fast asleep again.

Vincent stayed where he was, buried inside him, and breathed in the scents of Jasper, sweat, and sex. Eventually he pulled away, tossed the condom to the floor to deal with later, and went back to sleep.

HE WOKE with a start from Jasper's horrified yell, rolling over to find Jasper hopping on one foot while picking a condom from between his toes.

"You're disgusting," Jasper grumbled, shooting a dark glare at the bed. "My dick just shriveled up and died."

"Breakfast," Vincent said, ignoring the dramatics and closing his eyes again.

"At least that explains why my ass is sore again."

Vincent was instantly awake, lifting his head to stare at Jasper. "You don't remember?"

Jasper tossed the condom in the trash and turned back to the bed. "Not really," he said with a yawn. He raised an eyebrow. "Is that bad?"

Vincent took a slow breath and let it out. Shit. "It wasn't listed in your limits."

"What wasn't?"

"Somnophilia." When Jasper blinked in confusion, he explained, "Sex with someone who's asleep."

"Oh. Yeah, that didn't exactly come up when I was talking with Keith," Jasper said dryly. He tilted his head, moving back to the bed and crawling in next to Vincent. "Why do you look like you're about to be sick?"

Vincent flinched, annoyed that he apparently wasn't hiding it well enough. "I'm not," he lied, focusing on the warmth of Jasper's body nearly touching his own. If he was still comfortable being that close….

"Bullshit, *Sir*. I thought you weren't going to lie?" Jasper poked Vincent's arm. "It's not like you raped me, right? You asked and I said yes, even if I was half asleep."

"You don't know that," Vincent snapped, biting his tongue to keep from lecturing Jasper on being too trusting. That would be counterproductive—both to the point at hand and the fact they had a contract. His therapist would be so proud.

Jasper snorted. "I might not remember everything, but I do know that much. That's what you always do when you make me do something."

Vincent frowned, blinking as Jasper crawled closer and straddled his lap. He tipped his head back, watching Jasper as arms settled around his shoulders.

"If you want, I can add sumophil-whatever to the yes column."

"Somnophilia," Vincent corrected, trying not to be distracted by having Jasper in his lap.

Jasper smirked, leaning in and pressing a chaste kiss to Vincent's lips. "Kiss me, Sir," he murmured. "It's already Sunday."

That was enough to kill his lingering panic, and Vincent slid a hand into Jasper's hair to hold him close as he obliged. He toppled Jasper to the bed and pinned him, adding a few fresh marks to his neck and chest. When he finally pulled back, Jasper was flushed and dazedly wanton.

Jasper licked his lips and wiggled beneath Vincent. "We could skip breakfast and stay in bed."

Well. How could he possibly say no to that?

For once he didn't bother with restraints, and he was all too happy to indulge Jasper in making out and wrestling and coming in each other's hands. As if one of them wasn't three decades old and should have had better control of his libido.

When they'd cooled, he trailed his fingertips down Jasper's spine and over his ass. "Don't pass out," he said, giving the supple flesh a light smack when it wiggled.

Jasper laughed and snuggled closer. "Won't. Feel too good," he said, resembling a cat who'd gotten the cream, canary, and car rubs all at once. "Really good, actually. Better than good."

Vincent snorted and flexed his fingers in Jasper's hair. "Then you should shower and get started on breakfast."

Jasper gave an exaggerated whine and reluctantly pulled away. "Yes, Sir," he said, and Vincent couldn't resist pulling him in for a last quick kiss before sending him on his way.

Fuck.

No, later. Much later.

Jasper was right, it was already Sunday. Which meant he needed to switch perspectives from Dom to Responsible Adult.

He didn't even want to think about the mess waiting for him at the club after taking a weekend off. Which, to be fair, was realistically likely to be less of a mess than expected. He didn't make a habit of hiring idiots.

While Jasper used the bathroom down the hall to shower, Vincent used his en suite to take his own. Then he took his time dressing in a suit and fixing his hair. Finally he headed to the kitchen.

Where he found Jasper in his apron.

So much for controlling his libido.

Vincent pressed against Jasper's back and slipped his hands under the apron to slide across warm skin.

Jasper shivered and leaned into the touches. "I'm cooking, Sir."

"You're almost done," Vincent replied, but he pulled away. Busied himself with fixing a cup of coffee instead of molesting his sub. His so very molestable sub.

He'd have to find a way to deal with the urge to fuck Jasper every time he saw him, without actually fucking Jasper every time he saw him.

Once they sat down to eat, he checked the time. "My driver will be here soon." He snickered when Jasper grumbled. "Not missing your home yet?" he asked dryly.

Jasper shrugged, sopping up runny egg yolk with a piece of toast. "I like being here."

Vincent hummed and sipped his coffee. "Coming back next week, then?" he asked. Not that he was worried about the answer. The weekend had gone far better than he'd expected.

"*Duh,*" Jasper said, slanting an offended glare at him.

"Do you need to change anything on your limits?"

Jasper hesitated before shaking his head.

Vincent raised an eyebrow. That wouldn't do. Especially with the barely avoided disaster that morning. "Lying includes lies of omission, FYI."

Jasper rolled his eyes and finished the last of his food. "I didn't hate anything you did enough to say no to it. It's just…." He shifted in his seat, toying with his fork. "When I woke up on the couch alone. Can I add that you have to stay until I wake up?"

"Of course," Vincent replied. He raised an eyebrow when Jasper slumped with relief. "Anything else?"

When Jasper shook his head, Vincent pushed his chair back and motioned Jasper into his lap. "I'll expect you not to touch yourself without my permission," he said, pressing a kiss to Jasper's shoulder.

Jasper snorted, leaning into Vincent's chest. "So I can't get off until I come back? Great," he muttered.

Vincent pinched Jasper's ass. "Maybe not even then."

"You're—" Jasper started, then apparently decided against finishing that thought.

"Oh, you can learn." Vincent chuckled when that earned a glare, dragging his fingertips over Jasper's thigh. "Should I give you something to remember me by?"

Jasper shivered, shamelessly parting his legs. "Yes, Sir. You definitely should."

"Good. Go get my paddle." Vincent smirked when Jasper blinked at him. He ignored the grumbled curses thrown his way as Jasper headed upstairs and dumped the dishes in the sink for later.

So many laters on the list. It was dangerously close to becoming a theme.

When Jasper returned, Vincent bent him over the kitchen table and restored his ass to a nice rosy pink. Vincent spent a long minute groping him after, then sent him to dress.

The driver showed up ten minutes later, and Vincent joined Jasper in the back seat.

When they reached Jasper's place, he tangled his fingers in unruly blond hair. "Call or text me if you need me," he said. He tried to kiss away the pleased smile that settled on Jasper's lips, but that only made it worse until he had to threaten to kick Jasper out on his ass so they could part ways.

Chapter Twelve

Vincent's therapy session on Monday went like any other had the past few years, aside from it having started with him saying, "I think I made a mistake."

In her reflection in the window, Dr. Cohn raised an eyebrow. "You got rid of the flamingo?"

He turned away from staring at the fountain outside, relaxing despite himself. "You know I didn't," he said dryly. Why she'd suggested he get such a horrendous lawn ornament he still didn't understand, but it was basically a permanent fixture now. If she hadn't been his therapist for the last several years—the only one he'd been able to stand for more than two sessions—he might have written it off as a joke. But she'd been one of his sole pillars of support since the accident that nearly destroyed his life. Had shined a light into some of Vincent's darkest corners and never looked at him differently after.

He thought maybe the flamingo was meant to give him something outrageous to smile at every day, but even in the deepest depths of his pain and depression, it never elicited more than a strong desire to burn it. Now it'd been there long enough he was *almost* sentimental about it.

With a sigh, he sat in his usual chair and crossed his legs. "I've taken on a sub."

"Ah." If she hadn't been Vincent's therapist long enough to know every facet of his life, he might have been impressed by her lack of surprise. "The one you mentioned a couple of weeks ago?"

"Yes." He realized he was flicking his foot and forced it to stop. He curled his fingers into fists against the arms of the chair to avoid tapping them too. He was not going to fidget. Except a glance at Dr. Cohn told him he was already too late to hide whatever he was feeling.

Fuck.

"And yes, he's amazing," he said, before he could backtrack. If there was going to be a "later," now was the time. Even if he did want to keep Jasper to himself.

Sparing all the sordid details, Vincent let her drag out and help sort his complicated reactions to having a sub again.

Finding one who was compatible with him, at least on the level he needed, was exhausting enough he'd stopped searching ages ago. Or rather he hadn't even tried. He woke up the day after kicking Adam out, too tired and apathetic to try again. He'd offered a few contracts in the years since, but never a second to the same sub. His work was enough to keep him busy, and playing in the club took the edge off enough he could usually ignore the rest of his desires.

And to have that hope shoved in his face now, when he was least expecting it and the least prepared…. Well, that was what alcohol was for.

Too bad he didn't drink anymore.

They didn't exactly uncover any earth-shattering revelations, but Vincent felt better by the end anyway. More at ease. Not quite as fatalistic.

He'd touched base with Jasper to ensure he was holding up. Not that he didn't want to text more, but he had responsibilities, and Jasper had college. And he refused to be one of those overbearing Doms who tried to control everything. If Jasper needed him, he had to trust Jasper would reach out.

VINCENT MADE it to Wednesday before giving in.

He didn't need a reason to call Jasper, but he ordered a gift anyway. A pale yellow glass plug and a matching dildo, a bit larger than the one he'd used on Jasper at the club. As well as lube. The local shop was one he'd frequented and still did on occasion for items he didn't want to wait for in the mail. He knew the owner well enough to get same-day delivery by his own staff rather than a third party.

Once he got the notification that it'd been delivered, he called Jasper.

"Hello?"

"Try again," Vincent replied.

There was a pause, and then Jasper said, "Hello, Sir?"

"Better." Vincent sat back in his seat, absently flipping through his paperwork. "Did you receive my gift?"

"Yeah," Jasper said, the grin evident in his voice. "Can I open it?"

"Not yet." He'd teach Jasper patience even if it was teaching him to pretend. "How have you been?"

"Um. Fine?"

Vincent stifled a sigh, though he wasn't too surprised by the response. He wasn't one for idle chitchat either. "Pet."

"Sir?"

"Nothing interesting the last few days?" he asked, and he could practically hear Jasper's shrug.

"Not really. Aside from the shooter drill that happened this morning. It was before my classes started, though, so…."

Vincent frowned, unaware those even existed in colleges. "That sounds horrifying," he said, keeping his voice neutral. It might have been a reminder of the gap in their ages, but he was glad he'd finished school when such things were less common.

"Yeah. I guess." Jasper fell silent, and Vincent found himself at a loss for how to help. Thankfully he didn't have to. "Just sucks, y'know? 'Cause they don't announce it, so you never know if it's real or not."

"Fuck," he said, not really meaning to say that aloud.

Jasper let out a soft humorless laugh. "Yeah. Basically." And then he proved to be a master at changing the topic of conversation with, "Soooo, what's in the box?"

And Vincent wasn't heartless enough not to allow it. "Are you alone?"

There were a few moments of silence and the sound of a door closing. "I am now."

"Where are you?"

"My room."

"Good. Strip."

Jasper's breath caught, and Vincent was sure he'd tossed the phone on his bed. After a few curses and the sound of something being knocked to the floor, he was back. "Done."

Vincent chuckled. "Put me on speaker and open it." He stood and flipped the lock to his office, listening to the faint sound of the box opening and the rustling of paper.

"What the—*Seriously?*"

"Do you not like them?"

"I…." Jasper's voice grew louder as he moved closer to the phone. "You want me to use these?"

"Can you handle it?" Vincent asked.

Jasper snorted. "I think I can handle a dildo and a plug, Sir."

"Get to it, then."

There was a beat of silence. "Now?"

"Problem?"

"No, but… is this basically phone sex?"

"Yes. First time?"

"Yeah."

Vincent chuckled. "There's lube in there too. Get comfortable and then coat your fingers."

"Are you going to walk me through prepping myself too?" Jasper asked cheekily.

Vincent snorted. Jasper was lucky he wasn't there to smack his ass. "Do you need me to?"

"No. But I like listening to your voice," Jasper replied quietly, and Vincent could easily imagine the flush in his cheeks.

"Is that so," Vincent purred, pitching his voice lower. And was rewarded by Jasper's soft moan. "Are you ready yet?"

"Yes, Sir."

"Are you on your back?"

"On my knees. With my arm on my pillow."

Vincent leaned back in his chair as he pictured it. "Press a finger in." He closed his eyes as Jasper gasped, and gave him a moment to adjust. "Tell me how it feels."

"Awkward," Jasper murmured, the sound of movement on the bed following. He let out a soft grunt. "Ass doesn't sting anymore at least."

"I'll make it last longer next time."

Jasper laughed. "Can't make it worse than popping a boner in the middle of class."

"Did anyone see? And add another finger."

"No, I got rid of it be-before the lecture ended," Jasper said, ending with a hitched sigh. "Feels better now. Still awkward, though."

"Are you moving your fingers?" Vincent asked, absently palming himself through his pants.

"And rocking my hips." Jasper's voice was starting to sound strained. "Are you at work?"

Vincent hummed an affirmative. "Can you get another finger in?"

"Yeah." Jasper grunted softly, letting out a shuddering breath. "Done."

"Switch to video," he said, pressing the button. A moment later, Jasper's face came into view, his cheeks pink.

"Hello, Sir," Jasper said with a grin.

"Enjoying yourself, pet?" Vincent asked.

"Oh yeah."

"Good. Let me see you."

Jasper rolled to his back, lifting the phone above him as he stretched out on the bed.

Vincent raked his eyes over Jasper. Much better than his imagination. "Pinch a nipple," he ordered, palming himself again.

Jasper rubbed his hand over his chest before pinching his nipple and tipping his head back with a soft groan. As responsive as ever.

"Again," Vincent growled, pressing harder between his legs as Jasper arched into his own hand. "Let me see the rest of you."

The phone moved lower, over Jasper's stomach to his erection. If he'd suspected Jasper of exaggerating his enjoyment, he had ample proof of it now.

"Get the plug. I want to watch you put it in."

Jasper groaned, the phone showing the ceiling while he got the plug ready. Then he picked it up again, tilting it so Vincent could watch. He pulled his legs up and apart and reached between them.

"Lower," Vincent said, guiding Jasper into giving him the best angle. Once he had a clear view of Jasper's ass, he hummed. "Right there, pet. You can put it in now. Slowly."

He unfastened his pants as he watched, listening to Jasper's sighs and moans as he worked the plug in. "It looks good in you," Vincent purred, gripping himself and giving a slow stroke.

"Would feel better if it were you, Sir," Jasper moaned, seating the plug completely and rocking his hips against it.

Vincent chuckled, squeezing himself. He couldn't exactly deny that. "You like me fucking you?"

"Yes, Sir. Loved feeling you stretch me open. Loved feeling it the next morning." Jasper moaned, sounding breathless. "Will you fuck me again, Sir?"

"Let me see your face, pet." He pressed his thumb against the tip of his cock as Jasper came back into view, his lips parted and eyes dark. "Tell me how you want me to fuck you."

Jasper frowned. "Like, where?"

"If you could choose the scene and what I did to you. No dark fantasies you want to explore?"

Jasper licked his lips and fell silent as he considered. "If I could choose how it happened, I think I'd like to wake up to you kissing me and then… fucking me nice and slow. Without the spanking or restraints, and me being able to touch you, Sir," Jasper said quietly.

Well, that was unexpected. And Vincent couldn't deny it sounded nice, if dangerously close to something more than what he would have planned for their weeks together. Some part of him was still waiting for this to turn out like his other contracts. Brief weeks of amazing sex until they got on each other's nerves enough to break it off.

Jasper got under his skin, there was no doubt about that. But it wasn't the same as with Adam or the few after him. As much as he wanted to find out what made Jasper tick, there was also the need to hold him after. And the fact that Jasper let him, seeming to need more from Vincent than just the kink, was a bit terrifying.

Especially when combined with the annoying desire to give Jasper anything he asked for.

"I'll keep that in mind, pet," Vincent growled, ignoring the unreasonable urge to hang up when Jasper smiled at him. "How's the plug feel?"

Jasper grinned and lifted the phone enough Vincent could watch him wiggle. "Feels good, Sir."

"Good enough you can keep it in until you go to bed?"

Jasper moaned. "Yes, Sir."

"Without coming."

He moaned again, though it sounded more like a whine. "Yes, Sir."

"Good. Now let me watch you touch yourself. Start with your nipples."

Jasper did whine then, but he obeyed. He rubbed a finger over his nipple, pinching hard enough to make himself arch off the bed. And he hadn't even had to be told.

"Good boy." Vincent stroked himself as he watched, ordering Jasper to lick his hand and pump his own cock, slow and loose enough to keep him from getting too frustrated. "That's it," he purred. He let out a soft moan of his own when he was getting close.

"Are—are you jerking off?"

"Mm-hmm." Like he would let this opportunity go to waste.

Jasper moaned, turning the camera to his face. "Let me see, Sir. Please?"

Vincent raised an eyebrow, then lowered the phone so Jasper could see his cock, enjoying the whine that came through a moment later.

"Fuck, Sir. I wish I was there so I could get my mouth on you."

Vincent's cock twitched at the memory, and he swiped away the precum with his thumb. "Keep talking," he growled.

Jasper flushed, licking his lips. "I'd kiss your cock and suck it clean," he said, sounding unsure of what he was saying, but he seemed to gain more confidence once he started. "And let you fuck my mouth. Let you come down my throat. Fuck," he groaned. "Can I watch you come? Will you come for me, Sir?"

Vincent tipped his head back with a groan as he came, spilling into his hand. Fucking brat.

"That was hot." Jasper grinned, rubbing his hand over his chest.

Vincent's chuckle came out as more of a gurgle, and he silently cursed himself. "I'll see you Friday, pet," he said once he could speak properly. "Don't get off before then." He hung up as soon as he heard a "Yes, Sir," and tossed his phone aside.

Fuck. *Hot* was an understatement.

He cleaned himself up, fixed his pants, and slumped in his seat to enjoy a few moments of postorgasmic bliss.

Unfortunately the lack of a warm body against his own meant it wasn't as blissful as it could have been.

Christ. One weekend and he was already getting addicted.

With a curse, he pushed to his feet and headed out to make sure his club hadn't burned down while he was slacking off.

Chapter Thirteen

Jasper expected the worst part of the week to be going back to mundane life, with college and work and the occasional chat with Vincent, but no. The worst part was constantly getting aroused and not being able to do anything about it.

He *could* have taken care of it. Vincent wouldn't know unless Jasper told him, and it wasn't like Vincent could really do anything to keep him from masturbating. But the few times he actually started to, he hadn't been able to finish.

The thought of disappointing Vincent killed his boner every time. Not to mention the fact it could be considered lying if he didn't own up to the deed.

There had to be a good reason Vincent didn't want him masturbating. He knew Keith or Amber would probably tell him if he asked, but he couldn't bring himself to let them in on any of the sordid details of his sex life.

So he suffered in silence. Enough that his coworkers at the theater gave him shit about needing to get laid.

By Friday afternoon, he was more than ready for Vincent to tie him up and have his way with him.

His phone dinged with a text as he tossed his bag onto his bed. Jasper was sure Vincent had his schedule memorized, since he'd gotten home from his last class barely ten minutes ago.

Bring any schoolwork you have.

Jasper groaned. Did that mean they weren't going to be enjoying themselves this weekend? Then again, there'd been several hours last weekend where he hadn't done anything but watch TV while Vincent worked on his laptop. It'd been surprisingly peaceful.

Really, spending time with Vincent was something he looked forward to. Sex or not.

With a sigh, he turned on his music and grabbed a textbook. He had a couple of hours to kill, and he spent it making notes for the next chapter in his physiology course.

The car arrived at six, and he settled into the back seat with his bag. It didn't take long for him to realize they were heading towards the club rather than Vincent's home, and he straightened in anticipation. Was Vincent planning something new? Not that he was worried, even if Amber had warned him against jumping in too deep with the new experiences. He could handle a bit of experimenting.

There was an ambulance parked at the corner with its lights flashing when they arrived, and a small crowd had formed on the sidewalks. Inside, everyone had been kicked out of the dungeon and were lingering near the open bar. As soon as he neared the sitting area, one of the staff motioned for him and led him upstairs.

"Vincent is handling an emergency at the moment, but he should be done soon." And then they were gone, leaving Jasper alone in Vincent's empty office.

Well, so much for this being planned playtime.

He dropped his bag on the black leather sofa and eyed the wall covered with security feeds. Most showed the main floor, with a few on the outside by the doors, but the ones in the center were the private rooms.

He knew there were feeds from reading the membership application, but he hadn't known Vincent had them in his office.

He skimmed over the screens, but he didn't see Vincent anywhere. None of the cameras seemed to show the dungeon. And since he wasn't a perv, he turned away and poked around the office. Not that there was much to it. An expensive desk, a filing cabinet, an aloe plant, and another fluffy one that a quick Google search said was a ZZ plant.

The sofa had a glass coffee table in front of it, and across from that was a small bookcase. Most of the books were BDSM related, but there were also philosophy, poetry, and a few fantasy novels.

He grinned as he spotted a familiar large blue book. He pulled it out and thumbed through *Hitchhiker's* well-worn pages. At least Vincent had good taste.

The door opened, and Jasper quickly put the book back, turning in time to see Vincent stalk in. He was pissed. Which probably did not bode well for the weekend.

Vincent paused as he caught sight of Jasper, his shoulders releasing some of their tension, but he was clearly one wrong word from biting someone's head off.

"Are you okay?" Jasper asked.

"I'm fine." Vincent's voice was sharp as he moved to his desk. He pulled out a piece of paper and shut the drawer with a bit more force than necessary. "I need you to sign this to be in here. It's a standard confidentiality agreement, saying you won't repeat anything about what you see on the cameras."

Jasper nodded and picked up a pen, glancing over the form without really reading it before signing. He watched Vincent tuck it away in the filing cabinet in silence.

Vincent's shoulders were tense again as he shed his jacket and tossed it over the back of his chair. He took a slow breath, finally turning to Jasper and focusing on him. "Have you eaten dinner?"

"Not yet." He might have been hoping they would have dinner together.

Vincent rifled through his drawer again and handed over another paper. "I'm going to be stuck here a while. With the clusterfuck downstairs, I'm catering dinner for the staff from here tonight."

Jasper took the paper and inched towards the sofa, trying not to call any more attention to himself. Not that he was really worried about Vincent biting *his* head off. But old habits were hard to break, and older, angry men kicked his flight instincts into overdrive. He sat on the sofa and studied the menu for a restaurant down the street.

A few minutes later, someone knocked on the door. Vincent made an annoyed sound as he opened it to admit a slender blond woman in a pantsuit.

She closed the door behind her and smiled faintly at Jasper before focusing on Vincent. "The paramedics have gone. She refused to be admitted to the hospital, so they're going home."

Vincent made another annoyed sound, then sighed and sat on the edge of his desk. "You're sure it was an accident?"

"Yes, I saw it myself. She was fine until someone cried out on the other side of the room, and it looked like she instinctively started to get up, which caused the scalpel to cut deeper than intended."

Jasper winced. Vincent really hadn't been kidding about people using scalpels and needles?

Vincent pinched the bridge of his nose. "I'd rather all the medical and sharp instruments be moved out of the dungeon and to one of the playrooms." The woman pursed her lips, and he sighed again. "You disagree?"

Jasper spoke without thinking. "It might remove distractions, but it also adds time for anyone to help if something goes wrong," he said, immediately sinking farther into the sofa when Vincent stared at him.

The woman pointed at Jasper. "What he said."

Vincent grimaced and rubbed his forehead. "Fine," he said tightly. "I'm ordering from Lucio's if you can get everyone's order."

"Sure," she said, wiggling her fingers at Jasper as she closed the door behind her.

Vincent stayed where he was, fingers pressed between his eyes.

Jasper gave up pretending to read the menu and cleared his throat, refusing to back down even when Vincent turned to him. He was still pissy. Great. "Can I help with anything?"

After a long moment of silence, Vincent let out a slow breath and shook his head. "No, it should all be taken care of." He stood and moved around to sit in his chair, glancing at the monitors and then focusing on his laptop.

When the woman returned with a list of orders, Vincent phoned them in, along with Jasper's.

The silence was almost deafening, and Jasper only managed to read two paragraphs in his textbook before nerves and curiosity finally got the better of him. A quick glance at Vincent still showed a furrow of annoyance on his face, but at least he no longer seemed one step away from violence. "Do you wanna talk about it or something?"

Vincent let out an explosive sigh and slumped in his chair, which didn't even squeak with the sudden shifting of weight. "Not really. As much as I want to rave about people being idiots, everyone swears it was an accident."

"People playing with scalpels are idiots?" Jasper guessed, relaxing a bit when Vincent's annoyance shifted into amusement.

"Far be it from me to judge anyone's kinks," he replied dryly. "I wanted to forbid any kind of blood play in the common area, but too many members insisted on keeping it." He ran a hand through his hair, and Jasper couldn't help but grin when it mussed up the perfect styling.

He tossed his textbook to the other end of the sofa and moved to the desk. After he'd nudged Vincent's chair back enough to make some space, he pushed the laptop aside and took its place. "If it was an accident, why are you still pissy over it?"

Vincent frowned at him even as he curled his hands against the backs of Jasper's calves. "Having to call the paramedics to my place of business isn't something I appreciate. This is exactly the kind of thing I wanted to avoid."

"They knew the risks, though," Jasper said. "I read the whole membership packet." No medical equipment was owned by the club but could be bought. Anything used for blood play had to be purchased new or brought in and tagged at check-in.

Vincent's disgruntled expression was almost comical, but Jasper managed not to laugh. "I think I'm going to punch the next person who says you're a dick." Which was probably going to be Matt, but he had it coming.

Vincent blinked at him, his expression shifting into something Jasper couldn't quite name. "I'm going to be stuck here until we close," he said, sliding his hands up to rub his palms against Jasper's knees. "I can have the driver take you home to wait."

Jasper did not pout. "Do you want me to leave?"

"No," Vincent answered quietly.

"Damn right you don't." With a grin, Jasper leaned forward and kissed Vincent's nose, then hopped off the desk to avoid making that any more awkward. He grabbed his book and settled on the sofa again. "I'll wait here, then." At least studying could be done anywhere, and the sofa wasn't as uncomfortable as its price tag likely suggested. He dug out his earbuds, put one in, and started his music.

The hours ticked by in silence while he studied. Dinner was delicious and came with a slice of chocolate cake that earned him more than one heated glance when he moaned while eating it. Vincent was called out several times, though not for anything serious enough to piss him off again.

Jasper ended up dozing on the sofa by eleven. Which he didn't really mind. The office was at least kept cool enough he didn't stick to the leather.

His phone startled him awake at some point, and he fumbled beside the sofa for it. He answered it with a grumbled, "'Lo?"

"Jasper baby," came a familiar singsong voice.

Fuck.

Jasper sat up, almost instantly awake and hating it. "You don't get to call me that," he snapped, scrubbing at his eyes.

"Oh, baby, don't be like that," Shayne cooed, making Jasper grind his teeth. "It's been *ages*."

"It's been four months." Not that Jasper was counting.

Shayne made a protesting sound. "I miss you."

What the actual fuck? Jasper pulled his phone away and squinted at the time. Almost one in the morning. "Are you fucking drunk?"

"Lil bit."

Jasper rubbed his eyes, listening to the loud music and conversation in the background. A club or bar most likely. Shayne was always doing gigs in one or the other. Which had been hot at the time. Everyone fantasized about banging a guitarist, right? But no one ever warned him about the whole "musicians love their music more than anything and are always emotionally unavailable" bullshit. The whole attempted drugging so Shayne could share him with some "friends" was the cherry on the shit sundae, and a few hundred miles past his tolerance point.

"Can I see you?"

Jasper would have laughed if it hadn't been so messed up. "No. And don't call me again, you absolute cunt." He hung up as Shayne started to say something, groaned, and flopped back on the sofa. When Vincent cleared his throat, Jasper realized he'd been there the entire time.

Shit.

He dragged himself into a sitting position and looked up.

"We can leave now," Vincent said.

Oh, thank gods.

Chapter Fourteen

Vincent grabbed his suit jacket and locked up his office.

Jasper's annoyance as they headed out of the club was as tangible as water, roiling off him in waves.

Considering how this weekend had started, Vincent couldn't say he was surprised by the arrival of a new problem. That didn't mean he wasn't curious about the phone call. And he apparently wasn't worn out enough to keep his mouth shut and let it go for now. "Friend of yours?" he asked, once they were settled in the back of the car.

"No," Jasper replied tightly, slumping into the seat.

Vincent stifled a sigh and let Jasper brood in silence for a few minutes. Once they were on the highway, he tried again. "Ex, then?" he guessed, staring out his window. "Do you want me to make his life a living hell?" He watched the reflection of Jasper's head turn quickly and fought back a snicker. At least that got a reaction.

"What? No. I don't want anything to do with him anymore," Jasper muttered, sighing as he crossed his arms and slumped even more.

So it was an ex. Vincent turned enough to study Jasper directly.

"What?" Jasper asked, voice sharp. "Sir," he added, like it was a challenge. He glared hard enough Vincent expected his eyes to pop out. He pressed his lips into a thin line, but the silent "Fuck off" was clear.

"You have thirty seconds to convince me not to cancel this weekend."

Jasper somehow glared harder. A few seconds before Vincent's mental countdown ended, he finally turned away and spoke. "I don't want to talk about someone who used to fuck me with the guy who's currently fucking me."

"Okay," Vincent replied slowly. That was fair. "So why are you pissed at me?"

"I'm not…," Jasper started. He blinked and visibly deflated. "I'm not mad at you. I'm mad that he called me after four months to say he missed me."

"And you don't miss him?"

Jasper let out a sharp laugh. "He tried to roofie me, so no."

Vincent bit back a snarl and a demand to know the bastard's name. "I could still make his life hell, you know."

Jasper snorted, the rest of the tension easing out of him. He slid across to the middle seat and leaned into Vincent's side. "No, don't bother. Please just take me home. I've been waiting to see you all week."

Vincent sighed and forced his attention to where it belonged, resting a hand on Jasper's thigh. "Because you want to get off?"

"No," Jasper said, gnawing on Vincent's arm. "Because I missed your winning personality, obviously."

Vincent dug his fingers in with a long-suffering sigh, though he was too tired to make threats he had no intention of keeping. "Right back at you."

Jasper grinned, lifting his leg to drape it over Vincent's lap. He somehow pressed even closer and rested his head on Vincent's shoulder.

The rest of the short ride passed in silence, and it was nearing two in the morning when they finally trudged up the stairs to the bedroom.

Vincent took a pair of sweats and a shirt to his en suite to change. When he returned to the bedroom, Jasper was already in bed. Which was something he could too easily get used to.

"Night," Jasper murmured, curling into Vincent.

Vincent buried his fingers in Jasper's hair. "Good night, pet."

Despite his exhaustion, sleep did not come easily, and it wasn't restful when it did. His nightmares had eased off the last few years, but particularly stressful days were usually all the excuse they needed to revisit.

The silver lining was that they were always the same.

So when he woke, gasping for air, with phantom pain crushing his chest and smoke in his lungs, there was only tired resignation left behind. He stared at the ceiling for several long minutes, waiting for his heartbeat to slow. The warmth of Jasper's body and the steady rhythm of his breathing was as unfamiliar as it was comforting, but it did nothing to lull him back to sleep.

With a sigh he finally slipped out of bed. The clock showed it was after five, at least, though that still added up to only a few hours of sleep. He knew from experience he wouldn't be getting more, so he took a shower, letting the tepid water beat into his skin.

He pressed his thumb against the jagged white scar on his right arm. It connected his shoulder to his elbow in the shape of an amateur's botched attempt to carve the Nile. A spiderweb of red stretched across his chest, remnants of the fire he could barely remember.

He had the money; he could have at least tried to diminish their appearance, but he kept them as a reminder of the consequences of losing control. The half-dozen scars on his back were a reminder of the price he'd paid for his unhealthy attempt to cope with his pain and desperation.

He finished his shower and pulled his robe on as he slipped back into the bedroom for a fresh pair of sweats.

Jasper was still dead to the world.

Vincent left him sleeping and went downstairs to start the coffee.

Restlessness itched along his senses, so he busied himself with small tasks. Opening the curtains. Emptying the dishwasher. Making a list for the week's groceries. Starting a load of laundry.

By the time six thirty ticked by, he was on his second cup of coffee and making waffles. He still wasn't sure what he'd expected to come of having Jasper at the club, but it wasn't like he could stop working on all their busiest nights. Bad enough he intended to take Saturdays off for the foreseeable future. And with Jasper's schedule, weekends were their only feasible block of time.

He scrambled some eggs, making sure they were fluffy and cheesy. The waffles came out crisp and golden, and he plopped one on each plate.

Jasper stumbled into the kitchen a few minutes later, wearing nothing but his boxers, blond hair sticking in all directions. He pressed into Vincent's side with a yawn. "How do you make even eggs look gourmet?" he grumbled, rubbing his cheek against Vincent's shoulder.

"Practice," Vincent replied, dishing out the eggs and handing over a plate.

They ate in a not-quite-awkward silence, and Vincent's restlessness hadn't faded by the time they moved to the couch. He tapped his fingers against Jasper's thigh as he stared out the bay window, not paying the least bit of attention to whatever show Jasper found on TV.

Jasper sighed, covering Vincent's hand with his own. "What's wrong?"

Vincent forced his fingers to still, squeezing Jasper's thigh and rubbing his thumb back and forth instead. "Nothing."

Jasper snorted. "Liar," he said, crawling into Vincent's lap. He straddled Vincent's thighs, arms wrapping around his shoulders. "Something's bothering you. What is it?"

The truth was, Vincent wasn't sure. It wasn't the nightmare. They didn't affect him as badly as they used to, and the guilt that came with them was nearly a decade dull.

It might have been the news of Jasper's ex, but their phone conversation hadn't sounded promising for their getting back together.

"Sir?"

And that, apparently, was all Vincent needed. The simple reminder that, at least for the moment, Jasper was his. A tension he hadn't even noticed eased in his chest. The last time Jasper called him that had been in anger, and that was something he should have addressed last night.

Christ, he was out of practice.

"Just tired," he replied. It wasn't exactly a lie; the restlessness was already fading like fog beneath sunlight. He caught Jasper's lips in a quick kiss. "I need some fresh air. Get dressed."

Jasper eyed him with a pouty frown. He took a breath like he wanted to argue, but he sat back instead, trailing his hands down the front of Vincent's robe.

Maybe Jasper would have pulled away without trying to get his hands on skin, but Vincent reacted before he could find out. He grabbed Jasper's wrists suddenly enough to make him jump and gently tugged them away.

Jasper huffed. "Am I ever going to get to see you naked?" he asked dryly, sliding backwards off Vincent's lap.

"Maybe." It certainly wasn't something he planned to address in the next few weeks, though.

"I have time for a shower?" Jasper called from the stairs.

"Sure." He gave Jasper a minute to get in the shower, then headed up to change.

Maybe he should have mentioned his preference for the total power exchange dynamic before signing a contract, but he hadn't wanted to scare Jasper off. Besides, these two months were to see if they were as compatible outside the playroom as they were inside. If Jasper wasn't ready to walk away at the end, he could bring up the idea of an official TPE then.

He didn't bother with a suit, pulling on dark jeans and a long-sleeved shirt instead. He waited at the bottom of the stairs for Jasper, then grabbed his keys and opened the door to the garage when Jasper was ready.

He could have called his driver, but he didn't have any particular destination in mind. And there was no sense spending money on a sports car if he wasn't going to use it once in a while.

Vincent closed the door behind them as Jasper hurried around to the passenger side with a grin, running his fingers across the hood. Once they were buckled, he raised an eyebrow at Vincent. "You actually know how to drive?"

"No," Vincent replied. He backed out of the garage quickly enough that Jasper latched on to the door with something close to a screech.

"You really are a dick," Jasper grumbled, tightening his seat belt.

Vincent snorted. "I'm sure you were warned about that more than once." He stopped at the end of the driveway to wait for the garage door to close. He found his sunglasses and slipped them on, then backed into the street at a more reasonable speed.

Jasper settled into his seat, running his fingers over the leather and fiddling with the AC. "So where are we going?"

"Have a suggestion?"

"Not really." Jasper finally got the vents pointed how he wanted and sat back. "Unless you wanna go to the arcade or something. You could get your ass kicked by the common-class citizens," he added with a grin.

"Is that your way of saying you think I need my ass kicked?" He wasn't sure if he was more offended by Jasper apparently seeing him as some high-and-mighty millionaire, or as someone who'd never played a video game.

"Whaaaat? I'd never."

Vincent shot Jasper an unimpressed look. "That wide-eyed innocent expression isn't convincing."

"No? Do I need to flutter my eyelashes more?"

"You expect me to help you become even more of a brat?"

Jasper *hmm*ed, and Vincent could hear the impish smirk in it. "The contract says you'll provide anything I need for our time together."

Vincent laughed. Christ. How had Jasper not been scooped up yet? "Speaking of things you need...." If Jasper was going to be at the club as his sub, he needed to be dressed properly. "You need a suit." He would have suggested leather of some kind, but he doubted Jasper would be comfortable in any kind of fetish gear in public. Not yet, anyway.

"Whyyy do I need a suit?"

"Everyone should have at least one."

Jasper fell silent, and Vincent waited for some kind of protest that didn't come.

As far as second gifts went, it might have been a little expensive, but it was as much for his benefit as Jasper's. Maybe more.

Jasper was still oddly silent by the time they parked at a strip mall, but he got out and followed Vincent inside the small suit shop without hesitation.

Vincent watched from the corner of his eye as Jasper pulled a suit sleeve out, checked the price tag, and immediately dropped it and stepped back.

It wasn't until Vincent picked a suit off the rack and held it out to him that Jasper finally spoke. "I can't accept this."

"Then it won't be yours. You can think of it as another item I'm adding to the playroom."

Jasper squinted at him, apparently unconvinced, before eyeing the suit like it was a snake. He finally took it with a sigh and draped it over his arm.

"Dressing room is over there," Vincent said, pointing. He waited until Jasper trudged into the room and closed the door to turn back to the racks with his own sigh.

He had less than two months to convince Jasper to keep a damn suit.

Or maybe he should view it as less than two months to prove his instincts were right and he should sign Jasper on for longer.

Chapter Fifteen

Jasper closed the dressing room door and slumped against it with a groan.

This weekend was not going how he'd hoped or imagined. Not only had last night been a mess, but today wasn't going much better. At this rate the chances of Vincent tying him up before he left tomorrow were slim to none.

And what was with the sudden shopping spree? Vincent was about to drop more money on him than Jasper would likely be able to save in the next five years.

For a suit.

Why the hell did he need a suit? That wasn't a fetish thing. Or was it? He liked seeing Vincent in them, though he preferred the sweats and soft shirts Vincent slept in more. The jeans weren't bad either.

This was probably another Rich-Person thing he'd never understand.

He sighed and stripped off his clothes, tossing each item onto the bench. Then he carefully pulled on the button-up shirt and gray suit. Of course the shirt was silk. He didn't dare check its price tag; he could tell it was expensive by how nice it felt against his skin.

A glance in the mirror proved this was a terrible idea. The suit was horrible on him. Too long in the arms, and the gray made him appear jaundiced.

He opened the door to peek out, hoping Vincent gave this up as the terrible idea it was. Being in a high-end store like this made him feel entirely out of place.

Vincent was waiting outside and looked him over with a slight frown. "Try these," he said, handing over two more suits.

Jasper made a face, stifling a sigh as he took them. More gray. Awesome. He almost asked if this was really worth it, but then he spotted a store employee coming their way. He ducked back inside to let Vincent deal with the guy while he changed.

Through the door he heard, "Can I help you find anything?"

"Is Richard here today?" Vincent asked.

"He should be back from lunch soon."

Jasper hung up the first suit and pulled on the next one. The gray was a darker shade and didn't clash as much against his skin, but the jacket didn't sit right and the pants threatened to fall off without a belt. "This one doesn't work either."

"Neither one?"

Jasper grumbled and changed again. He couldn't tell the difference between them, but maybe he lacked the refined gray-tone eyesight Vincent had.

A digital bell announced someone entering as he got the second suit back on its hanger. He tilted his head as he heard Vincent's name and pulled on the third pair of pants.

"Time for a new suit already?"

"Not for me," Vincent replied, still close to the door. His words were followed by a quick knock.

Jasper tugged the jacket on and opened the door. This one fit better, but gray was *not* his color.

The man standing next to Vincent studied Jasper with a soft *tsk*. "No, no, he needs black."

Vincent raised an eyebrow. "Black is boring."

"Black is classic. And you do not waste such a gorgeous complexion on *gray*." The man shook his head and held his hand out to Jasper. "I'm Richard. Why don't we find you a better suit, hmm?"

"Jasper," he replied, shaking Richard's hand and glancing at Vincent. As much as he hated the gray, Vincent was the one paying.

"Actually, I have a new style that would look amazing," Richard continued.

Vincent sighed in obvious resignation. "You're the expert," he replied, tugging at Jasper's too-long sleeve with a frown.

Once Richard was gone, Jasper eyed Vincent. "You really don't need to buy me a suit…."

"I want to."

"But they're expensive."

Vincent released the sleeve to flick Jasper's nose instead. "If it bothers you, I'm doing this more for me than for you."

Jasper wrinkled his nose and swallowed the rest of his protests. "Is this a kink thing?" he asked, unable to stop himself.

"If it makes you feel better to think of it as one," Vincent replied with a soft laugh.

Jasper rolled his eyes. It was on the tip of his tongue to call Vincent an ass, but Richard was on his way back to them. He took the black suits into the dressing room and changed yet again.

The black was worlds better, and he was almost willing to say it—ha—*suited* him. Except for how it was too tight in the shoulders. The other jacket was the same but a size bigger, and while it fit in the shoulders, he was back to the problem of too-long sleeves. "This is ridiculous," he muttered, opening the door.

Vincent looked him over. Then did another take more slowly with a soft hum.

Richard smiled. "See? Black isn't so boring now, is it?" he asked with a wink at Jasper.

Vincent flicked his fingers. "It'll do."

Jasper flapped his sleeves at Vincent. "Really?" When Vincent gave an exasperated sigh, he stuck his tongue out.

Richard chuckled. "I'll fix those up for you over here." He turned, leading Jasper to a platform with mirrors.

Ten minutes later, the suit was adjusted enough that Jasper didn't feel like he'd borrowed Terrance's clothes.

"How's that feel?" Richard asked, straightening and checking his work.

"Better." Jasper turned, studying himself in the mirror. Unlike Vincent's suits, the jacket hem was jagged, asymmetrical in what he assumed was some fashion-forward style. He caught Vincent's eye in the mirror and raised an eyebrow.

Vincent offered a faint nod and returned to rifling through the ties. He selected a few, then joined Jasper on the platform to hold them up to Jasper's throat.

"You'll want the deeper, muted colors," Richard said, pointing to the dark purple in Vincent's hand. "Or we have some low-collar shirts if you want to forgo a tie."

"No," Vincent murmured, draping the purple tie over Jasper's shoulder before putting the others back.

Jasper settled the tie around his neck. Silk. Of course. He refrained from rolling his eyes and tugged on both ends. "I don't know how to tie these." He huffed softly when Vincent batted his hands away and tipped his head back to let him work. He wasn't quite prepared for the clench in his gut when Vincent tugged and tightened the tie into place. The quick, knowing look Vincent gave him only made it worse. Or better.

Richard cleared his throat, handing Vincent a slip of paper. "We should have it done within two weeks," he said, then disappeared to the back of the store.

Jasper glanced at his reflection again, toying with the tie and fighting a grimace. He never thought he'd be in a suit, and especially not one that wasn't even for work.

"You need shoes," Vincent said.

"Of course I do," he breathed, surrendering to the inevitable. He followed Vincent to the other end of the store and tried on shoes until they settled on a pair both Jasper's feet and Vincent could agree on.

"Do you do this for all your subs?" Jasper asked as he headed back to the dressing room. He glanced over when there was no immediate response, mentally kicking himself for asking about Vincent's exes. They'd finally gotten back to stable ground, and he had to go stick his foot in his mouth. "Never mind."

He reached the room and paused, turning and slowly backing into it. "You might need to help me get out of this suit, Sir."

Vincent raised an eyebrow, the corner of his mouth twitching. "I thought you could undress yourself."

"But it'd be more fun if you did it." He backed up a step as Vincent stalked forward, tipping his head back in invitation when Vincent stopped in the doorway.

With a hum, Vincent dragged his gaze over Jasper as he stepped into the room and closed the door behind him. "Public sex wasn't in your lists."

"I didn't exactly consider it a possibility," Jasper replied, hyperaware of Vincent's fingers brushing his throat as they worked his tie off. He'd had sex outside of a bedroom, but this was different. This wasn't a bathroom in some club with deafening music. This was an expensive suit shop where respectable businessmen could walk in. And while the idea of offending a snobby rich man's sensibilities amused him, at the moment he was completely out of his depth.

Vincent pulled the tie free with a whisper of silk and draped it over his arm. "And now?" he asked, sliding the jacket down Jasper's arms and settling it over the tie.

Jasper shivered, tipping his chin up as Vincent started unbuttoning his shirt. After a week of not having Vincent's hands on him, he was willing to do almost anything to keep even that little bit of contact. "Is public sex something you like to do?"

"It has its perks." Vincent slid his palm over Jasper's chest as he removed the shirt. Before Jasper could say yes to anything, Vincent stepped back. "Bring the rest when you're done," he said… and left.

"Wha—" Jasper stared at the door when it closed. He wasn't sure if he was more relieved or disappointed, but he hoped that wasn't a sign of how the rest of the day would go. With a sigh, he finished changing and took the pants and shoes to the register. He made the mistake of glancing at the price and couldn't help the strangled sound that escaped his throat.

Four figures. For a suit.

No wonder Terrance called Vincent a sugar daddy.

He took the bag with the shirt, shoes, and tie and let Vincent lead the way back to the car. He settled in his seat with his hands clasped between his knees, watching Vincent from the corner of his eye. He might have said never mind earlier, but he really was curious if this was something Vincent did for all his subs, or if Jasper was special.

Not that this was anything more than a couple of months of some amazing sex and getting his feet wet with the whole kink thing.

"Hungry?" Vincent asked.

"I could eat." He curled his hands into fists until his nails bit into his palms, silently counting to keep from saying something stupid. By the time they arrived at a café, he'd nearly bitten through his tongue to keep quiet.

He didn't need to know. It wasn't like he was eager to talk about his own exes.

They settled at a table, and Jasper pretended to be absorbed in the menu.

"Does it bother you that much?" Vincent asked.

Great. He'd managed to make a fool of himself anyway. Jasper silently cursed and peeked at Vincent. He needed some kind of excuse for his silence, but they all died on his tongue.

"I won't force you into something you don't want."

Jasper sighed. "It's not that." He liked the suit, but spending that much money on something he'd rarely wear…. "Do you do that with all your subs?"

"Only the ones who are okay with it."

"Who wouldn't be okay with you spending money on them without even caring about the price?" he muttered, ignoring the fact that was part of exactly what was bothering him.

Vincent set his menu down, brows drawn together in confusion. "The suit?"

That wasn't the reaction he'd expected. Jasper dropped his own menu to the table, giving up the pretense of reading it. "You weren't talking about the suit…." Of course he wasn't. Why would he be? But Jasper couldn't for the life of him think what else Vincent would be talking about.

"I am now," Vincent said, but then their server came for their order. Once they were alone again, Vincent turned his full attention to Jasper and studied him a moment. Somehow Jasper managed not to squirm beneath the intense gaze. "Is it the price or the suit itself that bothers you?"

Jasper opened his mouth to reply, but no words came out. Finally he managed a soft, "Neither?" When Vincent raised an eyebrow, Jasper shrugged. "It's just, that's a lot of money to spend on someone you barely know." He was tempted to say they probably wouldn't know each other for very long either, but stopped himself. Barely.

Vincent didn't respond immediately, tapping his thumb against the table instead. "Do you need to set a new limit?"

"For what?"

"The contract says I'll provide anything needed for our time together. I consider the suit an acceptable expense, but I've been told some of my tastes are excessive." He paused for a moment, but when Jasper didn't reply, he added, "If spending that kind of money makes you uncomfortable, then set a limit."

Vincent made it sound simple.

Maybe it was, but even after two and a half years of living with his cousin, the thought of asking for anything still made Jasper nauseous. He managed a nod anyway and instead asked, "What were you talking about, if not the suit?"

A hint of amusement tugged at Vincent's lips. "What we were discussing in the dressing room."

"Oh," he said before the words really sank in, then, "Ohhh." He cleared his throat, but kept silent as the server returned with their food. He pulled the toothpick out of his sandwich and took a bite. "I don't think I'd mind," he said after swallowing.

"Not interested in an 'I don't think,'" Vincent replied dryly. "Stop acting like I'll abandon you out of boredom if you don't try new things."

Jasper flinched. Matt's words had been haunting him since his first weekend with Vincent. He didn't think Matt was lying, but it was obvious something had happened between Matt and Vincent.

He took a breath to get his throat working again, dropping his sandwich to his plate when he nearly squeezed it into pieces. "Matt warned me you would," he said, surprised by how steady his voice came out.

Vincent paused with his drink a few inches off the table, then set it back down. "You know Matt," he said, though he didn't quite sound surprised.

Jasper shrugged. "He lives with Amber."

"Ah." Vincent sat back in his seat with a sigh. "Can't say I blame him for hating me."

He waited for some additional information, and dug his fingers into his jeans when Vincent fell silent. "Is what he said true, then?"

"That depends on what he said, exactly."

"That you're a dick," Jasper said, unable to help himself. That part at least he could believe to some extent, and he wasn't sure if it was a good or bad sign when Vincent didn't even try to defend himself. "And that you go through a lot of subs and don't have relationships."

Vincent hesitated but nodded. "I don't usually form romantic relationships with play partners. I fill in as a temporary Dom at the club when needed. Do you know what that is?"

"You hit people who ask you to?"

"To put it simply." Vincent gave him a bemused look, drumming his fingers against the table. "Someone wants to be spanked but doesn't have someone who can give them that, they can ask me. There's no relationship expected beyond that."

Jasper studied Vincent for a long moment. Matt had made it sound like Vincent left a string of pissed-off lovers wherever he went, but Jasper had basically used Vincent in that exact way. Before he'd signed a contract. "So," he started, his fingers aching where he clutched his knees to keep from fidgeting. "You don't offer contracts often?"

Vincent smiled, if only briefly. "Not often. If it makes you feel any better, it's been about a year since my last one."

He wasn't sure he should admit to feeling better about that, so he reached for a fry and shoved it in his mouth. "Can I ask why he hates you?"

Vincent crossed his arms in front of his plate. "I hurt him. Deliberately."

"Why?" He raised an eyebrow when Vincent eyed him with exasperation, waiting to see if he'd answer or tell him to fuck off.

After a long moment of silence, Vincent let out a slow breath. "I was in a bad place," he said quietly, picking up a chip, breaking a piece off, and dropping it. "It was the same day I'd gotten word my mother died. I was grieving, had a point-one-nine blood alcohol level, and he was conveniently available."

Jasper refrained from asking for more details, surprised he'd even gotten that much. He ate another fry as he mulled that over, wondering if Matt was a jilted lover. That would explain why Matt hated Vincent so much. Maybe he shouldn't give Vincent the benefit of the doubt when they barely knew each other, but surely Amber or Keith would have warned him off if Vincent was dangerous.

Vincent hadn't hurt him, which was all that really mattered at the moment. "For the record, I like trying new things," he finally offered. "Even if it's public sex," he added, snickering when Vincent nearly choked on his tea.

By the time they finished eating, things felt back to normal. Like the past twenty hours never happened. Especially when Vincent caught him on the way back to the car, backed him into the passenger door, and kissed him.

His lips were tingling as he climbed in and buckled his seat belt. "So does this mean you'll tie me up when we get back?" he asked, not even bothering to try and sound nonchalant.

Vincent glanced at him with a chuckle and a "We'll see."

LATER THAT evening, Jasper was naked and sitting on the coffee table, watching as Vincent wove rope around his right arm. His left arm was already done, a pattern of messy red loops chained together from his wrist to elbow. Maybe the messy part should have worried him, but he was almost giddy, seeing that Vincent wasn't perfect at everything.

The black loops forming on his right were neater and tighter, and he found himself mesmerized by the way Vincent's fingers moved. Quick and deft but unhurried. They seemed to brush against every inch of skin as they trailed down his arm, leaving goose bumps in their wake.

"So," he said, glancing at the cushion beside Vincent, where more rope, lube, nipple clamps, and a crop were laid out. "You're going to use all of that on me?"

Vincent's lips twitched, but he didn't slow in his task. "Objections?"

Jasper hummed softly, at least pretending to think about it. "Nope."

Vincent finished with Jasper's arm and picked up another bundle of rope, this one purple. He eyed Jasper as he unwound it. "I'm more interested in tormenting you tonight than getting off."

"Does that mean I'm not getting off either?"

"Can you handle that?"

He swallowed down the reflex to say he definitely could not handle that after an entire week. It might have sucked, but knowing Vincent was pleased with his restraint made it worth it. "Maybe."

"Maybe?" Vincent asked, sounding amused. He motioned for Jasper's leg.

Jasper shrugged, propping his foot on Vincent's knee. "I don't usually go this long without…." He flicked his fingers between his legs and rolled his eyes when Vincent didn't completely hide a smirk.

"Tell you what," Vincent said, securing the rope around Jasper's heel and ankle, "if you can handle not getting off tonight, I'll reward you in the morning." He tightened the rope and ran it up the outside of Jasper's leg before making a thick loop around his thigh.

The clench of heat in Jasper's gut forced a soft groan out of him. He might have wanted to experiment with orgasm denial, but he'd thought it would stop at the point of "no getting off through the week." "Okay," he said softly, switching his feet so Vincent could do his other leg.

Once all of his limbs were done, Vincent stood and put a sofa cushion on the table. "Kneel here," he said, tugging Jasper's legs as far apart as was comfortable once he was settled. He then proceeded to tie Jasper's ankles to the back table legs and his thighs to the front ones.

Jasper glanced back as Vincent moved behind him, his breath catching in his chest when Vincent pulled his wrists back. When Vincent was finished, Jasper's forearms were pressed together and tied to the same legs of the table as his ankles.

Vincent's fingers ghosted up the length of his arms. "All good?" he asked, squeezing Jasper's shoulders.

He tugged against the restraints and flexed his fingers. "I think so," he said, wrinkling his nose when Vincent flicked it. He watched Vincent pick up the clamps and crop and sat, expecting him to do something other than cross his legs and stare. He opened his mouth to ask what he was supposed to do now, then thought better of it. Not like he could do much of anything, even if he wanted to.

He shifted his weight, straightening until he felt the rope biting into him, soft and rough and only a little yielding. Judging from the way Vincent watched him, the squirming was appreciated. "Take a picture, it'll last longer."

Vincent raised an eyebrow. "Is that an offer?" he asked, leaning forward. He brushed the crop against Jasper's knee before lightly tapping it up the inside of his thigh.

Jasper stilled, all his attention focusing on the crop and the touch of leather on his skin. When it reached his balls, he instinctively tried to curl in on himself, but it was no use. His legs wouldn't budge, and he couldn't bend forward without feeling like he'd lose his balance. A small part of him expected Vincent to hurt him, to punish him for the mess of the past couple of days. Why else would he be more interested in torment than sex?

He didn't realize the crop had moved on until the edge of it scraped up his throat and along his jaw, coming to rest against his lower lip.

"Breathe."

Jasper squeezed his eyes shut as he forced a shuddery breath into his lungs. The crop beneath his chin was an insistent pressure he didn't resist. He tipped his head up, letting Vincent's lips distract him. The kiss was as unyielding as his bindings and was nothing but pure bliss. He leaned forward with a groan of protest when Vincent pulled back.

"Relax, pet. We're just getting started."

That didn't sound as much like a threat as it should have. If anything it sounded like a promise for a long night.

He licked his lips and took a slow breath, and then another, letting the cushion and restraints take his weight. "What do you plan on doing to me, Sir?"

"Give you a taste of a crop for starters." Vincent hummed and gave a light smack to Jasper's inner thigh. "Then we'll play a little game."

That sounded vaguely like a threat, but it still sent a shiver of excitement through him. He let out a slow breath and focused on Vincent's stomach. "Sounds fun."

"Good boy." Vincent buried his fingers in Jasper's hair and tightened them into a firm grip. He brought the crop down on Jasper's thigh with a sharp thwack.

Jasper jumped with an instinctive hiss before realizing it didn't actually hurt. The faint sting was already gone, but Vincent replaced it with another a moment later. The crop went down one leg and up the other, getting a little harder with each strike.

By the time Vincent moved behind him and started on his ass, the lingering stings on his thighs had dissolved into thrumming blossoms of heat. The pain was sharp but fleeting. Different from the dull impact of a paddle.

He was still trying to decide which he preferred when Vincent pressed the shaft of the crop against his lips.

"Open up, pet. You're going to hold this for me, without leaving teeth marks and without dropping it. Understand?"

Jasper tipped his head back. "Is this the game, Sir?"

Vincent chuckled and lightly tapped the crop against Jasper's lips. "The start of it."

He let out a slow breath, though it did nothing to calm the nerves twisting his stomach into knots. He opened his mouth and carefully bit down on the crop. The pop of the lube cap was his only warning, but it was enough that he didn't clamp his jaw against the crop when Vincent's finger pushed into him.

Vincent's hum of approval sent shivers down Jasper's spine.

Pleasure washed over him and erased any lingering pain from the crop. He renewed his struggling, enjoying the way the rope dug into his skin, but he was far more interested in helping Vincent's fingers than getting free. Especially when Vincent's lips found his neck, and fingers found his nipple. A muffled "Yeah," escaped around the crop, along with a bit of saliva.

Vincent took his time, alternating between one nipple and the other until Jasper was on the verge of whimpering. When the fingers finally disappeared, Jasper sagged in a mixture of relief and disappointment. He squeezed his eyes shut and struggled to catch his breath without dropping the crop.

And then dull metal bit into his nipples without warning. His entire body flinched and strained against the ropes hard enough the table should have ripped to pieces. It wasn't until the shock and almost-pain wore off that he realized the strange sounds he was hearing were coming from his own throat. And that the crop wasn't between his teeth anymore.

"Fuck," he whispered.

"Indeed." Vincent retrieved the crop with a soft *tsk* and set it on the couch. "Ready for part two?" he asked, picking up the last piece of black rope. He didn't wait for a response as he tied one end to the rope on Jasper's thigh.

Even when Vincent put the rope through the end of the chains on the nipple clamps, Jasper didn't quite comprehend what he was doing. It wasn't until Vincent put the other end of the rope through the loop on his other thigh and pressed Jasper down that he understood.

"No." His initial urge to get free ended as quickly as it started when the pressure on the clamps left him gasping.

Vincent tipped Jasper's chin up with a finger. "You'll need to give me a word I understand."

Jasper blinked, trying to breathe without moving too much. "What?"

Vincent crouched in front of the table and pressed a brief kiss to Jasper's lips. "A color, pet."

He blinked again and let out a shuddery breath. "Oh." He swallowed the instinctive urge to say red so Vincent would remove the rope. Now that the shock was wearing off, this wasn't too much. It was almost overwhelming, but in a good way. He wanted to see if it would feel even better. "Green."

Vincent's brief smile of approval caused a ripple of goose bumps on Jasper's arms. "Good. Then the scene ends when the clamps come off," he said as he stood up. "And I have no intention of removing them myself."

"What?" Something that wasn't quite panic formed in the pit of Jasper's stomach. He instinctively tried to straighten and ended up curling into himself with a hiss instead. With the clamps attached to his legs, he was effectively trapped in an upright fetal position. He saw Vincent move from the corner of his eye and braced himself, but the sharp sting of leather on his ass still made him flinch. Sparks of exquisite agony exploded from the clamps before reforming as heat between his legs.

Pain melded with and became pleasure as Vincent continued, landing the crop on Jasper's ass and thighs and occasionally his shoulders. His skin ached, and the ropes dug into his limbs, keeping him immobile. Unable to escape. Helpless to do anything but surrender to the hazy blanket of sensation settling over him.

He wasn't sure how long it lasted. It could have been only minutes, but it felt like hours. Long enough for coherent thought to slip beyond his grasp. His entire existence coalesced into the thrum of heat covering his body, interspersed with sharp tingles of pain or pleasure or both. He was distantly aware of cool fingers brushing over his abused flesh, but even those light touches were a mixture of agony and pleasure.

And then the crop was between his legs, a quick flick of leather against his balls. Then the hard, ridged, unyielding handle of the crop pressed into him, his body arching into it despite the sharp pleasure-pain-pleasure on his nipples. White-hot bliss followed, cascading through him as the agony of the metal snapping free of his nipples blossomed into torturous relief. Everything went dull and hazy after that.

Vincent was talking, but Jasper couldn't grab on to the words long enough to find their meaning. He thought the tone was reassuring, or approving, maybe. Soft and rough in a way that made him shiver.

And then Vincent's arms were around him, and he breathed in Vincent's cologne, his body warm and heavy, and nothing else mattered.

Chapter Sixteen

The moment Jasper came from his crop was the moment Vincent gave up any lingering hope of not becoming utterly captivated.

It wasn't so much the coming untouched that fascinated him. It was the way Jasper allowed himself to be bound so completely. How he freely offered his submission to Vincent.

He'd played with his fair share of subs, switches, and Doms, but Jasper…. Maybe it was Jasper's inexperience making everything new again, but this felt different. It felt like Jasper needed this as much as Vincent did.

He set the crop down and ran his fingers over Jasper's flushed skin, marveling at his responsiveness. He'd read books, even heard others talk about a perfect sub they'd found, but outside of the occasional fantasy, he'd given up on ever finding one for himself, much less in his own living room.

Getting Jasper untied and to the couch was easier said than done, but Vincent managed. He wasn't too surprised when Jasper settled across his lap and latched on to him like he never meant to let go. He'd caught glimpses of Jasper's clinginess already, especially after an intense scene, but he didn't mind.

It was a nice change from what he was used to.

He got comfortable, propping a foot on the edge of the table and resting his arms around Jasper.

It'd been years since someone had offered themselves to him so eagerly. Years since he'd experienced this strong a pull towards someone.

He trailed his fingers down Jasper's arm to his thigh, working the rope off with one hand. Then he did the same to the other leg and tossed the ropes and clamps tangled in them aside.

Jasper didn't react until Vincent tried to get the rope off one of his arms, tightening his grip and pressing his face into Vincent's neck with a soft whine.

"Okay," Vincent whispered, rubbing his palm against Jasper's arm. "It can wait. You're not going anywhere." Once Jasper settled again, he propped his cheek against Jasper's head to wait.

With the scene done, he was more surprised at the complete satiation spreading through his limbs despite not getting off himself. Working the floor at the club and doing the occasional scene took the edge off most of the time, but nothing could scratch the itch like having his own sub. And Jasper was proving to be far more amazing than expected.

Vincent's leg started going numb long before Jasper finally stirred, shifting his weight and nosing against Vincent's neck.

"All right, pet?"

"*Mmnngh.*"

He almost hated the burst of fond amusement in his chest, but he accepted it for what it was. "Can you sit up?"

Jasper tightened his arms around Vincent's shoulders with a whine of protest. A few moments later, he sighed and lifted his head enough to rest his forehead against Vincent's cheek instead.

Vincent squeezed Jasper's knee. "Good enough. Can I take this off now?" he asked, tugging at the rope still covering Jasper's arm.

Jasper sighed again, as though Vincent were being unacceptably demanding, but he lowered his arm so Vincent could get to it.

"Thank you, pet." He worked the rope off with one hand, dragging it through his fingers enough to untangle the cords as he went. When he was done, he dropped the rope to the side and brushed his fingers against the indentations in Jasper's skin.

Shibari was his favorite type of bondage, mostly because of the intimacy involved in putting it on and taking it off, but partly because of the marks it left behind. They might not last as long as others, but being able to feel them beneath his fingers after a scene took things to a different level.

He turned his head enough to kiss Jasper's forehead. "How about the other one?"

It took several long seconds, but Jasper finally sat up enough to offer Vincent his other arm. Once freed from the last of the rope, Jasper ran a finger over the marks on his arm.

Vincent watched in silence for a moment. "All good?"

Jasper licked his lips, rubbing his thumb against the line around his wrist as he nodded.

"Can you stand?"

That seemed to be too much to ask. Jasper slumped into Vincent's chest again with a quiet groan. "Five?"

Vincent stifled a laugh. "How about ten," he replied, resting a hand on Jasper's thigh. He traced his finger back and forth along the marks there, feeling the tiny grooves left by the rope.

As the minutes ticked by, he worried maybe he'd gone a bit too far, both too early in the relationship and too late in the weekend. This was the first time he'd seen Jasper so far in subspace, and he wasn't sure how long it would take him to recover.

But Jasper had been nothing if not responsive through the entire scene, and it was hard to resist the chance to explore his limits.

He suspected Jasper was impatient to experience everything Vincent could offer, but there was no need to rush. The last thing he wanted was to hit a plateau before their first contract was even up.

And he knew without a doubt he'd be offering a second contract. Two years ago, he'd resigned himself to having a sub for only a few months at a time. Either the chemistry faded, or their needs never quite aligned with his own. At some point he'd stopped searching for anything more than the occasional scene.

And then Jasper, the walking contradiction of shyness and naivete and brattiness, dared set foot in his club.

Jasper sighed and pressed his face into Vincent's shoulder, his grip on Vincent's shirt relaxing a bit. Even so, it still took a while longer for him to sit up. Then he glanced down at himself with a grimace. "Need a shower," he murmured.

"Go ahead. I'll be up in a minute."

Jasper nodded and slid off Vincent's lap, sat beside him for a long moment, then finally stood and headed upstairs.

Vincent winced as blood circulated back into his leg, waiting for it to wake up a bit until he dared to stand himself. He grabbed a bottle of water and a carton of apple juice from the pantry, then took care of the locks and lights. The mess could be cleaned up later.

The shower was still running down the hall when Vincent reached the bedroom. He tossed the drinks on the bed and grabbed some sweats and a T-shirt, using the en suite for his own quick shower and brushing his teeth. When he finished, Jasper was sitting on the bed with the straw of the apple juice in his mouth, his other hand tracing the marks on his arm.

He hoped that was as reassuring as it looked. "How do they feel?" he asked, settling in beside Jasper.

"Good." Jasper glanced up, setting the empty carton on the nightstand, then shifting to his knees and facing Vincent, twisting the sheet between his fingers. "I'm sorry."

Vincent paused, resisting the immediate impulse to catch Jasper's fingers with his own. "What for?"

Jasper stared at the sheets as he gripped them tighter. "I came without permission."

That was true enough, though he hadn't realized that had become their habit. "You did."

Apparently that was a bigger issue than he thought, because Jasper made a soft sound of frustration. "Shouldn't you punish me or something?"

Vincent tilted his head as he considered, tugging Jasper closer and getting comfortable. "If you want to add punishments to the contract, that can be done. But I didn't say you weren't allowed to come. I said if you didn't, I'd reward you in the morning."

Jasper inched closer until he could lie down with his head on Vincent's pillow. "You're not mad?" he asked, his fingers twisting Vincent's shirt.

"No." He almost asked why he would be but held his tongue. Instead he said, "You were amazing tonight."

With a soft sigh, Jasper pressed his face into Vincent's chest. After a moment he asked, "Sooo, does that mean I still get a reward?"

Vincent snorted and pressed a quick kiss against Jasper's hair. "No." He leaned back far enough to turn off the light before settling an arm over Jasper's side.

"What was the reward?"

"Maybe next time you'll earn it and find out."

"Jerk," Jasper grumbled.

Vincent pinched Jasper's ass, smirking at the sharp yelp it caused. "Go to sleep, brat."

DESPITE WHAT he'd said, it was difficult to resist rewarding Jasper. Especially when Vincent woke to a hand pressed against his morning erection. But rewarding Jasper for submitting was a slippery slope he couldn't let himself get near.

Jasper nuzzled into Vincent's neck, pressing a warm kiss there as he wiggled his fingers.

"Someone's feeling frisky," he murmured, trying to hang on to a thread of sleep.

"Of course I am. It's Sunday."

Vincent tried to follow that logic, but he wasn't awake enough yet. "And?"

Jasper huffed and grazed his teeth against Vincent's neck, lips curving into a grin when Vincent couldn't contain a soft moan. And then he did it again like the brat he was. "We haven't had sex in a week."

"Was that in the contract? Weekly sex?" he asked, stifling a yawn against Jasper's hair.

Jasper tightened his fingers against Vincent. "Yes," he said, a hint of a growl in his voice. "Once a week, bare minimum."

That might have been more amusing if the growl weren't such a turn-on. He let out a soft groan, finally giving up on sleep and shifting to find the lube and condoms. Once in hand, he tossed both to Jasper. He raised an eyebrow when Jasper stared at them. "Well?"

With a grumble, Jasper picked up the lube. "Why do you like watching me do this?"

"Because you haven't told me to stop."

Jasper glanced up, a frown tugging at his lips. He started to say something but seemingly decided against it. He stared at the lube in his hands as a flush crept into his cheeks. "How do you want me?"

Vincent reached for Jasper's leg and tugged until Jasper was facing him with his back to the foot of the bed. "However you like. So long as I can see."

"Such a—" Jasper muttered under his breath. He flopped onto his back, lying there a moment before popping the lube open.

"Such a…?" Vincent asked, amused. Jasper censoring himself was new enough to be intriguing. He sat up a bit and tugged Jasper's leg onto his chest to massage his ankle.

Jasper's foot twitched, but he didn't pull away. "Do you have a foot fetish too?"

"No. Do you?" He pressed his thumb into Jasper's heel, his lips twitching when Jasper moaned. "Maybe a little?"

Jasper grumbled under his breath, shooting a disgruntled frown at Vincent as he finally squeezed out some lube and got to work.

Vincent kept hold of Jasper's ankle as he watched, sliding his other palm against the inside of Jasper's thigh. "Good boy."

"Because I have my fingers up my ass?"

Vincent raised an eyebrow. "Having my fingers there instead is more praiseworthy?"

"You're so weird," Jasper scoffed, adding more lube to his fingers.

"Outside of last night, I think everything we've done so far has been rather tame. And I did warn you I was a voyeur." If Jasper thought this was weird, Vincent needed to decide if it'd be better to go slower or to hurry and give Jasper a taste of what the future could hold.

He slid his hand up to join Jasper's and pressed a finger inside between Jasper's two. "If it bothers you so much, you know how to stop."

Jasper failed to completely stifle his moan, his foot twitching in Vincent's grasp as he pushed into the extra finger.

Vincent held his finger still as Jasper moved his own, content to watch him squirm as his cock stiffened. Eventually he pulled his finger out. "Fetch me a belt from the closet," he said, blinking at the way Jasper immediately froze.

Jasper tugged his foot free and pushed up onto his elbows with a wary expression. "Why?"

"I was going to restrain you with it, but I can use something else." When Jasper's shoulders relaxed at that, he asked, "Tie or handcuffs?"

"Tie," Jasper said, rolling off the bed.

Vincent pointed him to the drawer with his ties and propped himself up against the pillows. He took the tie Jasper had picked out, trading the condom for it.

Jasper gave a dramatic roll of his eyes and climbed into Vincent's lap with a huff. "Do I have to do everything?" he asked, ripping the condom open. Then he hesitated, fingers hovering at Vincent's waist.

Belatedly, Vincent realized this was the first time Jasper had been in such a position with him. "Do you not want to?" he asked, resting his hands on Jasper's knees.

Jasper glanced up, lips parting like he was going to say something, then changed his mind again. After a moment, he visibly steeled himself. "I'll do it," he muttered and tugged Vincent's sweats down.

Before he could pinpoint what was bothering him, Vincent caught Jasper's wrist and secured one end of the tie around his forearm. The marks from last night were long gone, but maybe he'd reapply them soon. "Hands behind your back."

"I thought I was doing all your work for you."

"I changed my mind," he said, tugging Jasper's arm into place with the tie. It was easy enough to restrain him—Jasper seemed wired for any kind of submission—and the way he finally relaxed when he couldn't use his arms settled the flicker of concern in Vincent's chest. "Better?" he asked, trailing his fingers up Jasper's biceps and down his sides.

Jasper's answer was a wordless grunt and renewed erection.

Vincent fought a satisfied smirk and found the discarded condom. Once it was in place and lubed up, he settled against the pillows with his hands resting on Jasper's hips. A couple of tugs got Jasper inching forward on his knees, and then he was lowering himself onto Vincent. In this position, Vincent had a perfect angle to sit back and enjoy the view.

And what a view it was.

The hint of teeth on Jasper's lower lip. The warm flush spreading across his light brown skin. The strain of his thighs and stomach as he balanced himself without his hands. The way the crease between his brows finally smoothed out when he was fully seated on Vincent's cock….

Jasper let out a shaky breath as he shifted, curling forward with a groan when Vincent's fingers found a nipple and pinched. "Fuck," he hissed through clenched teeth.

Vincent slid his other hand up so he could properly torment Jasper with both hands. The way Jasper struggled and the tortured sounds he made went straight to Vincent's dick. Nothing else was needed for all the banked arousal from last night to spark and ignite.

"Get moving," he growled, his voice thicker than he'd expected it to be.

Obedient as always, Jasper shifted his knees. He ducked his head as he leaned forward and lifted his hips, effectively hiding his face.

That wouldn't do at all.

Vincent gripped Jasper's hair and forced his head up enough to get the view back.

Jasper's soft sound of protest dissolved into a deep groan. He leaned forward more as his hips sank down again, his eyes rolling back, either from the pressure on his hair or in his ass, Vincent wasn't sure. Not that it mattered. A few moments later, Jasper was using Vincent's hands on him as leverage, riding Vincent with abandon.

"H-harder," Jasper gasped, fighting Vincent's grip on his hair like he intended to pull it out by the roots.

Doesn't like pain, my ass, Vincent thought. Jasper only needed to be properly introduced to pain and its pleasures.

He loosened his grip on Jasper's hair a bit, making up for it by squeezing and twisting one nipple and then the other.

Jasper tried to curl in on himself once more, but Vincent tightened his fingers in his hair again, keeping him upright. "Please." Jasper's moan was desperate and frustrated as he rocked his hips, grinding down on Vincent's cock.

"Fuck, pet." Vincent surged forward, fastening his lips to Jasper's throat and pressing his tongue against the rapid pulse he found there. He licked his way up Jasper's neck, tasting sweat and the lingering scent of soap. "Please what?" he growled, sinking his teeth into Jasper's earlobe.

That earned a full-body shudder that Vincent felt all the way at the base of his cock.

"Please touch me. Please, Sir. Please."

Vincent tugged Jasper's head back farther and dragged his teeth against Jasper's throat, enjoying the strangled moan he felt beneath his lips. With his other hand, he made his way down Jasper's chest and stomach until he lightly brushed his palm over the head of Jasper's dick.

"Here?" he asked, swiping up the moisture gathered there and smearing it down the length with one finger. At the same time, Vincent found a nipple and sucked it between his teeth before biting down.

That was enough for Jasper to thrash against him, his hips bucking and a loud moan catching in his throat as he came. Mostly untouched. And without permission for the second time.

The miracles of youth.

Vincent shifted, rolling Jasper over onto his back. He planted a hand beside Jasper's head and settled the other on his ass. He took a moment to enjoy the dazed, half-lidded, well-fucked expression, then buried himself in Jasper's ass with a quick, hard thrust.

Jasper's eyes rolled back, and a loud drawn-out groan tore out of his throat as he shot what was left in him. "Yes," he gasped, and then again each time Vincent slammed into him.

He wouldn't last much longer. Not with Jasper's legs clamped around him and the sweet encouraging sounds he was making. Or the clench of his ass around Vincent's thrusts.

He moved his hand from Jasper's ass to his stomach, dragging a finger through the mess and up to Jasper's lips. They parted easier than the first time, and the press of a hot tongue curling around his finger, sucking it clean, pushed him to the edge. He leaned down and bit Jasper's throat, his hips stuttering as orgasm ripped through him.

Jasper moaned around Vincent's finger and continued sucking until Vincent pulled it away.

It took a few breaths for Vincent to find the strength to move. He sat up, tossed the condom towards the trash, and found one end of the tie. Once Jasper's arms were free, Vincent leaned over the edge of the bed for Jasper's discarded towel to wipe them both down. Then he stretched out on his own side of the bed, snagged the tie still attached to Jasper, and pulled him closer.

Jasper didn't need more coaxing to plaster himself to Vincent's side, one arm and leg slung over his body. He let out a deep sigh and went boneless, his head pillowed on Vincent's chest. "Mm."

Vincent echoed the sentiment, threading his fingers through Jasper's hair and closing his eyes. The promise of sleep hovered at the edge of his senses, and he didn't feel like fighting it. They had all morning to get Jasper back home, and he didn't have much to take care of before heading to the club. He was starting to drift off when Jasper spoke.

"Sir?"

"Mm?"

Jasper's fingers rubbed an absent pattern against Vincent's chest. "Can I ask why you never take your shirt off?"

Vincent tensed, then forced himself to relax. He stifled a sigh and gave up on getting back to sleep yet again. He'd expected that question sooner or later, and he didn't want to go into the second contract without answering it, but he'd hoped to put off opening that can of worms at least a *little* longer.

"Because of the scars," he said, trailing his fingers from Jasper's hair across his shoulders.

Jasper tipped his head back, a dozen questions evident in his expression. When he didn't ask any of them, Vincent sighed again and resigned himself to dealing with this now.

"I was in a bad car accident," he said, propping up his outside leg and enjoying the way it caused Jasper to shift against him. "It was a long time ago, but they're not exactly pretty."

"I don't care about that," Jasper said, and Vincent stifled a scoff. "Scars aren't supposed to be pretty."

Vincent let out a slow breath as he stared at the ceiling. That was the opposite of Adam's attitude. Every few weeks he had either subtly reminded Vincent that he had more than enough money to reduce the scarring or argued with him over why he chose to keep them as an ugly reminder.

Jasper crawled up Vincent's body until he could press his nose into Vincent's neck. "And I'm going to be a paramedic, remember? Open wounds don't bother me. Scars are pretty compared to those."

That earned a weak chuckle. "Do you have a scar fetish?"

"I dunno. I might have a Vincent's-scars fetish," Jasper replied, somehow sounding cheeky and genuine at the same time.

Vincent hesitated, rubbing his hand back and forth along Jasper's forearm before grasping his wrist. No point in waiting. If the scars had a chance of being a problem, he'd rather know now, not after he'd become even more attached. He tugged Jasper's hand down and then under the hem of his shirt.

Jasper lifted his head fast enough he nearly clocked his skull on Vincent's chin. He pushed up on his other elbow, staring at Vincent with wide blue eyes. "You're sure?"

He wasn't, but he nodded anyway.

Jasper's tongue flicked out, wetting his lower lip as he stared at their partially covered hands. He spread his fingers against Vincent's stomach and didn't try to shake off the grip on his wrist. "Really sure?" he asked, his thumb swiping down and poking beneath the sweats.

"It's fine," Vincent said, his lips twitching when Jasper frowned at him. He slid his free hand up to the back of Jasper's neck, tugging him down and pressing a kiss to his forehead. "Really," he added, meaning it. He wasn't bothered by the thought of Jasper touching his scars as much as he was Jasper's potential reaction to seeing them.

When Jasper's fingers walked farther up his stomach, he nudged them to the right, keeping his breathing steady when they brushed the edge of the scarring. He still had feeling in most places, but a spot over his ribs had suffered the worst of the damage. The ticklish, tingling sensation of fingertips on his skin vanished as they seemed to jump over that area.

"Is—Are these burn scars?" Jasper asked, his brows drawn together in concentration.

"Mm."

"Second or third degree?"

Vincent let out a shaky breath that was almost a laugh. "Second, mostly, but some areas were third," he said, watching Jasper's expression from the corner of his eye. He wasn't sure what he'd expected. Pity, maybe. Not this open curiosity, but maybe he should have expected that from someone planning to get a paramedic license. Jasper had mentioned that he was using his scholarship to get a BS in biology until he could afford the EMT courses—all while juggling a part-time job—and hoped to take the NREMT exam by the end of next year.

Vincent suspected their available time together would become even more constrained then, but for now, Jasper's blue eyes were focused on the path of their hands beneath the shirt, mapping out the extent of the damage.

His fingers twitched against Jasper's arm as he considered pulling his shirt off—he'd shared this much already—but the visual was far worse than they felt.

"All this from an accident?" Jasper reached the top of Vincent's chest, his fingers brushing the end of the scar on his shoulder. He tilted his head, tracing it down Vincent's arm as far as the sleeve allowed.

"It was a bad accident. I was drunk."

Jasper glanced up, the intense furrow of concentration still on his face. "Point-one-nine kind of drunk?" he asked quietly.

Vincent nodded, not really surprised that Jasper made the connection. "Same night." And his injuries and how he'd hurt Matt weren't even the worst part of that night.

And with that sobering thought, he reached his limit. "Breakfast," he murmured, releasing Jasper's arm to land a light smack on his hip.

Jasper slid his palm over the scarred area again as he pulled his hand out, pressing a quick kiss to Vincent's cheek. "What am I making?" he asked, rolling off the bed.

"Whatever you won't burn," he said, chuckling as he caught the pillow Jasper threw at him before it could hit him in the face.

"I'm not that bad at cooking," Jasper muttered as he disappeared down the hall.

Vincent slumped against his pillow, rubbing his forehead and failing to ignore the phantom touches lingering on his chest. He gave himself five minutes to breathe and sort his reactions, then rolled out of bed.

There was still the chance that seeing his scars could change Jasper's tune. At least his chest was more of a mess than his back.

By the time he showered, dressed, and headed downstairs, the eggs were scrambled and the bread toasted.

When Jasper finished eating, he shifted in his seat. "So… I was wondering."

"About?"

"If I could see you outside of the weekends."

Vincent glanced up, surprised yet again. After the rocky start Friday night and their conversation barely twenty minutes ago, he figured that request was still a couple of weeks out.

He already knew Jasper's class and work schedule well enough to know where he had a few chunks of time available. And he couldn't deny he liked the idea. Plus it would give him a chance to make sure Jasper wasn't suffering a sub drop.

"Dinner on Wednesday," he said, finishing off his toast.

Jasper grinned. "Are you cooking?"

"Do you want me to?"

"Absolutely." Jasper stood, pressing a quick kiss to Vincent's cheek before taking both their plates to the sink.

"That should give you enough time to decide if there are any more changes you want to make."

Jasper returned to the table and leaned against the back of Vincent's chair. "Like punishments?" he asked dryly.

"For starters," Vincent replied in the same tone, reaching up to flick Jasper's nose.

Jasper caught the finger between his teeth with a soft growl. "Can you make lasagna on Wednesday?" he asked, moving around the chair to sit across Vincent's lap.

"Maybe." Vincent found himself nuzzling into Jasper's neck without consciously deciding to, his hand settling on Jasper's thigh.

"Mm. We have time for another round, right?" Jasper asked, burying his fingers in Vincent's hair.

Vincent hummed as if he were considering it and fought back a smile. "We already hit your once-a-week quota."

"Technically we can start a new week right now," Jasper said with a wiggle of his brows.

Vincent sat back with a soft laugh. "Oh? You're going to wait until Sunday to have sex again?"

Jasper made a face. "No. I'm changing it to twice a week."

"You got off last night too."

"That doesn't count!"

"No?"

"No." Jasper bit Vincent's shoulder. "Only counts if you're inside me."

"Ah. So you giving me a blowjob counts, but not me giving you one. I see."

Jasper lifted his head and rolled his eyes. "Hilarious."

Chapter Seventeen

Monday took a page from Friday's book by turning into complete shit. Jasper woke up late and had to skip breakfast to catch the bus in time. As if that wasn't bad enough, he'd completely forgotten about his test.

Luckily, trauma care was one of the subjects he was most interested in, so he was sure he'd aced it, but it still left him rattled. He couldn't afford to lose his scholarship. He had barely two hundred bucks to his name, and that was needed to cover bus fare and lunches.

His day only got worse when he got to work and spilled half a machine of popcorn all over the floor. Then the slushy machine pissed lukewarm blue liquid all over him. He was tempted to bang his head against the wall as he cleaned himself up in the bathroom, but he didn't want to risk ending up in the hospital with a fractured skull. The only bright side was that their uniforms were black, so he only had to deal with being sticky and the sweet fake raspberry smell rather than also looking like he'd murdered a Smurf.

By the time Keith picked him up at the end of his shift, he wanted a shower and to crawl into bed for a week.

Thankfully the car was silent, at least until they hit the highway.

"Rough day?" Keith asked.

"Could say that," Jasper muttered, letting out a long sigh. Wednesday was a million years away, but it was the only thing keeping him sane at the moment.

"Wanna talk about it?"

Jasper slumped lower in the passenger seat. "Amber put you up to this?"

"Up to what?" Keith asked, sounding genuinely confused.

He made a face and let his forehead thunk against the window.

"No one put me up to anything. I asked because you seem worn out."

"I'm fine. Just need sleep," Jasper muttered. And for everyone to stay out of his business.

"All right." He felt Keith's eyes on him, and a few moments later he asked, "Thought any more about getting your driver's license?"

He squeezed his eyes shut with a soft groan. "I'll take care of it after I save enough money to afford the EMT course." He didn't have the money for the classes or tests right now, and he hoped his plans to take them next year weren't too ambitious. He'd have to pick up more than a few extra shifts to pay for the course and textbooks.

"You know we don't mind taking care of the driver's ed classes for you."

"It's fine," he said, managing not to snap. "You guys have done enough." No way was he letting them pay for his license on top of everything else. He wouldn't follow in his brother's footsteps—couch surfing, drugs, and planting the seeds for stage-three lung cancer by the age of thirty. Not a chance in hell. He'd make his own way, and he wouldn't rely on others for every damn thing.

Keith sighed with a soft "All right," and thankfully let it drop.

Once they were home, Jasper grabbed his bag and trudged up the stairs for a quick shower, then settled in to work on his assignments. Amber brought a plate of food up a bit later and set it on his desk. "Thanks," he murmured, glancing up when she leaned against the wall.

"Spill," she said.

Jasper sighed and turned back to his assigned reading on drug administration. "I'm fine. Just tired."

"Uh-huh."

His fingers twitched, and he curled them tight in his hair to keep from saying anything he'd regret. "Thanks for dinner. I have a lot of homework to do," he said, staring at his textbook without really seeing it. He ignored Amber until she sighed and left, then eyed the plate of chicken and veggies. The chicken was unseasoned, and the broccoli was undercooked. No doubt it was Matt's night to cook—his food was as insipid as his personality.

He managed to choke down two bites before his phone rang.

The sight of Vincent's name on the screen immediately made his day better. "Hello, Sir."

"Pet," Vincent replied, and that one word somehow popped the bubble of the dark mood he'd been trapped in since that morning. "What are you up to?"

Jasper eyed his plate with a soft snort. "Eating disappointing food."

"Oh?"

"Matt can't cook for shit."

"Some things never change," Vincent said with a soft laugh.

Right. He'd almost forgotten they all knew each other. Vincent had probably eaten Matt's food loads of times. He realized he'd never asked if they'd been together, and he really didn't want the answer.

"Sounds like that's the highlight of your day."

He snorted quietly. "Yeah, the rotting cherry on a shit sundae," he muttered, then winced. Vincent didn't want or need to hear about his horrible day. He opened his mouth to say he needed to finish studying so he didn't shove his foot any farther into his mouth, but Vincent spoke first.

"What happened?"

Jasper snapped his mouth shut, but not before a quiet strangled sound escaped his throat. It was on the tip of his tongue to say, "Nothing," but that would obviously be a lie.

As if sensing that intention, Vincent said, "Talk to me." It wasn't a request.

He let out an explosive breath, and then he spilled everything. From the test he hadn't properly studied for, to the clusterfuck at work, to the others hounding him about his driver's license. Not to mention the general sense of feeling utterly useless that'd been plaguing him all day.

When he finished, he slumped in his chair, somehow feeling even more drained than earlier.

There were a few moments of silence, and then Vincent asked, "Should I come over?"

Jasper blinked at the wall, sure he'd heard that wrong. "What?"

"Do you need me to come over?"

Yes, he thought, but he clamped his mouth shut. As much as he wanted to see Vincent, him showing up unannounced would only stir up drama. And he didn't need Amber kicking him out for not focusing on getting through college. "No," he said softly, "that's okay."

"You're sure?"

A faint smile tugged at his lips. "I have an assignment to finish, and then I'm going to bed."

Vincent hummed softly, as if he wasn't quite convinced. "Call me if you change your mind."

"Okay. Night, Sir."

"Good night, pet."

Jasper set the phone down after Vincent hung up. He was still exhausted, but at least he didn't have the urge to smash his head against the wall anymore.

TUESDAY WAS marginally better, but his two-hour lecture dragged on for *years*. He managed not to spill anything on himself at work, but then Amber texted to say she was stuck in a last-minute meeting and couldn't pick him up. And since Tuesday was date night for Keith, Matt, and Reiko, he was stuck taking the bus and then walking ten blocks home.

It was early enough in the year that the heat wasn't stifling, but he was still covered in sweat by the time he got inside.

For once, the place was empty, which meant no one to pry into his business. He dumped his bag in his room and took a shower, then made breakfast for dinner, relishing finally having some peace and quiet. Unfortunately it didn't last long enough for him to finish eating, but he shoveled the rest of the food into his mouth and escaped to his room before he could be bombarded with questions.

Maybe it was rude, but he didn't feel like dealing with anyone, so he settled in to study. He had a couple of tests next week, and he couldn't afford to flunk out.

He kept glancing at his phone, waiting for a call or text from Vincent, but none came. He told himself not to be disappointed. Vincent didn't contact him every day. Why would he start now?

Logically he knew there were any number of reasons Vincent wouldn't call him, but it didn't keep the hurt or doubt from creeping in.

AS HE was getting ready to leave for class on Wednesday morning, Vincent finally sent a text.

Can you be ready by 5?

He grinned and replied with *Definitely, can't wait*

His last class ended at two thirty, which gave him plenty of time to get home, even if he had to walk.

Good, see you soon.

Jasper's stomach tightened with excitement. He wasn't sure how he was going to make it through classes with five o'clock hanging over him, but he'd manage. Two days was too fucking long. Even worse than the five days he'd had to wait the last few weeks. How had he managed to wait that long?

Maybe he could talk Vincent into making Wednesday a part of the contract, or would that be too clingy? Shayne had started avoiding him the moment Jasper asked to see him outside of whatever gig he had going that week. Actually most of his relationships tended to follow that path.

It didn't help that the few guys he'd dated in high school had still had both feet in the closet or were "just experimenting." College was supposed to have been better, but since he didn't live on campus, he hadn't had many chances to hang out with anyone. He'd gone to some parties last year, which was how he'd met Shayne, so he wasn't too compelled to repeat that clusterfuck.

Maybe he should keep his mouth shut in case asking for more of Vincent's time ruined his chances at renewing the contract. And what kind of stupid arrangement was that anyway? Who actually used a contract in lieu of a relationship? Or was the point to *not have* a relationship?

Fuck. Why did he even care? This wasn't supposed to be anything more than a few weeks of great sex and experiencing being tied up. They weren't *boyfriends*.

Vincent had probably never had something as mundane as a boyfriend in his life. Jasper needed to get rid of that expectation now, before it ruined everything.

This was nothing but sex.

Hot, kinky, blow-your-mind sex.

That was way better than any kind of fucking relationship.

He'd even managed to convince himself of that by the time the driver dropped him off at Vincent's.

He knocked, then tested the doorknob and found it unlocked. He stepped inside after a moment's hesitation. "Sir?" he called, toeing off his shoes by the door.

"Pet."

He spun around and spotted Vincent at the top of the stairs, dressed in sweats, his hair tousled. "Did you just wake up?" he asked, grinning as he hopped up the stairs. He balanced against the banister as he leaned up for a kiss, only a little surprised when Vincent granted him one that tasted like toothpaste.

"I fell asleep."

"Bad sign when cooking tires you out," he said, his laugh turning into a moan when Vincent groped him in response. "How long until dinner's done?" he asked, hoping they had time for a quickie at least.

"It's done. It's keeping warm in the oven," Vincent replied, slipping his hands under Jasper's shirt.

He moaned and stepped onto the landing. "So we can work up an appetite first?"

Vincent's lips twitched as he nudged Jasper into the bedroom. "Mm," he said, backing Jasper into the dresser with a few kisses against his neck.

A surprised yelp escaped him when Vincent grabbed the backs of his thighs and lifted him onto the dresser. Mmm. Good height. He grinned and buried both hands in Vincent's hair, mussing it even further. He leaned in for another kiss, only to pull back in confusion when Vincent didn't return it. He started to ask what was wrong, but the expression on Vincent's face made the words die in his throat.

That wasn't a "ready for sexy times" expression. Usually that kind of look preceded some sort of serious conversation that tended to end with everything blowing up in his face. "I'm sorry," he said, panic fluttering in his chest. Fuck. No way was he getting dumped now after the shitfest of a week he'd already gone through.

Vincent pulled back, brow somehow furrowing even further. "For what?"

Jasper shrugged. "Whatever I did that pissed you off."

"You didn—" Vincent started, but he stopped and let out a slow breath. He shook his head, his fingers flexing against Jasper's hips as he took another breath. Then he reached back and pulled off his T-shirt, hesitating once it was over his head, before pulling it off completely and tossing it onto the dresser.

It took Jasper a moment to clue in enough to realize what it meant that Vincent was standing shirtless in front of him. His eyes dropped to Vincent's chest and the elaborate scarring there with a soft, "Oh shit." He vividly remembered the feel of those scars, rough and too smooth by turns, and he knew how gnarly burn scars could be, but seeing them with his own eyes was different.

He followed the angry red pattern of thick spiderwebbing with his eyes, medical curiosity distracting him for the moment. He tilted his head when he spotted a faint curved scar near Vincent's ribs. He slid his hand down and lightly traced a fingertip over it. "Skin graft?" he asked, glancing up when Vincent let out a shaky breath.

"Yeah."

"They did a pretty good job." He wouldn't have noticed if he hadn't known what one looked like.

More noticeable was the tension practically thrumming through Vincent's entire body. It wasn't anger at least, but it still didn't bode well, and not only because it meant little chance of getting lucky. He considered ignoring it and trying to seduce Vincent again, but that felt like a dick move. Even if they weren't in any kind of relationship, this was still something he couldn't simply shrug off.

With a sigh, he slid his palms up Vincent's chest, winding his arms around his shoulders again. "Are you okay?"

Vincent gave a neutral "Mm," in response, eyes fixed on Jasper's chest, but he didn't pull away.

He leaned back, brushing a thumb against the faint shadow beneath Vincent's eye. "Have you not been sleeping?"

"I'm fine," Vincent replied, finally moving enough to flick Jasper's fingers away.

It was on the tip of his tongue to say *If you were fine, you'd be fucking me right now*, but he bit the words back. He dropped his hands and braced them on the edge of the dresser, clamping his mouth shut against the hurt until it flared into irritation instead.

"Liar," he muttered, bracing himself when Vincent tensed. Panic slammed through his chest again, but he breathed through it, tightening his grip on the dresser to keep from running for the door. He was far too close to Vincent for that anyway, and his instincts knew it. Better to stay as still as possible and try to keep his mouth shut.

Confronting someone rarely turned out well for him, but he was getting better at it since moving in with Amber. It helped not being near his sperm donor anymore.

"They don't bother me," he murmured, his gaze dropping to Vincent's scars again, "if that's what's got you so on edge." Why Vincent even bothered to show him was a mystery. Not like seeing them changed their contract.

Vincent shifted back half a step and dragged his fingers through his hair. "I could have handled that better."

Jasper shrugged, not about to deny that. He'd already reached his limit by calling Vincent out.

"Sorry," Vincent said, resting his hands on Jasper's knees. "I had to know if it was going to be a problem."

Why would it be a problem? Jasper kept his mouth shut since he didn't know what the fuck he should say to that. He was pretty sure the offer to work up an appetite was off the table now, but this also didn't feel like something that should be a concern. They weren't dating, and their contract only had a few more weeks.

He straightened a bit as that really sank in. He didn't have much to lose at this point. "Make you a deal. I won't let the scars bother me if you don't let my clinginess bother you."

Vincent's lips tugged into a frown. "You haven't been clingy."

Jasper snorted softly and shrugged. Maybe not yet. But he would be, especially knowing this was going to end soon either way. That was inevitable when he liked someone. "Deal?"

Vincent studied him a moment, a bit of the tension easing out of his body as he nodded. He glanced down when Jasper offered his hand, lips twitching in amusement, but he took it in a warm grasp and shook.

That settled, Jasper slipped his arms around Vincent's shoulders and leaned in. "Good. Now feed me." He gave in to the impulse to kiss Vincent's nose, then hopped off the dresser. He glanced back as he reached the door and couldn't read Vincent's new expression to save his life, so he winked and hurried downstairs.

VINCENT TOOK a moment to breathe once Jasper left the room, leaning all his weight against the dresser with his head hanging between his shoulders. He wasn't certain if he'd completely fucked everything up or only gotten close. He hadn't even meant to pull his shirt off. Last night he'd finally decided to wait until the last week of the contract to bring his scars up again, but… he couldn't wait that long.

He was already getting far too attached, and if Jasper had looked at his scars with even a hint of disgust, he would have had to spend the last few weeks of their contract distancing himself. Waiting even a few more weeks for his answer wasn't worth the prolonged stress or potential heartache.

Except now he needed a plan to figure out Jasper's reactions, because even sleep-deprived and stuck in his own head, he was intimately familiar with a response of panic. That and the way Jasper froze when he'd asked for a belt made him wary. And then the way Jasper spoke on the phone the other night, like he was aching for contact yet refused Vincent's offer to come over.

Was that what he'd meant by being clingy? Was Jasper holding himself back, afraid of asking for too much? Even if Vincent could understand the sentiment, it still didn't sit well with him.

He dragged his fingers through his hair and pulled his shirt back on, then headed downstairs for damage control. Jasper had already pulled the lasagna from the oven and filled two plates. Vincent caught up with him as Jasper was grabbing forks from the drawer and hooked an arm around Jasper from behind. He pressed his lips against Jasper's neck with a quiet, "Thank you, pet," and meant for more than getting the table set.

Relief flooded him when, after a few moments of silence, Jasper relaxed into his chest. He took the offered fork, using his other hand to turn Jasper enough for a proper kiss—slow and thorough, like he should have done from the beginning. It took longer than he liked for Jasper to relax with a soft, sweet sound of surrender.

"Every day," Jasper murmured against Vincent's lips.

"Hmm?"

Jasper's fingers twitched where they'd latched on to the front of Vincent's shirt. "Contract. Sex every day."

He pulled back with a soft laugh. "What happened to once a week?"

"Not enough."

"Hmm. I suppose I'm open to negotiation," Vincent said, pressing a light, quick kiss to Jasper's forehead before moving to the table.

He wasn't willing to agree to an every-day clause—not only was it impractical, he didn't want sex becoming a chore. Jasper wanted more than a once-a-week guarantee, which was fine. By the time they finished eating, they'd agreed not to part ways without being satisfied, barring emergencies or unexpected situations.

Once the dishes were cleared and the leftovers put away, he nudged Jasper back upstairs to the bedroom, where he took his time unbuttoning Jasper's shirt, brushing his fingers against every inch of exposed skin.

Jasper shivered, clutching Vincent's hips. "Should undress me more often, Sir."

"I should," he agreed, finally reaching the last button. He splayed his hands against Jasper's stomach and slid up his chest, catching his thumbs on Jasper's nipples and savoring the audible catch in his breathing. He slipped the shirt off Jasper's shoulders and let it fall, then unfastened his pants. He found the warm skin of Jasper's neck with his lips as he inched the jeans and boxers down until gravity caught them. "Lie back," he murmured.

Jasper stepped back and sank onto the bed, stretching out with an enticing arch of his body. His skin flushed under Vincent's gaze, his cock swelling.

Vincent found himself spellbound by how responsive Jasper was, especially to something as simple as a heated glance. He slid his palm along the inside of one of Jasper's thighs as he sank to a knee between them and leaned down. He claimed Jasper's lips in another slow kiss, making it the entirety of his focus, reveling in the eager reciprocation. In the flex of fingers on his arm and in his hair. In the way Jasper whined with impatient need and squirmed beneath him. He pulled back, rubbing a soothing hand against Jasper's chest. "Patience, pet."

Sex wasn't enough to make up for his idiocy earlier. Not nearly enough to thank Jasper for being Jasper. For not looking at him with disgust or horror. Or for not suggesting some kind of cosmetic surgery.

"Roll over," he murmured, reaching into the nightstand for the massage oil. He paused long enough to appreciate the sight of Jasper stretched out on his stomach, all lean limbs and sun-kissed skin. He settled over Jasper's thighs and poured oil into his hands, rubbed them together, and slowly spread the oil across Jasper's shoulders.

Jasper tensed, with a sound of surprise. "Sir?"

"Relax, pet," Vincent replied, gently digging his fingers into tight muscles.

Jasper didn't relax at all, but when Vincent hit a knot and dug in, his body twitched with a sharp groan before melting. "Oh fuck."

"Good?" he asked, stifling a soft laugh when his only answer was a strangled moan. He focused on the tension in Jasper's shoulders, finding more knots and tight spots than he liked, but the soft sighs and the way Jasper unwound further each time he soothed one into releasing was gratifying.

How long had it been since he'd laid hands on someone without sex or service to the club being the primary focus? Apparently far, far too long.

He slid his hand up, unable to resist curling his fingers tight in Jasper's hair, and was rewarded with a deep sigh.

"Feels so good," Jasper slurred.

Vincent chuckled, alternating between massaging Jasper's scalp and tugging his hair. "You're an overgrown cat."

Jasper let out a startled laugh. "What does that make you, then?"

"Hmm. Your owner."

A warm flush spread across the back of Jasper's neck, and he buried his face deeper into the pillow. "At least I found a good one."

Vincent smiled and dragged his thumbs down either side of Jasper's spine, spreading his fingers as he slid his hands back up and across his shoulders.

Jasper was as responsive as ever, his eyes closed as sighs, groans, grunts, and whimpers of pleasure guided Vincent's hands.

His cock gave a valiant effort to rise to the occasion, but the antianxiety pill he'd taken earlier made that all but impossible. He didn't take them regularly anymore, but the endless list of—mostly horrible—possibilities of what could happen if he showed his scars to Jasper had forced his hand. He wouldn't be getting it up anytime soon, but that's what toys were for.

And he'd even bought a few new ones recently that he'd been meaning to try out.

He reached into the nightstand again, snagging the vibrating prostate massager. Jasper's moans turned eager as Vincent poured more oil into his hands and slid them lower. "Insatiable, aren't we?" he murmured, rubbing his fingertip against Jasper's entrance before pressing inside.

Jasper hiked a leg up and pushed his hips back. "More."

Vincent clicked his tongue and landed a light swat to Jasper's ass. "Is that any way to ask for something?"

There was a pause as Jasper went still, his fingers curling against the sheet as he answered with, "Wasn't asking." His face was mostly hidden by his shoulder as he peeked at Vincent with one eye.

Relief eased some of his lingering tension. If Jasper was comfortable enough to be bratty again, they were on the right track. "My mistake," he replied dryly, adding another finger. Never let it be said he couldn't give a sub exactly what they asked for.

Once Jasper was a writhing, moaning mess, he grabbed the prostate massager and lubed it up, then took his time slowly pressing it inside. Jasper shifted his knees wider with a moan, rocking his hips in search of something more. When he was nearly to the point of begging, Vincent turned it on.

Jasper let out a sharp, keening yelp, his back arching as he eagerly pushed his hips back.

Vincent hummed and settled his free hand on Jasper's hip, holding the massager steady with the other as Jasper fucked himself on it. A soft litany of curses and pleas grew more incoherent by the minute as Vincent experimentally cycled through the various vibration and speed settings.

Jasper pushed onto his arms and knees, his chest and head pressed to the mattress, his skin slick with massage oil and sweat.

Vincent might have seen Jasper lost to pleasure numerous times by now, but seeing it without the haze of his own arousal or the focus of an intense scene was entrancing. Sex seemed to be the one thing Jasper let himself freely and fully experience, and Vincent hoped that freedom would find its way to the rest of their time spent together.

He'd made a mistake earlier, and he wasn't young or naive enough to think it'd be the last, but Jasper continued to prove that taking an interest in him hadn't been a mistake, and Vincent was finding it harder to keep from going all in.

He slid his hand from Jasper's hip to his cock, gripping tight as he leaned over to graze his teeth against the back of Jasper's neck.

Jasper shuddered with a gasping whimper, ineffectually thrusting into Vincent's hand. "Please."

Vincent pressed the button to cycle to the triple pulse and long vibration pattern Jasper seemed to enjoy the most, biting a little harder. Once he'd left a mark there, he ordered, "Come." He loosened his grip enough to let Jasper thrust, and it only took twice before he shuddered through his orgasm with a long-drawn-out moan. Vincent pressed against the massager, grinding it into Jasper's ass and stroking him until he whimpered from overstimulation. Only then did he turn off the toy, but he left it in place. After a few moments, Jasper shifted to the side and collapsed, chest heaving and eyes closed.

He leaned down to press a quick kiss to Jasper's shoulder and got up, letting his fingers drag lightly down Jasper's leg to his ankle, then lift away as he headed to the bathroom. He washed his hands and returned with a warm, damp cloth. Jasper offered no resistance as Vincent carefully pulled the massager free and cleaned him up. Only after he'd tossed the toy and cloth aside and stretched out on the bed did Jasper move, rolling over to press into Vincent's chest.

Vincent tugged him close, contentment seeping through his limbs. He pressed a kiss to the top of Jasper's head, more than willing to doze until it was time to take him home and head to the club.

Chapter Eighteen

Jasper whined as the house came into view, turning his best puppy eyes on Vincent in one final effort to stay with him. "Really no chance of taking me back home with you?"

Vincent glanced at him with a faint smile. "You have an early class, and I need to get to work."

He failed to stifle a sigh. That might be true, but he could skip. Once wouldn't hurt anything. Except Amber might kill him for skipping if he wasn't sick. Especially if he did it to stay with Vincent in the hopes of having sex. "Fine," he muttered, reluctantly pushing the door open. "Night, Sir."

"Good night, pet."

Jasper glanced back when he reached the house, waved, and watched the car pull away before dragging himself inside. The few hours of bliss had been nice, but now all the stress of the week was threatening to suffocate him again.

Matt glanced up from the couch, his legs sprawled across Keith's lap. "Nice date?"

Jasper hesitated. "Yeah," he said, unsure why the question felt like a trap.

Matt squinted at him a moment, his lip curling with disgust. "It's been over a month. You're still interested in him?"

Jasper frowned, glancing at Keith, but he seemed to be actively ignoring their conversation. "Why shouldn't I be? He's"—*the best thing to happen to me in a long time*—"amazing."

"*Amazing?*" Matt asked, staring at him like he'd grown a second head. "Did you seriously call that sociopath *amazing?*"

"Did you just call him a *sociopath?*" Jasper clenched his hands into fists as he stepped into the room. "What the fuck is your problem?"

Matt dropped his feet to the floor and stood with a sneer. "My *problem* is you're falling in love with someone you know nothing about."

Jasper froze, his breath whooshing out of his lungs. Falling in love? He wasn't… falling in love. This was nothing more than a two-month thing where he could get laid and actually feel like someone gave a shit about him for once.

Which might not have been fair, considering how much Amber and the others had done for him. Taking him in, giving him safe harbor, helping him get to or from campus and work. But they all had each other, and he didn't have anyone. He hadn't even really spoken to his own brother since he was thirteen. Not since Noah moved out and left him to deal with their father on his own.

"I'm not," he whispered, taking a step back.

Except he was. He totally was, and everyone could fucking see it.

Could Vincent see it? Did Vincent see how desperately Jasper wanted something more than *just sex* with him?

"Nice job, dumbass," Keith muttered to Matt.

Jasper glanced up from where he'd backed into the wall, latching on to Keith's arms when Keith planted his hands on Jasper's shoulders. "I'm not," he said again, wishing he could make that true by saying it.

"Breathe," Keith said, taking a deep breath.

Jasper whimpered and clutched at Keith's shirt like a lifeline, coughing as he tried to match his breathing. It hurt, and the walls continued threatening to close in on him, but Keith stayed with him, and his voice managed to keep Jasper grounded long enough to calm down. The panic finally ebbed back after an eternity, and he slumped beneath a wave of exhaustion. "Sorry."

"Good now?" Keith squeezed his shoulders with a sympathetic look. "Tea?"

Jasper nodded, followed Keith to the kitchen, and collapsed into a chair at the table. He scrubbed his palms against his face with a shaky breath. What the fuck was he supposed to do now? "I'm screwed." He was *so* screwed. How the fuck was he supposed to walk away now?

Keith huffed a laugh. "A little."

Jasper glared at Keith before sighing, crossing his arms as he resisted the urge to bang his head on the table. "Why aren't you all pissed off at me like Matt?"

Keith didn't answer immediately, glancing towards the living room, but Matt had vanished like the cowardly little shit he was. He sighed softly and brought two cups of hot tea to the table. He sat across from Jasper. "What has Vincent told you?"

"That he hurt Matt. He didn't exactly go into detail."

"I won't either. I know most of what happened, but Matt hasn't told me everything. If I were him, I'd probably hate Vincent too." He paused, drumming his fingers against his cup. "I know people can change. That they can learn from their mistakes. I've seen Vincent at the club, and I've never seen him hurt or abuse anyone. But I still know what he did to Matt. I'm not going to tell you not to trust him for something he did nearly ten years ago, but I'm not going to encourage you either. You're an adult. You can make your own choices."

Jasper stared at Keith as his brain tried to wrap itself around all that, surprised that Keith wasn't trying to tell him what to do or not do. Now that he thought about it, even Amber hadn't tried to interfere too much, which was surprising considering she'd been bossy to the point of tyrannical when they were kids. He'd never forget the time she thwacked him with a tree branch until he kissed her shoes.

Looking back now, that was probably the first hint of her Dominatrix manifesting, and he felt a brief twinge of sympathy for Terrance, but he quickly shoved those thoughts away. He did not need those mental images of his cousin.

He took a small sip of his tea and let out a slow breath. "Thanks."

"Sure. We're here for you, Jas. You may be Amber's cousin, but we're all family."

Jasper swallowed and refused to acknowledge the sting in his eyes. He nodded faintly, not trusting himself to speak, especially considering he'd been kind of a dick to them lately.

Keith stood and reached across the table to squeeze his shoulder, then headed upstairs.

Once he was alone, he let out an explosive breath and scrubbed his face again.

Fuck. He needed to get his shit together. And he definitely had to get his fucking infatuation under control, because he was absolutely certain the quickest way to ruin everything was for Vincent to realize he was developing feelings.

He sipped a bit more of his tea before dumping the rest in the sink and heading up to bed. All he wanted was a quick shower and to pass out, but the sound of sharp voices brought him up short, years of avoiding drawing attention to himself making him freeze.

"—to get over your problem with Jas," Keith said.

"Over it," Matt snapped.

"Really. 'Cause you've been a dick to him for weeks."

Matt's sneer was evident when he said, "He deserves it for getting involved with that motherfucking bastard!"

Jasper nearly jumped at the venom in Matt's voice, a twinge of unease tightening his stomach. He'd assumed Matt was pissed that Vincent had dumped him, but that was a lot of hate to hang on to for so long if that's all it was.

"Still being a dick."

Matt snarled something under his breath, and Jasper couldn't resist inching closer to hear despite the nervous pounding of his heart.

"Don't you think it's time to let this grudge go?" Keith sounded like he was getting irritated.

"You don't know what all he did!"

"How can I when you've never trusted me enough to tell me?" Keith shouted back.

Jasper flinched. He really shouldn't be listening anymore. His room was only a few steps away, but Keith's door was open, and if he moved now they'd definitely know he'd been listening.

Matt let out a frustrated, wordless yell, and then silence.

Keith sighed and sounded weary when he spoke again. "You know I love you, so don't take this the wrong way when I say I can't deal with this right now."

Shit, shit, shit.

Jasper tensed as he heard someone moving towards the door, standing still and hoping if it was Matt that he turned and went farther down the hall. Of course as soon as Matt stepped out, their eyes met.

Matt's eyes were bright and red-rimmed. He stared at Jasper a moment before a twisted smirk settled on his lips, his voice eerily calm when he said, "Whatever you think you have with him, it means nothing to him. He'll take what he wants and leave you for others to break whatever's left."

Jasper blinked, hardly able to think of a response. He slumped against the wall as Matt's door slammed behind him, rubbing a hand against his chest, trying to steady his rapid heartbeat. What little comfort he'd gotten from Keith was shattering under Matt's absolute certainty that Vincent would never care. Somehow this felt different from all the other times Matt said Vincent was a dick and not worth Jasper's time.

Maybe he'd deluded himself by thinking there could be something between them. Everything seemed to become sort of hazy and surreal when he was with Vincent. Like time stopped existing until they had to part ways. That was probably because he was seeing everything through lust-colored glasses.

He shoved off the wall towards his room, ignoring Keith calling him, and shut his door.

This was fine. He'd known from the start this was nothing more than a fling. He could deal with that. Take what he could and learn from it. If nothing else, he'd at least discover a few new kinks before the end.

Even telling himself that, he couldn't shake the doubt that seemed to grow by the hour and the day. His nerves twisted themselves into knots so tight he could barely pay attention in class or eat. By the time Friday came around, he'd managed to stress himself sick. And for once, the thought of seeing Vincent didn't spark joy, so like a complete and utter ass, he sent a text saying he wasn't feeling well and asking if they could skip this weekend.

The response came a few minutes later, a simple: *Do you need anything?*

Which only added guilt to his already muddled emotions. If Vincent were really as bad as Matt said, he did an amazing job of pretending to care.

No just going to sleep it off sorry

Then he turned his phone off, and when he failed to lose himself in his assigned readings, he went to bed.

Chapter Nineteen

Vincent stared at his phone with a frown, completely willing to blame it for the fact there were no new messages from Jasper. It was still early, far too early to be awake on a Saturday, but having his weekend disrupted meant no Jasper in his bed, which meant he'd slept as poorly as usual. He knew he shouldn't read more into a text than what was there, but Jasper's last message seemed off. And since he *definitely* knew he shouldn't assume the worst, he sent a text asking if Jasper was feeling better and if he needed anything.

That done, he dragged himself out of bed and dressed. With his weekend plans shot, he took his time making breakfast and drained three cups of coffee. Not like there wasn't plenty of work he could do, but he wasn't feeling it.

His phone chimed when he was settling on the sofa, debating on a movie or a game, and he immediately checked the message. He raised an eyebrow at the single-word text from Jasper.

No

He tossed his phone aside so he didn't immediately respond, letting his head fall against the back of the sofa. It didn't mean anything, even if it *felt* like Jasper was pushing him away. It didn't have to be a bad sign. Maybe he was trying not to be clingy. He let out a slow breath, but then he was up and moving before he'd fully decided on what to do.

Two and a half hours later, he found himself knocking on Jasper's door, a large bowl of hot homemade chicken noodle soup in hand.

Keith answered the door mid-yawn, still in a T-shirt and boxers, and squinted at Vincent in confusion. "What happened?"

"Jasper said he was sick," he replied, lifting the bowl a bit.

A long, drawn-out silence followed that. "Huh," Keith finally said, turning and motioning Vincent to follow. He bypassed the kitchen and headed upstairs, where he knocked on the second door. "Jas, you in there?" he asked, glancing at Vincent and pointing for him to stop where he'd be out of sight of the door.

That wasn't foreboding in the least. He pushed his sunglasses to the top of his head and shifted his hold on the soup as the door cracked open.

"What?"

"You sick?"

"No, why?"

Vincent tensed and somehow kept himself from stalking forward.

Keith raised an eyebrow at Jasper with a frown. "You sure? Why aren't you with Vincent?"

"Fuck off," Jasper snapped. "It's none of your business."

"But it is mine," Vincent said, managing to keep his voice steady. Why Jasper had felt the need to lie to him was something that would need to be addressed, but that wasn't the bigger issue right now. He breathed through the anger twisting his stomach, the silence from the other side of the door speaking volumes.

Keith shot Jasper a look that clearly said *Good luck digging yourself out of this one* and stepped back.

Jasper sucked in an audible breath, then stepped out of his room. His eyes landed on the bowl, and he glanced up in confusion, though he quickly turned his attention to the floor. "I said I didn't need anything."

Vincent fought down an incredulous laugh. "That's what you're going with?" He waited a moment for Jasper to offer anything else, an excuse or explanation—*anything*—but Jasper stared at the floor with a stubborn set to his shoulders.

He was well-versed in the signs of someone who wasn't willing to talk, but he couldn't understand what had happened. He'd been sure things were going well, that they'd settled their misunderstandings and moved on, but maybe he'd missed something.

It certainly wouldn't be the first time.

He stepped closer to hand over the soup at the same time another door opened down the hall. He glanced up and met Matt's eyes with the same sinking dread he felt every time they met.

"The fuck?"

"I'm leaving," Vincent said, not at all willing to stick around an openly hostile environment. Jasper could reach out to him when he was ready to talk. Or not. He didn't like the thought of Jasper cutting things off without even an explanation, but if that was how he wanted to play this, they wouldn't have made it past a second contract anyway.

Before he could even get to the stairs, Keith poked his head out of his room, where he'd obviously been listening. "Or maybe you two could finally put this shit behind you."

Vincent hesitated and glanced at Matt. He'd offered an apology years ago, and Matt had made it abundantly clear he would never forgive or forget.

"You're a fucking cuntass bitch," Matt snarled at Keith. Then he turned his attention to Vincent, his gaze snagging on Jasper. His expression shifted with sadistic delight, and Vincent braced himself to have the entire story laid out for everyone. "But sure. *Jas* deserves to know what he's getting into."

"Matt," Vincent said tightly, "I'm sorry I wasn't able to give you what you wanted—"

"You think I give a fucking shit about that?" Matt yelled, slamming his fist against the wall hard enough a picture frame fell and shattered on the floor. "You fucking. Left. Me," he snarled. "I let you tie me up, and then you *left me* there. Did you really think no one would find me like that?"

"I—What?" No, that wasn't what happened. "I untied you."

Matt laughed and stepped forward, the broken glass crunching beneath his socked feet. "No you fucking did not." He stopped in front of Vincent, leaning close and pitching his voice low enough Vincent could barely hear him. "Do you know how many guys found me like that? Three. And they were all too happy to do what you were too fucking chickenshit to do."

No. He'd untied Matt before leaving him in that room. He'd been sure of that. Except he'd been so drunk he didn't even remember getting from that room to his car, and he'd never understood the depth of Matt's hatred and anger.

Vincent flinched, nausea quickly slicing through his disbelief. "Matt," he whispered. "I'm so sorry."

"Die and go to hell!" Matt shoved past him and down the stairs, with Keith hurrying after him.

He clutched the banister for balance, struggling to get a decent breath. He swallowed hard, forcing down the roiling emotions threatening to overwhelm him.

When he looked up, Jasper was still in his doorway, watching him with wide eyes. How much of that had he heard?

Not that it mattered. Whatever he'd done to make Jasper distance himself from him paled in comparison to Matt's bombshell. Fuck, he wouldn't even want a contract with himself right now. "I'll consider our contract void," he managed to say. He could at least spare Jasper the trouble of ending it himself.

He stepped back, nearly tripping down the stairs when his feet refused to work properly. He barely got the door to his car open, but it was probably a good thing he couldn't get the key in the ignition. His fingers refused to cooperate, enough so that the keys finally clattered to the floorboard, and he couldn't bring himself to try again. He gripped the steering wheel and pressed his forehead against it, struggling to keep his breathing even.

All these years he'd blamed himself for hurting Matt and ruining their friendship, and he'd never understood how much damage he'd done. He never should have let Matt talk him into tying him up. Even drunk he'd known it wouldn't satisfy either of them. Matt didn't submit easily, and Vincent had never been interested in anything less than a full-time lifestyle. But he *never* would have left Matt there without untying him. Never would have left him naked and powerless. At a frat party of all things.

He remembered reaching for the ties, pulling the knots free. But nearly every other memory of that night was a black nothingness or a blur, and there was little more than flashes of sense memory or disconnected images from the moment he left the party to waking in the hospital.

The sickening self-loathing he'd felt when he learned his accident had nearly killed someone returned with a vengeance. Somehow it was even worse now, fueled by a decade of ignorance and the fact Matt was living with that trauma because of Vincent's careless mistake.

He should have died in that accident. There was no reason he should have survived. He didn't deserve to be alive. He certainly didn't deserve to be free, with a nice home and thriving business, all because of his grandfather's money and expensive lawyers. Once he'd healed enough to be discharged, he'd completed his mandatory counseling while finishing his degree at Oxford. It was only when he'd returned to the States with Adam in tow that he'd found Dr. Cohn to ensure he never reached that low point again.

Footsteps smacked against the pavement, and he lifted his head to find Jasper standing near the car. "Sorry," he said, clearing his throat when his voice came out rough. "I'm leaving." He swiped his arm across his face and fumbled for the keys with one hand, tugging the door shut with the other. He looked up again when the door didn't shut, eyeing the hand gripping the top in confusion.

Jasper pulled the door open farther and stepped around it, expression somewhere close to furious. "What do you mean the contract is void?"

Vincent pulled back, unsure how to respond to that as he struggled to switch his focus from Matt to Jasper. "It's fine," he finally said. "You don't need to worry about it. I won't contact you anymore."

For some reason that only seemed to piss Jasper off further, but a moment later his expression shattered. "Just like that?"

Fuck. He apparently couldn't do anything right today. "Trying to keep a contract when one party isn't committed is a breeding ground for resentment and abuse. I won't make that mistake again."

"Who said I wasn't committed?"

Frustration swallowed the dozen replies that got tangled in Vincent's throat. Instead of trying to voice any of them, he forced in a breath until his lungs ached, then slowly let it back out. "If that's true," he finally said, sliding the key into the ignition, "we can talk about it later."

For now, he needed someplace quiet. When he tugged on the door again, it shut easily, and he didn't think too much of it until the passenger door opened as he was buckling his seat belt.

Jasper slid into the car, slammed his door shut, buckled in, and sank into his seat without so much as a glance at Vincent. "Go."

JASPER LINGERED by the front door of Vincent's house until Vincent disappeared into his bedroom, then released a slow breath. He'd fully expected to be thrown out of the car and wasn't even really sure what had made him get in to begin with. He knew he'd fucked up—had known he was fucking up the moment he decided to avoid Vincent— but the thought of everything crumbling between them because of that?

Fuck no. Like hell he'd let something like *irony* play a part in their breakup. When Vincent finally dumped him, it would be because Jasper tried to strangle him with his octopus tentacles of clinginess.

He slipped his shoes off and wandered into the living room, immediately turning towards the kitchen when he smelled something cooking. A large pot of soup was keeping warm on the stove. The same chicken noodle soup Vincent had brought him. Because he'd said he was sick.

That more than anything reassured him that what had happened with Matt was a misunderstanding. At worst a terrible accident. The horror on Vincent's face when Matt had whispered to him was proof of that. Vincent hadn't hurt him on purpose.

Vincent *made Jasper soup* because he'd said he was sick. Even Amber had never done more than toss him a sleeve of crackers.

He swallowed against the tightness in his throat and filled a bowl with chicken noodle soup, then sent a quick text to Keith asking him to put the bowl he'd left in his room in the fridge. No sense in letting it go to waste.

He ate two bowls, then settled on the couch to channel surf. Vincent didn't make an appearance after an hour, but Jasper waited another forty minutes before giving up and creeping up the stairs. He poked his head into the bedroom to find Vincent lying on the bed, one hand on his stomach, his other arm thrown over his eyes.

Jasper hesitated after one step into the room. He knew he had to suck it up and fix things or they'd only get worse, but he wasn't sure how. He was relatively confident in his ability to patch a person together well enough to keep them alive if they had a minor stab wound, but relationships required skills he'd never managed to develop. But he'd try. He could only hope trying would be enough for now.

He inched into the room and onto the bed. When Vincent didn't tell him to fuck off, he risked pressing closer, resting his head on Vincent's thigh. "Hey," he said softly, settling his hand on Vincent's stomach. "You awake?"

Vincent sighed. "Yeah," he murmured, his voice rough.

"You okay?"

A longer sigh and a moment of silence. "I don't know."

Jasper rubbed his hand back and forth. "Anything I can do?"

Vincent let out a soft hum that wasn't really an answer.

When nothing else followed, Jasper slid his hand down farther, intent on distracting him with sex, but Vincent caught his hand as soon as he reached for the button of his pants. He winced and pulled his hand away, only for Vincent to tighten his grip and hold it in place.

"Stay."

Jasper let out an explosive breath and slumped into Vincent's warmth. If they weren't having sex, that left talking. He needed to apologize, but the words were stuck somewhere near his gut, and he had to find a way to vomit them out. Two simple words. How could they be so hard?

His fingers twitched in Vincent's hold, and he closed his eyes, taking a steadying breath. "'M sorry."

Vincent squeezed his hand. "Sorry for what?"

"For lying." He swallowed hard in the silence that followed, wondering if he'd gotten it wrong.

"Okay," Vincent said quietly, his thumb brushing against the back of Jasper's hand. "Though I'd like to know why you felt the need to lie in the first place."

Jasper shrugged, pressing his face into Vincent's stomach. "Matt," he said, regretting it when Vincent immediately tensed, but he quickly forced the rest of the words out. "He said this would never mean anything to you. That you'd take what you wanted and then leave."

"And you believed him."

"I guess," he said, wincing when Vincent let out another sigh. That one sounded aggravated.

"It's not like I can blame you," he said after a moment, and Jasper lifted his head with a frown, not liking the new tone in his voice. It was almost defeated. He didn't like that Vincent's arm was still covering his eyes either.

Vincent cleared his throat. "I would understand if you wanted to end the contra—"

"No!" Jasper moved without thinking, dread fluttering in his chest as he straddled Vincent and tugged his arm away from his face. Those gorgeous hazel eyes were wide and red-rimmed as they stared at Jasper.

"I don't care," he choked out, his fingers clutching Vincent's shirt. "Whatever happened with you and Matt, I don't care. It was ages ago, and you've never hurt *me*." And Vincent obviously regretted it, or he wouldn't be up here alone instead of taking advantage of his sub. "You're not getting rid of me that easily, asshole."

Vincent raised an eyebrow, his lips twitching into a ghost of a smile. "My mistake."

Jasper huffed and relaxed, unable to maintain eye contact and focusing on Vincent's lips instead. "I really am sorry," he murmured. "I thought… maybe space would be a good idea." Especially after Matt so helpfully pointed out he was in love. Maybe it was lust? Wouldn't it be better if he was merely obsessed and it faded after exploring a few more kinks?

He blinked at the light touch to his cheek, risking a glance up.

"I forgive you." Vincent sat up and slid both of his hands into Jasper's hair, tugging enough to force his head back. "Can you promise not to make this mistake again?" he asked, dragging his lips across Jasper's exposed throat, which was more than enough to completely distract Jasper.

Why had he thought denying himself this for a weekend was a good idea? He tilted his head to add some pressure to Vincent's grip and moaned, twisting his fingers tighter where he had latched on to Vincent's shirt. That felt so good. How had he never realized how good a sprinkle of not-quite pain could be? The intense tingles along his scalp were like their own tiny orgasms.

"*Jasper.*"

Jasper blinked his eyes open, unsure when he'd even closed them, and managed to focus on Vincent. "Huh?" What was with the exasperated look?

Vincent's lips twitched. "I asked if you could promise not to do this again."

Could he promise that? He knew he had a bad habit of getting stuck in his own head, overthinking things, and then making things worse with his decisions. "I can try."

Apparently that wasn't good enough. Vincent shifted his grip, considering Jasper as his thumb traced beneath his lower lip. "Can you promise to tell me that you need space rather than making up a lie?"

He swallowed hard, the anxious energy that had started to build up fading at having a clear path to follow. That would be far easier. "Yes," he whispered. He could do that.

Vincent nodded as if that were settled and returned his lips to Jasper's neck. Jasper stared at the ceiling, his stomach a mix of giddy relief at getting through that without making it worse and a niggling worry that it had been too easy or wasn't enough. "Shouldn't I be punished or something?" he whispered, hoping he didn't end up regretting that when Vincent stilled and pulled back to study him.

"Do you want me to punish or discipline you if you make a mistake?"

No! was his initial reaction, but he wasn't *completely* naive when it came to this stuff; he'd done some deeper research the past few weeks. Besides the draw of being tied up and helpless, he wanted the assurance of being with someone who would tell him when he did something wrong rather than decide he wasn't worth the trouble anymore. "Yes?"

He shivered as Vincent's eyes darkened, as if the thought of punishing Jasper was a huge turn-on. Or maybe he was wanting to give that assurance as much as Jasper craved it. His stomach swooped like the ground had disappeared, but somehow he couldn't imagine regretting this particular decision.

Vincent dragged him in for a kiss, and Jasper moaned at the intensity of it. Every time, Vincent proved to be an amazing kisser, and this one was no different. Vincent kissed him like he wanted to claim Jasper's very essence with his lips.

That was almost as distracting as his next thought that made him pull back with a grin. "Does this count as makeup sex?"

Vincent laughed and tumbled him to the bed. Once he'd pinned him down, he showed Jasper how absolutely mind-blowing makeup sex could be.

CHAPTER TWENTY

JASPER'S SUIT arrived earlier than expected. As soon as his driver dropped Jasper off at the club, Vincent sent him up to his office to change into it while Vincent walked the club. The evening was already busy, a steady flow of members coming in for a quick scene, and several who lingered for the community. Applications continued piling up—to the point he'd need to hire extra staff soon, both to curate and process applications, and to monitor the floor.

Members stopped him to chat as he made a round through the play area. Some even asked after Jasper, which surprised and pleased him, and left him bemused. He hadn't made any effort to keep his contract a secret, but he'd forgotten how quickly gossip spread; he'd been blissfully free from it for years.

And like that, fate answered his temptation with a loud and clear *Fuck you.*

He stepped out of the dungeon and glanced towards the bar, freezing as he caught sight of Adam.

Tension seized every one of his muscles, the familiar fight-or-flight instincts warring against each other.

As if sensing him, Adam turned and smiled, all bright white teeth and sanctimonious green eyes. He sidled up to Vincent's side before Vincent had fully accepted that he was real. "There you are," he said, taking the liberty of clasping his fingers around Vincent's wrist. "You've been ignoring me."

That touch was enough for it to sink in that Adam had really found a way into his club, despite not being a member and having never been active in the local community. He stared at the offending fingers until they released him, then finally managed to pull himself together enough to stare at Adam.

He hadn't changed much, and Vincent wasn't sure if that was disappointing or not. After four years together, he would have liked to think his absence had left some kind of mark, but Adam was obviously as skilled at getting his needs met now as he had been while living with Vincent.

Adam took his silence in stride and raised an eyebrow. "You're not still mad, are you? I expected you to call me *ages* ago."

Vincent couldn't do more than blink as he fought against the sensation of the walls closing in around him. Come again? Why in the ever-loving-fuck would he do that? Why was Adam *here*?

"Don't look at me like that. I know you missed me. We were so good together." Adam touched Vincent's wrist again, tilting his head and adding one of his seductive smiles. The one that had rarely failed to make Vincent drop everything, including his pants. Except it wasn't so seductive now. More like a starving piranha spotting a drowned elephant. "You can't tell me you haven't missed me."

"Sure I can," he replied, as surprised as Adam looked and more than a little relieved he'd managed to get the words out.

Adam recovered quickly. He even had the audacity to inch his fingers up Vincent's arm, skirting around the area of his scars with a familiar avoidance that set Vincent's teeth on edge. "What I'm *saying*," he said in a slow manner Vincent remembered all too well, "is that I'll take you back."

Vincent twisted out of Adam's grip with as much grace as he could manage when all he wanted was to scrub his arm with bleach. He struggled to find something, anything, to say, but his mind was blank. Then Jasper slipped between them, pressing into Vincent's chest and tipping his head back in an obvious demand for a kiss. Without hesitating, he leaned into Jasper's warmth, tugging him closer with a hand on his hip, and kissed him.

Jasper grinned when they broke apart. "Hi."

"Hello, pet," he replied, pressing his lips to Jasper's temple and inhaling. He felt like he'd just surfaced after being underwater for hours and could finally breathe again. If he'd doubted for a moment that breaking things off with Adam had been a mistake, the warmth he felt in Jasper's presence was a stark reminder that it'd been the right choice. The effect each of them had on him wasn't even comparable.

When Adam cleared his throat, it was obnoxiously loud.

Jasper raised an eyebrow at Vincent, tilting his head inquisitively. He must have found some kind of answer on Vincent's face, because he turned to Adam. "Dude," he said, "even I know desperation when I see it."

Adam's eyes widened, and his face flushed with splotches of red. "Excuse me," he said, somehow managing to sound politely curious while his eyes promised violence, "who are you?"

Vincent couldn't see Jasper's expression, but he didn't need to when Jasper replied, "An upgrade, and I'm the only one allowed to touch Master Vincent."

Vincent didn't quite manage to stifle the noise that came with the jolt of surprise and pleasure at hearing *Master* on Jasper's lips. His arm slid around Jasper's waist of its own volition, keeping him close.

A muscle in Adam's cheek twitched as he eyed Jasper in clear disdain. "I see," he said, deliberately dismissing Jasper and turning his attention back to Vincent. "I'd like to speak with you. Alone."

"I'm busy," Vincent replied, trying to sound apologetic. He missed and landed somewhere closer to "Go fuck yourself."

Adam appeared crestfallen, but Vincent suspected it was as fabricated as everything else about him. "I'll come back later." He eyed Jasper with a faint sneer before adding, "It's important. Don't try my patience." The threat might have been amusing—Adam held no power or leverage over him, not anymore—but Vincent wouldn't put it past him to have found something he thought he could use.

He'd have to contact his lawyers to make sure he hadn't missed anything when he'd cut Adam out of his life.

Once Adam was gone, Vincent blew out a long breath. First order of business was to deal with Adam's access to the club and find out if he'd come in as a guest. Then put him on the banned list. The drama that was sure to follow him had no place here.

Jasper shifted, pressing into Vincent's chest and turning his head. "Sir?"

Vincent turned his attention back to where it belonged for the moment, noting the uncertainty in Jasper's eyes and tightening his grip in response. "You were amazing, pet."

"Yeah?" Jasper grinned and let Vincent take most of his weight. "That guy had douche canoe written all over him."

Indeed. "Hopefully you won't have to meet him again." He had no hopes of that for himself. If Adam was back, he was after something, and he wasn't the type to give up because he'd been told no. He noticed Jasper's questioning look and sighed softly. "That was my ex."

Both of Jasper's eyebrows went up. "Not a past sub?"

"He was. He's the reason I started using actual contracts." He could see the questions forming, but this wasn't the time or the place. He'd figured he would have to tell Jasper all this at some point if they moved beyond the first contract, but he never expected to have to deal with Adam in the flesh. "I'll tell you whatever you want to know at home," he said, pressing a kiss to Jasper's temple when he relented with a nod.

"How's the suit fit?" he asked, pulling back enough to enjoy the sight. He wasn't too worried about it; Richard did amazing work. And the suit design really did look breathtaking on Jasper. He dragged his fingers down the length of the tie with a smile, as pleased that Jasper had learned to tie it as he was disappointed at not having an excuse to do it himself. He glanced up as Jasper's breathing hitched, a smirk settling on his lips as he gave a light tug.

Maybe he should consider getting a collar and leash.

Before he could get too carried away, he let go and smoothed the tie back into place. "Come on," he said, turning to continue walking the floor. Having Jasper beside him in the club, dressed in a suit like Vincent, was its own kind of thrill. His last few subs had preferred fetish gear, which he thoroughly enjoyed, but there was something about a sub in a suit that lit up some of his buttons. And the way Jasper responded to the members who stopped to chat—nervous but polite, even with the subs, and openly curious—filled him with a pleasant hum of approval.

By the end of the night, he wanted nothing more than to pin Jasper to the wall, kiss and tease him senseless, and leave him disheveled and begging for release.

He made a stop at the security room to request the feed for the evening be logged and sent to him so he could review it later, added Adam to the No Entry list, sent a message to his lawyer requesting a meeting on Tuesday afternoon, then took Jasper home.

"Tonight was nice," Jasper said softly, stretched out and utterly relaxed in the passenger seat.

"You didn't mind being stuck at work with me?"

"Uh-uh. I liked seeing you like that, and… it was nice. Knowing everyone there knew I was yours."

Vincent glanced over with a smile. "I liked it too." He certainly wouldn't mind if it became a regular occurrence.

Once he'd parked in the garage, he shut the engine off but made no move to get out. "If you have questions," he started, fighting a grimace at the thought of talking about Adam, "I'd rather answer them here." Adam had no place in his life, and he certainly had no place in Vincent's home, especially now that it was starting to belong to Jasper.

Jasper unbuckled and shifted in his seat. "You said he was the reason you started using contracts. What'd he do?"

"A lot of small things." He'd gone over and over the details with his therapist, pinpointing all the manipulations and toxic behavior. "He forgot to do things I'd asked. All the time. Used sex as a bargaining chip. Insisted on eating at the most expensive restaurants and going to exclusive events so he could schmooze the elite. Refused to meet any of my needs until I was near a breaking point."

He paused, debating on whether he should even mention the scars, but Jasper had already seen them and hadn't brought them up since. "I think the worst was him constantly arguing with me to get cosmetic surgery on my scars."

"That *son* of a mother*fucker*!"

Vincent nearly jumped at the vehement response, eyeing Jasper in surprise.

"If I see him again, I'll punch him in the face." Jasper leaned across the center console, fisted a hand in Vincent's shirt, and yanked him closer to crush their lips together. "There's nothing wrong with your scars," he growled, nearly biting Vincent's lip.

Relief and gratitude unfurled in his chest. He slid a hand into Jasper's hair and pulled him into a deep kiss. "Thank you," he murmured against Jasper's lips.

Jasper nuzzled against his cheek. "What was he trying to talk to you about?"

Vincent shook his head with a sigh. "I have no idea. Hopefully my lawyers can figure it out before there's an issue." Hopefully Adam had only sought him out in a moment of desperation after his latest victim kicked him out.

"Any other questions?" he asked when Jasper remained silent.

"Not really. He's a little bitch, and you looked disgusted by him, so I don't think I have anything to worry about."

"You really don't. And please don't hit him first if you see him again."

"No promises," Jasper replied as he climbed out.

With a soft laugh, Vincent let them inside, slipped his shoes off, and headed upstairs. Inside the bedroom he turned and grasped Jasper's tie, using it to tug him towards the bed.

Jasper let out an eager moan and followed, resisting enough that Vincent had to tighten his grip to keep hold of the tie.

He switched on the lamp on the nightstand and turned his attention to removing Jasper's clothes. "You were amazing tonight, pet."

"You weren't so bad yourself." Jasper reached for Vincent's tie, tugging it free and draping it over Vincent's arm with a cheeky grin. "But I thought you said you did scenes when people asked?"

"I do." Vincent set the ties on the nightstand before slipping his hands under Jasper's jacket and down his arms to slide it free. "Why?"

"That woman asked you for a spanking, and you had someone else do it."

Vincent folded the jacket and draped it over the ties as he considered that. Taking up the role of a temporary Dom for others when he'd been getting the club off the ground had been a matter of course. But now he had enough staff that he wasn't needed regularly. And with Jasper he wasn't desperate to scratch a few itches to stay on the right side of miserable. "I didn't want to make you uncomfortable. Or jealous."

"I wouldn't have been *jealous*," Jasper huffed.

He didn't bother commenting on the defensive tone and started on Jasper's shirt buttons. "You want to watch me spank people, then?" he asked, his lips twitching in amusement.

"I dunno. Maybe." Jasper stared at Vincent's chest as if he were trying to burn a hole through it to the wall. He barely even blinked when Vincent finished with the shirt and dropped Jasper's pants.

Vincent tipped Jasper's chin up and flicked his nose to get his attention. "What are you thinking?"

Jasper sighed and wrinkled his nose. Instead of answering he pushed Vincent's jacket off his shoulders, stepped out of his pants, and took the jacket to the closet to hang it up.

The oblivious domesticity of the moment almost hurt with how badly Vincent had been craving it without realizing. When Jasper was within reach again, Vincent pulled him closer and kissed him until they were both out of breath.

Jasper licked his lips when they broke apart, eyes a little glazed, which was a fantastic look on him. "What was that for?"

Vincent shook his head, unable to put it into words even if he'd wanted to. It was far too early to make declarations of open-ended contracts and suggestions of permanent collars. "For being you."

Jasper flushed, an endearing, confused smile on his lips. Before he could ask what he'd done, Vincent pressed him back until his legs hit the bed.

"Lie back, pet."

"Do I get another massage?" he asked, deliberately making a show of wiggling onto the bed. He stretched out with his arms above his head, then rolled over and lifted his ass.

Vincent brought his hand down in a solid swat. "Not tonight," he said, stifling a soft laugh. He needed more than sex tonight. The roller coaster of the past few weeks had left him raw in ways he hadn't felt in years, and while the makeup sex had been more than satisfying, it'd been too long since they'd done a proper scene.

He couldn't deny he'd been tempted to handle some of the requests for scenes at the club in order to scratch that itch. It was too late for an elaborate scene tonight, but he could at least indulge a little.

He grabbed the lube and a condom and tossed them to the bed. He took a moment to enjoy the view as he untucked his shirt and unfastened the top few buttons, trailing his other hand down Jasper's body from shoulder to ankle and removing one sock then the other. Then he hooked his fingers in Jasper's boxers and tugged them off to toss to the floor in a soft rustle of fabric. "On your back."

Instead of going for the ankle restraints, he tugged the larger ones that were closer to the middle of the bed out from under the mattress and secured them around Jasper's thighs above his knees.

Jasper's breathing stuttered as he watched, fingers twisting in the sheets as he shifted on the bed, testing the restraints. "Fuck," he breathed, a warm flush spreading over his cheeks as his legs remained pinned on opposite sides of the bed.

Arousal sparked in Vincent's groin, hot and sharp enough to momentarily steal his breath. He finished unbuttoning his shirt and let it fall to the floor, followed by his pants, leaving him in his undershirt and boxers as he climbed onto the bed. He slid his hands up Jasper's thighs before gripping his hips and tugging him closer, forcing his legs a bit higher and farther apart.

Jasper gasped, blue eyes going nearly black as he reached for the front of Vincent's shirt and pulled. "Mark me," he murmured, hooking both arms around Vincent's shoulders when he leaned over.

Vincent didn't hesitate, fastening his lips to Jasper's neck, kissing with tongue and teeth and suction. He didn't pull away until the skin was flushed dark enough to last a few days. Only mildly mollified, he moved down a few inches to leave another, then another in the hollow of Jasper's throat. More across his chest, paying special attention to each nipple until Jasper twitched and shuddered with a desperate moan.

He reached Jasper's stomach and the mess of precum smeared there, pausing as he stared and questioned every rule and limit he'd set in place. They hadn't been tested, and he knew the risks, but in that moment he didn't care. He wanted his mouth on Jasper, wanted to taste him, feel the heat of him on his tongue. He *wanted* in a way he never had with anyone else.

That, more than anything, was enough to pull him back from breaking his own limits. They were there for a reason, and if he broke them now, it would only be easier to break others, and that was a pattern he couldn't let himself fall back into.

Jasper's fingers on his cheek brought him back to the moment, and he glanced up, tilting his head to nip at Jasper's palm. "Hands above your head."

Jasper blinked, a soft whine escaping him as he obeyed. "I'll be good...."

Vincent moved up the bed with an amused snort. "Oh, have you been bad?"

There was a profound silence as Vincent found the smaller cuffs near the corners of the bed. He secured one around Jasper's wrist before glancing down.

Jasper's face was flushed with more than arousal, his bottom lip nearly white between his teeth.

"Pet?"

Jasper sucked in a sharp breath, lifted his eyes up briefly to meet Vincent's, but then he quickly closed them. "I've… been very bad, Sir."

That was certainly news to him, but he'd bite. "Oh?" he asked, stroking his fingers along Jasper's other wrist as he secured it as well. That done, he sat up on his knees to take in the full sight of Jasper, bound and naked and splayed open for the taking. He snagged a pillow and put it beneath Jasper's hips, then settled his hands on Jasper's inner thighs, circling his thumb against his exposed hole.

When there was still no answer forthcoming, he prompted, "How so?"

Jasper swallowed hard enough his throat clicked. He shifted, tugging against his restraints as he squirmed. "I've been… thinking about you," he finally said. "Imagining you naked." He cracked his eyes open and briefly met Vincent's eyes before lowering his gaze somewhere near Vincent's chest. "Getting my hands and lips on every inch of you."

Vincent let out a slow breath, trying to ignore how much those words affected him, knowing Jasper had seen his scars and yet somehow sounded eager to touch him. "What else?" he asked, hating the hoarseness of his voice.

Jasper whined and tugged harder at his restraints, turning his head and pressing his face into his arm. "Thinking of being with you, Sir. All the time," he whispered. "You're all I can think about when I'm away from you. When I'm in class, all I want is for it to be Friday so I can see you again."

He let out a shuddering breath, trying to press his face farther into his arm, but the restraints kept him from hiding completely. "Sunday is the worst day of my week, because I know we have to say goodbye, and all I want is to be yours. Every day."

Vincent focused on breathing, telling himself that wasn't a declaration of love. It couldn't be, considering they'd only known each other for a few weeks. But the fact Jasper felt the pull to be together as strongly as he did? It was both gratifying and terrifying, and he wasn't about to miss out on seeing where this could go.

He slid a hand up Jasper's chest and into his hair, forcing him to stop trying to hide and meet his gaze. "You're mine," he said firmly, dragging his thumb across Jasper's lips before following with his own.

Jasper's whimper was full of relief, echoed in the way his entire body relaxed as he opened to the kiss. "Yours, Sir." He sighed when they broke apart, lifting his head to press his nose against Vincent's cheek. He fell back with a grin and gave a full-body wiggle. "Now claim me."

"So demanding," Vincent murmured, catching Jasper's lips again even as he got the lube open with one hand. He sat back to get his fingers coated, working one and then two fingers into Jasper. He took his time adding a third, content to watch Jasper's spiral into pleasure. It didn't take long—it rarely did—and he hummed in appreciation when Jasper used the restraints for leverage to match the rhythm of Vincent's fingers. "Christ, you're perfect," he whispered.

Jasper's breath hitched, either from Vincent's words or the sudden loss of Vincent's fingers inside him as he got the condom open and rolled into place. "Yes," he groaned, "fucking finally."

Vincent snorted and lined himself up. "Oh, is this what you wanted?" he asked as he pressed inside.

Jasper tossed his head back with a hissed, "*Yes.*"

Vincent had to pause as he pushed into Jasper's heat, his arousal making itself known with a visceral intensity that stole his breath. "Fuck," he hissed, unable to stop his hips from slamming the rest of the way home.

He had a brief moment of worry that he'd moved too fast, but Jasper keened, his eyes popping open to stare at Vincent with a rushed out, "Don't you dare fucking stop."

Vincent gripped Jasper's hips and gave up any thought of going slow or being gentle. For several hard, quick thrusts at least, until he careened towards the edge of bliss and managed to haul himself back. He slowed his thrusts despite Jasper's incoherent protests, peeling his fingers away from the start of bruises he'd left and sliding a hand up Jasper's chest instead. He swiped his thumb over Jasper's nipple, enjoying the full-body shiver it earned.

Jasper flexed his wrists against the restraints with a devastated whine. "Vinc—Siiiirrrr."

The near slip of his name made him chuckle. "Yes, pet?" he asked, leaning over and dragging his nose up the side of Jasper's throat.

"Please stop being a dick and fuck me," Jasper gasped, straining against the thigh restraints enough Vincent worried he might hurt himself.

He slid his hand up to rest on Jasper's throat, pressing his other palm to Jasper's thigh, retracing the path of his nose with his tongue. When he pulled back, Jasper had taken the hint and gone still, breaths quick but deep as he stared up at Vincent. Much better.

"You're mine," he said softly, voice firm. He raised an eyebrow when Jasper didn't respond, felt the movement of his throat as he swallowed.

"Yes, Sir," Jasper whispered.

Vincent hummed softly in approval and leaned down again, tracing the same path up Jasper's throat, this time with his teeth. When he reached Jasper's ear, he bit lightly on the lobe. "Then stop fighting, and give me a color."

Jasper swallowed again, a soft high-pitched sound escaping him. "Green."

"Good." He bit at Jasper's ear again and slid his hand from Jasper's thigh all the way up his body. He braced himself with his palm on the bed beside Jasper's head, his other hand resting lightly on Jasper's throat as he finally started moving again. Slow thrusts, far slower than the rabbiting of Jasper's pulse beneath his fingers.

Jasper's wrists flexed again, his breath stuttering every few breaths, but he stopped fighting the restraints and moved with Vincent instead. "Please," he gasped, arching beneath Vincent with a soft whine that bordered on frustrated.

Vincent kept his eyes on Jasper's face as he obliged, picking up the pace and force of his thrusts again, gradually giving in to his own burning need. He curled his fingers tight in the sheets, sliding his thumb along Jasper's jawline, then dragging his fingers down Jasper's body, tweaking a nipple on the way down to grasp his leaking cock.

"Fuck!" Jasper shuddered and bucked into Vincent's hand. His eyes rolled back as Vincent gave a few quick, tight strokes, and he fell over the edge with a shout.

Liquid heat spilled over Vincent's fingers, the sharp scent of Jasper's cum and the tighter grip on his own cock pushing him to his own orgasm. He bit Jasper's shoulder with a loud groan, holding on with his teeth for a long moment before carefully pulling back. He made quick work of the restraints and condom, then slumped to the bed to finish catching his breath, unsurprised when Jasper immediately rolled over and latched on like an octopus.

He stroked his fingers through sweat-damp hair. Jasper responded by pressing his entire face into Vincent's chest and nuzzling his way up to Vincent's lips. The easy affection still took him by surprise, especially after sex. This was something he'd been denied so long, he'd almost forgotten how much he craved it.

The kiss was lazy and sweet and lasted until they were both long past recovered. Until their bodies cooled and the postorgasmic bliss faded.

He wasn't sure when they'd ended up on their sides, with Jasper's leg thrown over his hip, his own tucked between Jasper's thighs, but it was nice. Jasper's fingers lazily flexing in his hair like a cat as he fought against sleep was nice. The pert flesh of Jasper's ass beneath his hand was more than nice. The warm breaths ghosting over his cheek between sleepy, satiated kisses were nice.

Being with Jasper was a bit like a dream. Like he'd been underwater for years and was finally breaking the surface to breathe again.

He tightened his fingers to give a light tug on Jasper's hair, his other hand curled over Jasper's wrist, listening as Jasper's breathing slowed and deepened. As usual, Jasper easily passed out after sex. Vincent tried not to be envious.

Once Jasper was out, he carefully slipped out of bed long enough to clean them both up and change, then settled back in, counting Jasper's steady breaths like sheep until he fell asleep.

Chapter Twenty-One

Jasper hummed as he held his hand under the spray of the shower, waiting for it to heat up to get in. He'd been riding a high all weekend, nearly giddy with the fact Vincent had practically made love to him. *Twice.*

The fact he'd admitted to almost all his secret little desires still filled him with mortification, to the point he wanted to curl up in a ball and die, but Vincent hadn't recoiled. Hadn't called an end to the weekend or their contract. Hadn't called him clingy or too much or naive. If anything, Vincent had seemed *pleased.* Not that Jasper could point to anything in particular that made him think so. But something had changed between them, and he couldn't deny he liked it.

He toweled off and pulled on his boxers, deciding against other clothes, and heading downstairs.

Vincent was on the couch with his phone and glanced up briefly as Jasper stepped into the room, then looked up again with a raised eyebrow. "Why aren't you dressed?"

Jasper grinned and settled himself in Vincent's lap, inordinately pleased when Vincent set his phone aside and rested his other hand around Jasper's waist. "We don't have to leave yet."

"Didn't you say you had assignments to finish?"

He wrinkled his nose and pressed his face into Vincent's neck. He did, but that didn't mean he wanted to focus on them anytime soon. "Maybe."

"Uh-huh." Vincent rubbed his hand over Jasper's arm before lightly pinching the back of his thigh. "I'm not going to be responsible for you failing your classes."

Jasper whined and burrowed closer. He didn't want to leave. The thought of going back home was torture. Here the house was quiet, he loved Vincent's company, and obviously, there was amazing sex. At home there were five other people, and finding a bathroom that was free or didn't smell was a miracle most of the time.

"Jasper."

He tensed despite himself. Vincent sounded more amused than angry, but still. "Jas," he corrected softly.

Vincent hummed and dragged his fingers through Jasper's hair. "You didn't seem to like it when Matt called you that."

Jasper made a face against Vincent's neck. "'Cause he's a prick, and I don't even like talking to him."

"Jas, then," Vincent said, and Jasper sighed softly in bliss. "I've got to get to the club for an interview soon."

And there went the blissful peace he'd been relishing all weekend. With a sigh, he pushed himself up, resignation burning in his chest. Vincent had a life and a job that didn't include him outside of the weekend.

"Right," he muttered, sliding off Vincent's lap and trudging upstairs to find his clothes. His eyes stung as he dressed, and he scrubbed a hand against them with a silent curse. Fuck. What was wrong with him? He knew the deal. Slutty sub on Friday and back to his pumpkin on Sunday.

And he'd even gone and told Vincent how far he was falling. He groaned and braced his hands on the dresser as his mind happily replayed him vomiting his feelings all over Vincent.

He'd never intended to bring his feelings into this. Not like that, anyway. Even if Vincent had promised not to let Jasper's clinginess bother him, basically declaring his love would have definitely ruined any chance of this lasting past their contract.

Fuck, fuck, *fuck*.

He swallowed another tortured groan and pulled his clothes on. Sucked in a deep breath. Failed to smooth his hair into something presentable. Finally dragged himself back downstairs.

A small part of him wondered if maybe this was the sub drop Keith and Vincent had warned him about, but suspecting that didn't help keep the crushing dread from overwhelming him as he reached the bottom step. Even through the tears threatening to blind him, he knew he was being ridiculous, but his body didn't care. "Please don't make me leave," he gasped, clutching the banister with one hand and his chest with the other.

He didn't even hear Vincent move, but suddenly he was there. Strong arms wrapped around him, and he buried his face against Vincent's chest, failing to stifle the sobs.

Gods, could he get any more pathetic?

VINCENT TIGHTENED his hold on Jasper as he took a deep breath, pushing aside the panic and guilt. Panic because it'd been years since he'd handled a truly distraught sub alone. Guilt because he was sure this was a delayed drop, and he really should have noticed the signs earlier.

There'd be plenty of time to beat himself up over that later. For now he rubbed a hand against Jasper's back and guided him to the sofa. Several long minutes passed as Jasper soaked Vincent's shirt with tears. He checked the time on his phone and sent a text to the person he was supposed to be interviewing to let them know something had come up and he might be running a bit late, but someone would be available to let them in if they arrived on time.

He continued running his fingers through shower-damp hair, hoping the tears were at least cathartic. When Jasper finally fell quiet, he snatched a few tissues from the box beside the sofa and passed them over.

He tuned out the loud sniffling and nose blowing as best he could. When it stopped, he tugged lightly at Jasper's hair. "So," he said quietly, "here's what we're gonna do. You're going to drink either some water or juice, and then we're going to have a chat about what just happened. Any objections?"

Jasper sniffled again and lifted himself off Vincent's chest, scrubbing at his face before shaking his head.

"Okay." Vincent headed to the kitchen for two bottles of water and an apple juice. He passed one of each to Jasper and settled next to him again. First things first... "I'm not upset, and I don't have to send you back home tonight." He watched Jasper as he sipped the water, noting the way he practically sagged with relief at hearing he could stay. The desire to find what was causing that kind of tension so he could fix it burned in his chest, but he'd get his answers soon enough. "Other than staying another night, is there anything else we need to address?"

Jasper fiddled with the bottle lid, turning it over and over between his fingers. "No. I'm sorry I freak—"

Vincent lifted a hand to stop him. "You never need to apologize for an emotional reaction, pet." He tapped his finger against the bottle to get Jasper to take another drink. "Can you tell me why you don't want to go home?" When Jasper shrugged, he asked, "Is it safe there?"

That at least got a soft huff and a roll of his eyes. "Yes, it's safe. I just—" He swallowed hard and took another sip of water.

Vincent took a breath and a drink of his own water to keep himself silent, waiting for Jasper to find the words he needed.

He might have had his suspicions, but he'd been wrong about someone before—so very wrong—and he wouldn't put words in Jasper's mouth. But when a few minutes passed, he gently prodded, "Just?"

Jasper shrugged and closed his hand around the bottle lid. "It's crowded at home."

That seemed like an understatement. The thought of living with more than one other person made his skin crawl, let alone five of them. He lifted his hand, running his fingers through Jasper's hair. "Is that all?" he asked, shifting closer. He settled his arm around Jasper's shoulders, unsurprised when he leaned in.

"I like being here. With you," Jasper told Vincent's shoulder.

"I enjoy having you here, pet." He tightened his arm in a brief hug. When the silence settled again, he asked, "Are you sure there's nothing else? This weekend was a bit more intense than usual." More like far more intimate than he'd intended, but Jasper's confession had pushed them down that path. Jasper had surrendered to him in a completely different way than usual, and he wasn't sure Jasper realized that.

"I liked it," Jasper murmured, keeping his face buried.

"Me too," he said, pressing a kiss to the top of Jasper's head. He waited a few minutes to see if Jasper had anything else to say, then let the subject drop for now. Jasper was calmer; that's all that mattered at the moment. "If that's everything, I really do need to get to the club."

Jasper sighed but sat up, and it only took a few minutes to get on the road.

"We'll stop by your place, and you can get what you need for tomorrow."

"Sorry for being a pain."

"I don't think you're a pain." He thought Jasper was touch-starved and still figuring things out, but he kept that to himself. He glanced over to see Jasper chewing on his bottom lip.

"What's the interview for?"

"A chef." He smiled faintly when Jasper made a noise of surprise. "I want the staff to have a chance to eat an actual meal, and maybe have a dinner option for those who reserve a private playroom." He'd been catering in food for those who worked the longer shifts for the past several months. He didn't mind the expense, but it would certainly help if he could get someone on staff instead.

"Huh."

"What?"

Jasper shrugged. "That's…."

He raised an eyebrow when Jasper trailed off. "Not as dickish as you expected?"

"I don't really think you're a dick," Jasper said softly.

Vincent turned his full attention back to the road, a pleased smile tugging at his lips. His free hand found its way into Jasper's hair, threading through the soft strands.

Maybe Jasper wasn't the only one a bit touch-starved.

THE DOUBT and anxiety that had fucked off all afternoon and evening finally tried to wriggle back into existence as they returned home that night. Jasper thought he'd hidden it well, but as soon as they reached the bedroom, Vincent tugged him around to face him.

"What's wrong?"

Jasper groaned and buried his face in Vincent's chest. He bit his tongue against a reflexive "Nothing" and let out a long breath. "I'm wondering what happens, I guess. After our contract ends." They only had a couple of weeks left, and he wasn't sure he could say goodbye yet.

"I was thinking of offering a new one. A longer one—for a year maybe." Vincent said the words easily, like he hadn't shaken Jasper to the core.

He squeezed his eyes shut, his breath shuddering out of him. He hated how relieved he was by that simple answer. Even if he hadn't meant for this to be anything more than a few weeks of fun, he couldn't deny he wanted it to last. Vincent was the best thing to happen to him since Amber took him in.

"So what exactly would that make us? If I sign again."

"What do you mean?"

Jasper swallowed hard. *Don't do it. Don't ruin it.* "I mean, will I still be a pet, or…?"

"Ah." Vincent tightened his arms around Jasper. "Will we be boyfriends or lovers?"

Jasper nodded against Vincent's chest, even though he was terrified of the answer.

"Is that what you want?"

More than anything. "I guess." He blinked as Vincent nudged him back a step and tilted his chin up.

"Honesty, pet."

He leaned back, barely resisting the sudden urge to slap Vincent's hand away. "What about you?" he snapped. "Why do I always have to say what I want, but you don't?" His chest seized, and he held his breath, clenching his hands into fists as he braced for Vincent's anger.

Vincent blinked at him before letting out a soft breath. "You're right."

Jasper stared, his breath sticking in his lungs before survival instinct forced him to breathe again. "What?"

"I may have been holding back, but in this case, the label doesn't matter to me. A contract says you're mine. I'm willing to offer a longer one if that's what you want. Some kind of relationship is to be expected with that, and I would require us both to be tested in that case. Which label would you prefer?"

"Uh," was Jasper's intelligent response. He was still trying to process being told he was right, let alone the idea of a longer contract with an actual relationship attached. "Boyfriend?"

"All right."

No way was it that easy. He should have left it at that, but he couldn't help but ask, "Boyfriends means dates, then, right?"

Vincent's lips twitched towards a smile. "It can."

Jasper nodded, reaching for Vincent's shirt and curling his fingers into the material. "Wednesdays," he said decisively. No way was he going back to waiting a whole week to see Vincent again. "And holidays. Do birthdays count as holidays?"

"If you want them to."

He rolled his eyes. "Of course I want them to. You're spending my birthday with me."

Vincent laughed and settled his hands on Jasper's waist. "And when is your birthday?"

"In June." After their contract was supposed to end. He might have hoped Vincent would still be around then, but he'd never let himself picture it. He hoped he didn't screw things up anytime soon.

"I'll be sure to make myself available for your birthday spankings."

Jasper grinned and leaned his weight into Vincent. "Does that mean I get to spank you on yours?"

"You're hilarious."

He smirked but quickly turned it into a pout. "Why can't you admit you find me adorable?"

Vincent raised an eyebrow. "Adorable?"

"You did call me a kitten."

"I called you an overgrown cat," Vincent corrected. "One of those cats that stick around even though it's mangy and missing an eye."

Jasper spluttered, pointing at Vincent with wide eyes, lips twitching as he fought a grin. "Maybe if you stopped feeding it, it wouldn't come around," he shot back. "But even an old, decrepit bastard needs some kind of companion."

Vincent narrowed his eyes. "Decrepit?"

"Yeah, you heard me." Jasper lifted his chin. "Old man."

Vincent lunged.

Jasper laughed as he hit the bed, managing to keep Vincent from pinning his arms. He got a knee in Vincent's stomach that made him roll away with a groan. "Ha!" He bounced off the bed and ran for the door.

"You shouldn't fight those who are younger and more flexible than you, Sir. It's really bad for your hea-eeee!" He bolted as soon as Vincent got to his feet, jerking the door shut behind him. He didn't have time to make it down the stairs, so he ran down the hall instead, slipping into the playroom a moment before he heard the bedroom door open.

"You better hope I don't find you, pet," Vincent called. The bathroom door opened, then closed a few moments later. "Because when I find you, I might wash your mouth out with soap and send you home with marshmallows in your ass crack."

Jasper couldn't quite hold back the shocked laugh, clamping a hand over his mouth and pushing away from the door. It was too dark to see, but he knew the room well enough to make it to the couch. Or so he thought until he slammed his shin into the table and stumbled with a yelp. He held his breath until he heard another door open.

"Or maybe I should tie you down on the dining table," Vincent continued, sounding closer to the stairs. "Pour honey all over you and jerk you off with some mint leaves. Ever enjoyed a cool burning sensation on your dick?"

Gods, did people really do that? Vincent had to be making shit up to fuck with him. No way was that an actual punishment. It sounded more like something he'd find in a smutty book.

He limped behind the couch and quickly dropped down as he heard Vincent at the door, wincing and holding his breath as the light came on.

Shit, shit, shit. He was so in trouble. The door slammed shut and he jumped, staying where he was as he strained to hear Vincent walking away.

Too late, he realized Vincent was still in the room and tipped his head back to find Vincent leaning over the back of the couch.

"Boo."

Jasper scrambled back and to his feet, glancing at the door with a soft whimper. He swallowed and slowly inched around the other end of the couch. "You wouldn't really do those things, would you?" he asked, not entirely sure if he was horrified or maybe a little turned on at the idea.

Vincent raised an eyebrow. "You were a disrespectful little brat," he replied, stalking after Jasper. "Why shouldn't I punish you for it?"

Jasper swallowed a smartass response as he reached the table and bolted for the door. He cursed as he found it locked, ignoring the hammering of his heart as he flipped the lock and yanked the door open, only for Vincent to slam his hand against it before it opened even an inch.

"Oh no, too slow," Vincent taunted.

Jasper whimpered and stared at the door as Vincent's arms caged him in. "Please don't set my dick on fire."

"No?" Vincent chuckled, settling his hands on Jasper's hips and turning him around.

He peeked up through his lashes. "Sorry I called you decrepit?"

"Are you," Vincent replied dryly.

He couldn't help the grin as he shrugged. "Your back does pop every time you stretch."

Vincent snorted. "Give it ten years and you'll be in the same boat," he said, tugging Jasper away from the door to open it.

Jasper hesitantly leaned into Vincent's side as they walked back to the bedroom. Despite the threats, Vincent didn't seem intent on punishing him. At least not tonight.

He stripped, changed into a pair of sweats, and crawled into bed, settling on his side facing Vincent. He blinked as Vincent reached over and tugged his bottom lip from between his teeth, unaware he'd been biting it.

"Can I see you Wednesday?" Jasper blurted. "You could come over," he continued in a rush, before Vincent could say no. "Amber and Terrance are out of town until Thursday. Matt switched to working nights, and Keith and Reiko have been getting back late."

Vincent's thumb brushed back and forth against Jasper's bottom lip. "You want me to come over for dinner?"

"Yes?"

"Will you be cooking?"

He shrugged. "I can try." He'd watched and read some cooking tutorials in his spare time, but it wasn't like he had a lot of chances to practice. Even if he'd had a car of his own, he didn't have the spare money for ingredients that might end up in the trash.

"Why don't I bring what we need to make something together?"

Jasper grinned and licked Vincent's fingertip on its next pass. "Deal."

Chapter Twenty-Two

Going back to regular college life in the morning was a special kind of torture. Jasper couldn't deny that Vincent letting him stay the night had helped ease the anxious knot in his gut, but he wished he hadn't had a complete and utter emotional breakdown in the first place.

He really needed to work on not overthinking things.

But he was glad to finally get everything out in the open and know where they stood with each other. Even if he was still falling hard, at least now he knew Vincent reciprocated on some level.

Knowing he'd be able to start another contract when this one ended was as much a relief as it was exciting. And terrifying. What if Vincent changed the rules this time? Not that he thought Vincent would do anything *too* drastic, but something would change, right? Surely he'd ask for something more… kinky? He was fairly certain everything they'd done so far was pretty tame. They didn't even use the playroom that often, and there were some contraptions in there they hadn't used at all yet.

Vincent had mentioned punishments a few times, and he couldn't deny he was curious, but marshmallows? Seriously? He hadn't dared ask if Vincent would actually follow through on that threat, but surely not. Right?

Should he tell Vincent he was okay with being punished? He knew better than to say he was okay with being punished for anything, but how the hell was he supposed to know what was a punishable offense? What if he'd been making so many mistakes that he'd end up being punished every day if he agreed to it?

Jasper closed his eyes and took a breath. He really needed to stop overthinking things; that was how he fucked things up. So he forced himself to breathe and focus on his classes and assignments and work, and allowed himself to text Vincent at least a few times each day.

Then it was Wednesday, and the agony of the past two days was worth it when he headed out of his last class and saw Vincent's car waiting for him. Not the one the driver used, but the sports car Vincent drove himself.

He climbed into the passenger seat and leaned over to kiss Vincent's cheek. "Hello, Sir."

"Hello, pet. How were classes?"

"Educational," he replied, grinning when Vincent snorted. He glanced in the back seat at the groceries and shifted in excitement.

Vincent would be spending the rest of the afternoon and hopefully evening with him. Maybe even spend the night. At home. Granted, it was Amber's place, but he earned his keep by doing laundry twice a week and odd chores to keep the place clean. So long as he kept his grades up he didn't feel too guilty about not paying rent, and his part-time job gave him enough cash he never had to ask for much.

He'd stayed up last night, after finishing some required reading, making sure the kitchen and dining room were spotless and ready for them to cook.

He was more than thrilled Vincent had agreed to see him outside of his own home. It made this feel more like a relationship. He had to bite his cheek to keep from grinning like a madman despite the ever-present fear of everything blowing up in his face.

Jasper leaned over to prop his head on Vincent's shoulder. "Missed you, Sir," he said softly. It'd barely been two full days, but it was the truth. He closed his eyes as Vincent ran fingers through his hair before getting them on the road.

When they got home, he helped Vincent carry in the bags and emptied their contents onto the counter. He tossed his backpack on the dining table and put away the items that needed to go in the fridge, rolling his eyes when he found the apron. Vincent really meant it when he said he'd bring everything he needed.

He laid out two cartons of mushrooms, parsley, onion, garlic, parmesan cheese, broth, chicken, and a fancy-looking box of rice. "Sooo, what're we making?"

"Mushroom risotto." Vincent paused as he set a knife down on the cutting board. "Do you like mushrooms?"

Jasper grinned. "Love mushrooms. Hate olives."

Vincent groaned. "Heathen."

He laughed and snatched one of the onions to peel it, but he'd only gotten half of it done when he realized he was still dressed. He shifted on his feet as he debated stripping. They weren't in Vincent's home, but no one else was here, and it wasn't like he hadn't seen the others in various states of undress. But this was different.

"Pet?" Vincent asked, eyeing him as he finished washing the mushrooms.

Jasper sighed and set the onion down, quickly pulling his shirt over his head before he could second- and third-guess himself. His fingers hesitated a beat on his jeans, but he pushed those down too. When he straightened and risked a peek, Vincent had his arms crossed and was propped against the counter with an amused look.

"I'm not complaining, but are you sure?"

He swallowed and gave a sharp nod, snatched up his clothes, and dashed upstairs to toss them in his room. Then he had to take a moment to breathe. It wasn't like he was *naked*; he still had his boxers on, but that wasn't enough to keep his heart from skipping like a kid stealing ice cream as he headed back downstairs.

Vincent was still where Jasper had left him, closing the oven on the chicken. He held up an apron when Jasper stopped beside him.

He wrinkled his nose and shook his head. "Defeats the purpose if I cover up your view, doesn't it?"

Vincent tipped his head back with a laugh and draped the apron over himself instead.

Jasper couldn't help feeling smug as he picked up the onion and got back to work. When he moved to the cutting board to start chopping, Vincent shifted to stand behind him, his arms resting lightly around Jasper's waist. He shivered and tilted his head to the side as Vincent's lips found his shoulder.

He stared at the onion for a moment, surprised by the casual affection. Maybe he shouldn't have been. Even from the beginning, Vincent hadn't been stingy with his touches, but he hadn't really expected it here.

"Pet?" Vincent asked, propping his chin on Jasper's shoulder.

He shook his head and cut the onion in half. "Just thinking," he murmured, focusing on dicing the onion, but he couldn't keep from thinking about punishments. Again. "Sir?"

"Mm-hmm?"

"I've been thinking," he started but then couldn't quite get the words out. What was he supposed to say, that he wanted to try being punished? He didn't want to give Vincent the wrong idea: that he wanted to make it a thing. He didn't want to say yes and be stuck with the consequences if he didn't like it.

"Jas," Vincent murmured wryly.

Jasper sighed and let his head thunk against Vincent's shoulder. "You've mentioned punishments a few times."

Vincent hummed against his neck. "And?"

Jasper shrugged his shoulder. "I might be curious about what it would be like?"

"How are you imagining it would be?"

Wasn't that the million-dollar question. "Spanking?" he guessed, rolling his eyes as he felt Vincent's lips curve in a smile against his neck.

"Sounds more like a reward."

Jasper huffed and scooped the diced onion into the bowl before starting on the next one. "Well, it's better than marshmallows in my ass," he muttered.

Vincent laughed and tightened his arm around Jasper's waist. "That's a different kind of punishment."

"Of course it is."

"What are you worried might happen?"

"I dunno…. Being punished for no reason?"

Vincent shifted behind him, grasping Jasper's wrist and sliding to his hand to press it against the cutting board until he released the knife, then he nudged Jasper around to face him.

"Look at me, pet," he murmured, waiting until Jasper flicked a glance up to continue. "None of this is a game to me. Punishment is just another type of scene. I'd never discipline you for something without you understanding why and agreeing the discipline is suitable."

Jasper swallowed, a knot of worry in his chest loosening a bit. "I know," he murmured.

"Do you?"

He flicked his tongue against his lips and toyed with the bottom button on Vincent's shirt. Vincent had done nothing except exactly what he'd said he would from the start. He hadn't lied or hurt him, and he went out of his way to give Jasper what he needed, which was more than anyone else had ever done, aside from Amber giving him a place to live. He'd never so much as raised his voice, even when he had reason to.

"Yes," he said softly, meeting Vincent's eyes. "I trust you."

Vincent tilted his head, studying Jasper a moment before his lips curved in a small smile. "Thank you," he said, pressing a kiss to his nose.

Jasper huffed softly and kissed Vincent's lips, then turned back to the cutting board. He cleared his throat and ignored the heat creeping into his face as he said, "Sooo, I guess we can experiment?" he asked. "At least once?"

Vincent settled his hand on Jasper's hip, lightly rubbing his thumb against the base of his spine. "I can give you a taste of punishment for being a complete brat the other day."

"So long as it doesn't involve marshmallows."

"I think I can come up with something," Vincent replied dryly.

"Okay." Jasper tried to ignore the flush of excitement, but warmth still pooled low in his belly as he wondered what Vincent would do to him. He reached for the mushrooms to start slicing and frowned as he noticed how many ingredients were laid out. "Isn't this too much food?"

"No. There's enough for your family if they show up."

Jasper wrinkled his nose. He really hoped they didn't show up. The last thing he wanted was his time with Vincent interrupted.

Vincent pulled his phone out and put on some quiet music, and Jasper smiled.

This was nice. This was something he'd always wanted. Someone he could simply exist with. The sex was great, but this was something that fed a deeper craving.

Vincent kept close, hands on Jasper's hips or guiding him through making a recipe that seemed far more tedious than it should be.

By the time the risotto was nearly done simmering, a storm was rolling in. A thunderstorm that quickly turned the sky dark and formed tiny *chink-chink-chinks* of what sounded like hail against the windows.

He glanced out the back door and watched the rain come down fast and hard, then turned back to watch Vincent. He was working on a blueberry compote to go with the store-bought sponge cake and can of whipped cream. With a hum, he went to prop himself against Vincent's side, shook the can, and sprayed a generous amount in his mouth.

"Really?"

Jasper tipped his head back with a grin. A shiver of heat went through him when Vincent glanced at him and leaned in to swipe his tongue against the corner of Jasper's mouth.

"Mmm, crème à la Jasper."

Jasper swallowed a soft moan, suddenly wanting more than he was comfortable doing in Amber's kitchen. "Fuck," he whined, biting Vincent's shoulder when he snickered.

He wasn't prepared in the least for the front door to swing open.

"Jas?" Amber called. "Whose car is in the driveway?"

Jasper froze, hearing a strange wounded-animal sound before realizing it was coming from him. No, no, no. *Why*? They weren't supposed to be back until morning. Not walking in while he was practically naked in the kitchen!

He whimpered as Vincent stepped back, clinging to him and blinking when Vincent put the apron on him.

"Jasper?"

Jasper made that strangled sound again as Amber and Terrance walked into the kitchen. They were both soaked. And staring at Vincent in surprise. "Hey. You're back early."

"The storm hit the lake this morning, so we headed back," she replied, still watching Vincent.

Terrance turned his attention to Jasper with a smirk. "Are you naked?"

Jasper flushed, clutching the apron against himself. "No! I'm… going to get dressed," he muttered, glancing at Vincent.

Vincent nodded. "Are you joining us for dinner?" he asked, glancing over his shoulder.

Jasper backed out of the kitchen and then bolted up the stairs and slammed his door behind him. He yanked the apron off and wadded it up into a ball that he threw against the door.

Stupid Terrance. Stupid Amber. Stupid storm. He should have known better.

Why couldn't he get a damn break?

He ran his hands over his face and sighed before pulling his clothes back on. So much for a quiet date at home.

He grabbed the apron and shook it out as he trudged back down the stairs. He passed the apron back to Vincent and focused on stirring the risotto. "Isn't this done yet?" he asked, even though he wasn't hungry anymore.

"Yes." Vincent moved the pan of blueberry compote to a different burner before picking up two plates. He filled them with risotto and passed them both to Jasper, then grabbed two more from the cupboard.

Great. Their dinner was being invaded then. Of course.

He stifled a sigh and took the plates to the table, setting one in front of Amber and the other in front of Terrance. He grabbed four glasses and poured the sweet iced tea Terrance liked to keep in the fridge, then sank into a chair across from him.

Amber sat to his right at the head of the table, and Vincent set a plate in front of Jasper as he took the seat to his left.

He could feel their eyes on him, but he ignored them both in favor of poking at his food.

"Vincent said you're going to sign a new contract. For a year," Amber said, her voice carefully neutral.

"Yes," Jasper said, his fingers tightening around his fork as his heart rate picked up, expecting some kind of fight. She might not have tried to interfere before now, but who knew what Matt had told her.

"Finally found yourself a sugar daddy. Nice job," Terrance said with a soft laugh. He winced as Amber likely kicked him under the table.

"It's not like that," Jasper muttered, glancing at Vincent. He wasn't sure what reaction he expected, but the wry amusement was at least better than a glower.

Terrance cleared his throat. "This tastes great, Vincent."

"Yes, thank you for dinner. Even if we crashed it," Amber added with a smile.

"Jasper made it."

Jasper felt heat creep up his neck as both Terrance and Amber looked at him in surprise. "I just followed your directions, Sir," he murmured, shifting in his seat when Terrance's eyebrows shot into his hairline. He turned his attention to his food, then nearly jumped when Vincent rested a hand on his knee, gave a light squeeze, and didn't pull away.

"Huh. Learning to cook, getting your first real taste of kink. Little Jas is growing up," Terrance teased.

Jasper made a face at him and rolled his eyes. "You're such a dick."

"I'm starting to think that's an endearment coming from you," Vincent said.

He turned to Vincent with a grin. "Yeah, maybe," he said, reaching over to pat his leg. He couldn't quite resist the temptation to let his fingers slide farther north, his grin turning to a smirk when he felt a bulge against his hand.

Well, at least it might be easy to get Vincent to stay the night.

VINCENT SPORTED an erection all through dinner. It'd started the moment Jasper took his clothes off and only intensified when he first called him Sir in front of Terrance and Amber. The brat's hand constantly touching his thigh hadn't helped either.

And once Jasper noticed, he'd made a point to touch his leg every chance he got.

Damned brat.

Since he couldn't exactly stand without giving himself away, he made Jasper serve the dessert.

It surprised him how drama-free dinner was. He'd expected some kind of fallout from Matt's revelation, but apparently Matt hadn't shared with anyone else, or they were pretending it was none of their business.

Seeing Jasper interact with someone besides him was interesting, though it was obvious Jasper wasn't completely at ease, even in his own home. He told himself it was far too early to even think of getting involved in such personal issues, but he could at least satisfy his curiosity.

"How did you end up living here?" he asked Jasper when they'd finished eating. He sat back with his arm resting along the back of Jasper's chair, fingers lightly brushing against his shoulder.

Terrance paused, sharing a look with Jasper before gathering up the rest of the dishes.

Jasper shrugged but kept his eyes on the table as he answered. "My dad was drunk. Like, *always*. Usually it wasn't too bad, but he'd just lost his job." He said it like that was a valid justification.

"Someone heard him yelling and called the cops, and Kris from next door called Amber. She saw my black eye and brought me here. And then she refused to let me go back home, even after Dad got released. I was, like, a week away from turning eighteen, so I kinda ended up staying here."

Vincent stared at Jasper a moment before turning to look at Amber. When she only shrugged, he looked at Terrance, who was studiously washing the dishes. "I see," he finally said.

Amber cleared her throat and stood. "Thank you for dinner, Vincent." She mussed Jasper's hair and took her glass to the sink, groping Terrance on her way to the stairs.

Vincent fixed Jasper's hair without thinking, ignoring the stupid smile Jasper gave him in return. He leaned in close enough to steal a quick kiss, a thrum of satisfaction settling in his limbs when Jasper let out a soft needy whine.

Jasper chased after him when he pulled back, pouting when he didn't get another kiss. "Will you stay the night, Sir?" A flush spread across his cheeks. He shot a quick glance towards Terrance, who was still at the sink, and lowered his voice. "You could… you know."

Vincent raised an eyebrow, settling his palm against the back of Jasper's neck. "Mmm, do I know?" he asked. His fingers rested near enough to Jasper's pulse to feel the quick, excited beat.

"Don't be a dick," Jasper whined.

"I thought you liked it when I'm a dick," he said, feigning shock. "Don't you?"

Jasper groaned and let his forehead thunk against Vincent's shoulder.

Vincent laughed softly and tilted his head, pressing his lips against Jasper's ear. "Am I punishing you for being an absolute brat?" he whispered, relishing the shudder that went through Jasper.

His erection twitched with interest, and he curled his fingers tight in Jasper's hair, tugging his head back and taking in the warm flush and darkened eyes. He hummed in approval and let go. "Lead the way," he murmured, snorting softly as Jasper lurched to his feet, practically ran out of the room, and thundered up the stairs.

He bid Terrance a quick good-night as he followed.

When he reached Jasper's bedroom, he stepped inside and closed the door quietly behind him. There were clean piles of clothes on the dresser; textbooks, notebooks, and a laptop in a mess on the desk; and a few posters of a violinist he didn't recognize on the wall.

Jasper sat on the edge of his bed, hands clenched in the blanket as he watched Vincent. His breathing audibly stuttered when Vincent flipped the lock, his tongue darting out to wet his lips.

Vincent let him sit there a moment before stepping farther into the room, then came to a stop in front of Jasper and lifted his chin with a finger. "Do you know what I'm going to do to you, pet?"

Jasper's breathing hitched again and sped up. "Punish me?"

"Mm-hmm. And why am I punishing you?"

That pink tongue flicked out again. "Because I was a brat?"

"You were a brat," he agreed. "You had the audacity to call me old and decrepit." He raised an eyebrow when Jasper bit his lip; it did nothing to hide the twitch at the corners of his mouth as he fought a grin. He *tsk*ed and stepped back. "Strip and lie down on your back, pet."

Jasper stood and peeled out of his clothes with eager but clumsy efficiency, then flopped onto the bed, wiggling until he was stretched out on the far side.

Vincent let his eyes wander over every inch of exposed flesh as he leisurely removed his own shirt. He tossed it over the back of the desk chair, then toed off his shoes and slowly unfastened his pants, aware of Jasper's eyes watching his every movement. He snagged the condom and lube packs from his pocket before draping his pants over his shirt, leaving him in his undershirt and boxers. The packs he tossed to the bed as he stretched out beside Jasper.

He slid his palm down Jasper's arm, grasping his wrist and guiding it up to press into the bed above his head. Then he settled his hand lightly around Jasper's throat, holding his chin between his fingers. "That tongue of yours has gotten you into trouble," he murmured, leaning down to nip Jasper's lower lip. "So now you get to deal with the consequences. Starting with: You don't come unless I tell you to. Understand, pet?"

Jasper swallowed and let out a soft moan. "Yes, Sir."

"Good. I might test your limits as a result. You know what to do if it becomes too much." He waited for Jasper's nod, then pressed a kiss to his lips and licked his mouth open. He drew the kiss out long enough to get Jasper worked up before finally pulling away to replace his tongue with his index finger. It slipped past Jasper's lips, pushing in all the way and lazily tracing all along the outer edge of Jasper's tongue, from one side to the other and back again.

Jasper's breaths came hot and quick until he sealed his lips around the finger and swallowed.

"That's it," Vincent murmured, pressing his finger against the center of Jasper's tongue and holding it down. "Now touch your nipple."

Jasper jerked as if the order itself had sent pleasure through him. He swallowed again and whimpered in protest but lifted his hand from beside him and slid up his chest.

Vincent looked down to watch as Jasper circled his own nipple, absently rubbing his fingertip in a small circle against Jasper's tongue. "Pinch," he ordered.

Jasper sucked in a sharp breath through his nose as he obeyed.

With a soft *tsk*, Vincent tapped Jasper's tongue. "Harder, pet," he said. This time Jasper's body jerked, and he tried to turn his head away with a moan. Vincent tightened his grip on Jasper's jaw. "You can do better than that."

Jasper whined, but he pinched himself again, squirming on the bed as his breathing turned ragged.

"Like this," Vincent murmured, pulling his finger free of the wet heat, dragging it down Jasper's chin and chest to his nipple. He circled it twice with lazy flicks of his finger, then pinched it tight with a sharp tug. He hummed when Jasper arched off the bed with a gasp. "Better," he said, brushing Jasper's fingers away so he could provide the other nipple with the same treatment. Then he shifted down far enough to get his lips around the first one, swirling his tongue a few times until it hardened completely, then sank his teeth into the sensitive flesh.

Jasper let out a choked cry and buried his fingers in Vincent's hair. "Fuck," he hissed.

"Touch yourself," he ordered, "and remember not to come."

Jasper whined and tugged on Vincent's hair before releasing his grip. His hand hesitated near his stomach, fingers twitching as they continued lower.

Vincent bit each nipple again, then pulled back to watch Jasper stroke himself, eyes fixated on the sight of his long golden fingers stroking over his hard and leaking cock. "Good," he said, his voice rough, pressing two fingers into Jasper's mouth this time. He rubbed Jasper's tongue between them in time to Jasper's strokes, the slick sound of his hand moving over flesh filling the spaces between his ragged breaths. He was captivated by the spreading flush and darkening eyes and soft moans that grew more and more desperate.

"Close?" he asked after several minutes, grazing his teeth against Jasper's ear.

Jasper's whimpering sound of affirmation almost made Vincent go easy on him. But a punishment was a punishment, even if it was a trial run. He wouldn't be doing Jasper any favors by relenting early, and he wouldn't do him that kind of disservice.

"Both hands above your head," Vincent ordered, pulling his fingers free and grabbing the condom and lube. He settled himself between Jasper's thighs as he got the condom in place, and then he coated two fingers and pressed them inside for a quick, proprietary prep. Enough to prevent injury. He smeared the rest over himself, then gripped Jasper beneath each knee, pushing his legs up and over Vincent's shoulders.

Jasper tossed his head back with a hiss as Vincent slowly pressed inside, his fingers twisting in the pillowcase with enough force it was a wonder it didn't rip.

With a groan, he seated himself fully in the nearly-too-tight heat of Jasper's ass. He turned his head and sucked a bruise into Jasper's thigh, grinding his hips forward to coax a continuous stream of gasps and choked-off moans.

"Sir! I'm gonna—"

"No," Vincent said, giving Jasper's balls a rough tug, making him twist with a sharp cry. "You're going to be a good boy for me, aren't you?" he asked with a gentler squeeze to his balls.

Jasper shuddered and nodded, his chest heaving with uneven breaths.

"Good." Vincent released his hold and wrapped his fingers around the base of Jasper's dick with a tight grip instead. He shifted to let Jasper's legs slide off his shoulders and leaned over him, pressing his free hand into the bed near Jasper's head. He leaned down to trace his tongue over Jasper's ear. "Good boy," he whispered, before giving a hard thrust.

"Sir!" Jasper cried, wrapping his arms around Vincent's shoulders and burying his fingers in his hair.

Vincent didn't bother scolding him, too focused on keeping a tight grip on Jasper's cock as he moved, and the bite of Jasper's grip felt good. "That's it," he murmured. "Take it, pet. Such a good boy for me."

Jasper wrapped himself tighter around Vincent, whimpering into his neck. If this weren't a punishment, he might have fucked Jasper through an orgasm until he reached a second. Since it was, he focused on his own pleasure. There was no headboard slamming against the wall, but the bedframe squeaked with his thrusts, a counterpoint to the slick sound of their bodies coming together.

"Yours, Sir," Jasper whispered, a moment before orgasm slammed through Vincent.

His vision whited out, and he let out a breathless grunt, his hips stuttering in their rhythm as he rode out the most intense orgasm he'd had in a while. He stayed stretched over Jasper for a long moment as he caught his breath, then pressed a kiss to Jasper's temple and pushed upright.

Jasper lay sprawled beneath him, still flushed with need, his stomach coated with enough precum that Vincent would have assumed he'd already come despite the painful-looking erection.

Vincent growled softly in approval, carefully pulling out as he slowly released his grip on Jasper's cock. "Good boy," he purred when it merely twitched. He tossed the condom in the trash and cleaned himself up with a tissue before doing the same for Jasper. Then he settled beside him again and grasped Jasper's jaw, guiding him into a leisurely kiss. He trailed his fingers down Jasper's chest, over his nipples, to his stomach, dragging them through the fresh mess already forming there and pressing two into Jasper's mouth.

"Do you think you've been good enough to come tonight?" he asked.

Jasper whimpered and sucked hard on Vincent's fingers, swiping his tongue over every inch of them as if to prove how good he'd been.

Vincent hummed thoughtfully and pulled his fingers away. He dragged them back down Jasper's body, this time going past the mess and palming his erection. Jasper bucked into his touch as a mantra of soft "Pleases" and "Sirs" fell from his lips.

He squeezed the base of Jasper's cock and stroked up to the tip. "You can come, pet," he said, releasing his hold and lightly brushing his palm down the hot length to give another stroke from base to tip, denying him the downward friction he needed to get off.

Jasper gasped and thrust his hips, trying to fuck into Vincent's hand, but he loosened his grip each time.

He *tsk*ed and rubbed his thumb over the leaking tip. "Don't you want to come, pet?"

Jasper whined in frustration and reached for his cock, but Vincent caught his wrist and pinned it to the bed.

"I didn't say you could touch yourself."

"Please," Jasper whispered. "Please, please let me come, please, Sir," he said, his voice breaking on a sob, and then another as tears filled his eyes and spilled over.

There it was. He was only a little surprised Jasper hadn't tapped out. He kissed away the tears with a soft, "Shh, pet. Deep breath and I'll let you come." He waited for Jasper to take a cleansing breath before he started stroking again, tight, quick strokes from base to tip, twisting against the head, then stroking tip to base.

Jasper choked on a groan and gripped Vincent's shoulders, thrusting into his hand twice and throwing his head back with a loud moan as he came, and came, and came some more, shuddering through an orgasm that seemed to last an endless minute until he slumped bonelessly to the bed, gasping for air.

"Good boy," Vincent murmured, pressing a few kisses to Jasper's cheek and forehead, brushing his other hand through the hair at his temple. He leaned back far enough to grab more tissues, cleaning Jasper up then pulling him close. "All right, pet?" he asked softly.

Jasper made a sound that was close to an "Uh-huh."

Vincent got the covers over them, reaching back to turn off the light. "Is your alarm set?"

Jasper nodded and burrowed into Vincent's chest. "Stay?" he whispered.

"I'm not going anywhere, pet."

Jasper noticeably relaxed, and Vincent tightened his hold on him, rubbing a hand against his back. "You were perfect, pet," he murmured, pretending not to notice the hitch in Jasper's breathing or the dampness seeping into his shirt. "Absolutely perfect."

And beautiful in his submission, as always.

Jasper sniffed and took several slow breaths. After a long moment, he said, "I guess that wasn't so bad."

"Glad to hear it," Vincent replied with a soft breath of amusement. "But take a few days to decide if we're adding punishments to the table."

"Okay." Jasper yawned against Vincent's shoulder. "Good night, Sir."

"Sleep well, pet."

WHEN MORNING came, alarms screeched, doors opened and banged shut, toilets flushed, and showers ran. Keith shouted for Reiko to shut off her alarm, which was getting louder by the second. Terrance yelled up the stairs that breakfast was nearly ready.

Vincent groaned and rolled over, burying his head under the pillow. How the fuck did Jasper deal with this every day? He preferred his mornings to be late and quiet.

"Sorry they're so loud, Sir," Jasper mumbled, still half asleep. He curled closer, fingers and arm warm where they settled on the back of Vincent's neck and across his shoulders.

Vincent grunted and tried to fall back asleep, but it was no use. Especially when there was a knock on the door.

"Jasper. Breakfast," Keith called. There were a few moments of silence, then, "Vincent, you can join us too."

Vincent sighed, removing the pillow and cracking his eyes open to find Jasper watching him. "What time is your class?"

"Nine."

Vincent sighed again, rolling onto his back. A quick glance at the clock said it was barely past six, but there was no point in trying to get back to sleep now. "Get ready, then. You need a shower."

"And whose fault is that?"

"Yours," he replied as he dressed in yesterday's clothes. He shot Jasper an annoyed glare when a pillow hit his head, ignoring the laughter that followed as he headed downstairs.

Terrance looked up from the stove when Vincent trudged into the kitchen. "Sleep well?" he asked with a grin.

He managed a soft grunt as he eyed the coffee maker. There were only some dregs of liquid left, but it was hissing and spitting as it brewed a fresh pot.

Terrance snickered. "I forgot you were a nightmare when you had a morning class."

Vincent turned bleary eyes on him and silently flipped him off. The last thing he wanted to think about this morning was college life. Most of that time was overshadowed by his mother's illness and death and then the car accident that turned his life upside down.

Terrance shook his head and grabbed a cup, switching it out with the pot and letting it fill up before handing it over.

"Bless you," Vincent muttered, ignoring Terrance's snort as he sipped the coffee, not even caring that it was black and too bitter for his taste. He was halfway through it before he was coherent enough to glance at the table to find Amber and Keith finishing their breakfasts.

He tilted his head as he turned back to Terrance. "Aren't you off today?" Jasper had mentioned he and Amber weren't due back until today.

"Yeah," Terrance answered, scooping a fresh pan of scrambled eggs onto a plate. He shrugged when Vincent eyed him like he was crazy. "We're always up this early. Not all of us have a vendetta against sunlight."

Vincent wasn't awake enough to argue, so he focused on his coffee. He heard a door shut upstairs, and then Jasper clamored down the stairs and rounded into the kitchen with a grin. He shook his head, not understanding how anyone could have that kind of energy in the morning.

Terrance wiggled the coffee pot in offering, and Vincent readily held his cup out for a refill. He'd need another three in order to get through the morning until he could get home for a nap before opening the club.

Jasper's smile faded into a frown when he saw the cup in Vincent's hands.

The little furrow between Jasper's eyebrows deepened as Vincent took a sip of coffee. He doubted Jasper was even aware of his reaction, much less recognized that specific type of jealousy for what it was. That could become a problem, but it could wait until he was more coherent.

"Eat up. You must be starving after last night," Terrance said, smirking as he handed Jasper a plate full of eggs, bacon, and toast.

Jasper scowled as he took the plate. "Ass."

Terrance laughed and mussed Jasper's hair. "Why're you so cranky? Did Vincent kick you out of your own bed?"

"Amber should teach you to mind your own business," Jasper said, slapping at Terrance's hand.

Vincent raised an eyebrow, not missing the shift in moods around the table.

Amber glanced up, phone in one hand and toast in the other, hovering halfway to her mouth. She met Vincent's eyes before setting her toast back on her plate and straightening in her seat. "I need to do what?"

Terrance winced and stepped away. He turned off the stove, grabbed his own plate, and took it to the table.

Apparently they'd be dealing with Jasper's jealousy now.

Jasper's cheek twitched as he gritted his teeth, staring at his plate and scuffing his foot against the floor. "Nothing," he finally said, setting the plate aside. "I'm not hungry. Can we go?"

"No," Vincent replied, ignoring Jasper's sneer.

"Why? Is there some rule that says 'Keep your mouth shut when someone's sub oversteps with your Sir'?"

Terrance sputtered and turned to Jasper with wide eyes. "I what?"

"You heard me!" Jasper clenched his fists and shoved away from the counter.

Vincent frowned. "Jasper."

Jasper stopped at the edge of the kitchen, though he refused to turn around.

With a sigh, he glanced at Amber. "Sorry. I'll take care of it." Amber nodded as he dumped his coffee in the sink and guided Jasper out of the kitchen with a hand on his shoulder.

Jasper grabbed his bag on their way out the door. When they reached the car, he slumped into the passenger seat, staring out the window with his arms crossed.

Vincent let him stew. There were a dozen ways he could approach this, though he wasn't sure which would be best. Jasper wasn't stupid, and he picked up on things quickly enough, but the issue was finding the real root of the problem.

He pulled into a café near the college twenty minutes later and held his card out to Jasper. "You're not going to class on an empty stomach," he said when Jasper eyed him in confusion.

Once Jasper was out of the car, he let out a slow breath. He probably should have expected this with how Jasper reacted to Adam, but he never expected that kind of reaction with his own family. Then again, Jasper hadn't interacted much with others in the lifestyle. Even in the club, he stayed in Vincent's office or at his side.

Maybe he should remedy that once Jasper's finals were out of the way.

He took his card back when Jasper returned with a breakfast sandwich and orange juice. "Jasper."

Jasper sighed and jammed his straw into the juice carton. "I know. I'm sorry, okay? I know I was a dick."

"I'm not the one you need to say that to. I'm more interested in why."

Jasper shrugged, tearing off a bite of his sandwich without eating it. "I wanted to get your coffee, even though our coffee sucks. I know it's stupid—"

"It's not stupid," Vincent said firmly. "It was stupid to act like a dick about it. You're my sub, Jas. It's okay if you don't want others serving me."

"Really? It feels stupid to get mad over something like that."

Vincent considered that a moment. "Are you more upset that I was served by someone else, or that it was Terrance who gave me the coffee?"

Jasper opened his mouth to respond, but closed it a second later. He took a bite of his sandwich and chewed in silence. "That it was him, I guess," he finally said.

"Why?"

"I don't know. I know he and Amber are happy together, and he's not gay. But you have history with them, and you barely know me."

"I did know them in college, but that has nothing to do with the relationship I have with you. I know you well enough. Enough to extend our contract." He reached out to press a finger beneath Jasper's chin and turned his face enough to look at him directly. "You're mine as much as I am yours, pet, so if you want to keep service between us, we can."

Jasper swallowed, his tongue flicking out to wet his lips. "Okay," he finally said.

"Okay?"

He tilted his head into Vincent's hand. "I don't want others serving you, but I think I'd be okay with you doing scenes at the club, so long as there's no fucking."

Vincent studied him in surprise at the distinction. "All right," he replied slowly. "That's something we can discuss later."

Jasper nodded and finished his breakfast as Vincent drove to the campus.

"Just to be clear, this is something that I would discipline you for."

"Are you going to punish me for it?" Jasper asked softly.

"Discipline, not punish. And should I?"

"I guess?" Jasper finished his sandwich and crumpled the wrapper into a tiny ball. He drank the rest of his juice until the straw gurgled on air.

"Why don't you consider it and let me know this weekend, and what kind of discipline you think would be appropriate."

Jasper made a face, his brow furrowed as he glanced at Vincent. "You're going to let me decide the punishment?"

"Yes."

"What if I say a blowjob makes it all better?"

Vincent shot him an exasperated look and pulled onto campus. "Discipline is nonsexual."

Jasper scoffed. "Says who?"

"Says me." Vincent followed where Jasper pointed and parked near the building he needed for class. "Discipline is not punishment, pet. My punishments are for things like being a brat, or deliberately refusing to do as told without safewording. They're another level of play. Discipline is for disrespect, to correct behavior. It will never be sexual," he said firmly. "Understand?"

Jasper gave a jerky nod. "Yes, Sir."

"Good." He grasped Jasper's chin again and coaxed his head up. "I'm not angry with you. You made a mistake, and you'll correct it, and we'll move on. Nothing has changed, and I will still work on the new contract for you."

Jasper blinked rapidly and let out a shaky breath. "Thank you, Sir."

"Of course, pet." He leaned in to press a quick kiss to Jasper's forehead and then his lips. "Are you good?" When Jasper nodded, he let go and sat back. "Then I'll pick you up this weekend. Let me know how things go tonight."

Jasper grimaced as he unbuckled. "You could come over and see for yourself."

"You need to work it out between yourselves, and I need to be at the club early."

Jasper pushed the door open with a sigh. "Thanks for breakfast, Sir. I'll call you tonight."

CHAPTER TWENTY-THREE

JASPER TRIED to focus on classes, but his mind kept wandering to last night and that morning. He still wasn't convinced jealousy was, in fact, an acceptable response, and over a fucking cup of coffee, no less. Vincent wouldn't have lied to him, but he was starting to wonder how far Vincent's patience would go. Surely he wouldn't want to spend the next year dealing with Jasper's shortcomings as a sub.

He had to do better. He didn't want Vincent getting fed up with him before he had the chance to really explore any of this—kink and relationship both.

After his classes, Jasper set up in his bedroom to study. He put his headphones on with some violin music and tried not to think about the conversation—that is, lecture—that would likely happen during or after dinner. He hated having to apologize for being a dick, though at least it was happening less often than a couple of years ago.

There was a knock on his door a few hours later. "Jasper," Amber called. "Dinner."

"Coming." He closed his notebooks and took a breath. He didn't mind tough conversations exactly, but he had a feeling it would be more embarrassing than anything.

Once in the kitchen, he filled a plate with broccoli-and-cheese casserole and settled at the table. Reiko and Matt were missing, but Keith was there with Terrance and Amber. He poked at his food, waiting for the others to get settled before speaking. "I'm sorry I was a dick this morning."

Terrance cleared his throat. "And I'm sorry if I overstepped. I didn't know you had service as part of your contract."

He shrugged, feeling even more like an ass. "I didn't until this morning."

Terrance raised an eyebrow and shared a look with Amber. "You're really jumping all in."

"Is that bad?"

"It's not *bad*, but…." Amber trailed off with a sigh. "There is such a thing as escalating too quickly. You can get overwhelmed or burn yourself out trying everything all at once."

"I'm already overwhelmed," Jasper muttered, stabbing at a piece of broccoli.

"What do you mean?" Keith asked.

He grimaced as he jabbed at his food again. "I keep fucking up." This morning was the worst fuckup so far, and he was sure he'd only get worse. He could already feel the helpless panic scratching its way up his spine. The anxious knot in his stomach wasn't nearly as bad as when he'd broken down in front of Vincent, but it was there.

No matter what Vincent said about still giving him a new contract, sooner or later he'd fuck up so bad there was no recovering. He didn't even get why Vincent wanted him to begin with. He was a decade younger, he deliberately pushed Vincent's buttons, and he wasn't a decent sub. He didn't even know what all he liked or didn't like yet.

"He should hate me by now." None of his relationships had ever lasted this long, contract or no.

His father had made it abundantly clear he was worthless, that he'd never amount to anything. It wasn't surprising that it extended even to being a sub or having any kind of relationship.

Before he could follow that thought into a downward spiral, Keith tapped his fork against his mostly empty plate. "You're still figuring out what works for you. That takes time."

"Also, you can't 'fuck up' being a sub unless you completely give up on your Dom," Terrance added, complete with air quotes.

Keith nodded. "No one can tell you how to be a perfect sub, Jas. Every relationship is unique."

"You're lucky you've found someone you're comfortable exploring it with." Amber sat back as Terrance cleared her plate. "As for this morning, apology accepted. But talk to us going forward. We're in this together."

Jasper ducked his head and nodded. "Sorry."

"Now eat up so you can go report to Vincent," Keith said, sounding amused.

Jasper looked up to see Keith smirking at him and rolled his eyes. "Is that common protocol or something?"

"Communication?" Keith asked with a soft laugh. "I'd be worried if it wasn't."

He poked at his food with a frown and forced himself to eat. When he finished he headed back to his room to sit on his bed and stare at his phone for several minutes.

He wasn't sure why he felt hesitant, or why there was a nervous flutter in his chest, but he finally took a breath and called.

Vincent answered on the second ring. "Hello, pet."

"Hello, Sir," Jasper replied, a smile tugging at his lips. The nervous fluttering vanished at the sound of Vincent's voice. He shifted back on the bed and settled against his pillows. "How was your day?"

"Much quieter than this morning."

Jasper rolled his eyes with a soft laugh. "Speaking of… I talked to them. We're good now," he said, picking at the frayed hem of his shorts.

"Good." When Jasper didn't say anything else, he asked, "Did something else happen?"

"No. Not exactly." He sighed and pulled his knee up, tipping his head back to stare at the ceiling. As much as he loved being with Vincent and finally experiencing things he'd only fantasized about, he couldn't help feeling overwhelmed the moment they were apart. The more time they spent together, the more he realized how little he really knew about how all this worked and how misleading all the porn was. Obviously.

"Keith said there's no such thing as a perfect sub?" He hadn't meant it to sound like a question.

"That's true." Vincent snorted softly. "Not everyone enjoys a mouthy brat."

"But you do," Jasper said, voice quiet. He found himself holding his breath as he waited for Vincent's response.

"Yes, pet," Vincent replied, just as quietly. After Jasper let out a loud, shaky breath, he continued. "That's part of why we work so well."

"Even though I keep messing up? You can't possibly enjoy dealing with me." He had to know. If Vincent was frustrated with his lack of experience—with kink and relationships both. If he really wouldn't rather have someone like Keith, who knew who and what he was and was comfortable with himself.

Vincent was silent for a moment, and Jasper could practically hear the little frown Vincent likely had. "If I wasn't prepared for the work needed for you to learn all this, I never would have agreed to that first dinner."

Jasper clamped a hand over his mouth, but not quickly enough to stifle the soft choked gasp as a wave of relief crashed over him.

Vincent sighed. "If you've been worried that I'll get bored or tired of teaching you, stop it," he said firmly. "You have no idea how——"

Jasper bit his lip, waiting for Vincent to finish that sentence, but several long seconds passed without another word. "Sir?"

He almost expected Vincent to brush it off, to say it was nothing and change the subject, but Vincent surprised him yet again with how willing he was to be honest about everything.

"You have no idea how incredible it is, finding you before you've been told how you should act or think as a sub," Vincent said. "I don't expect you to change who you are, pet. I only expect you to be willing to explore your depths with me."

Jasper blinked back the tears of relief and gratitude that Vincent was the one he'd ended up with his first night in the club. He'd really have to make sure he didn't fuck all this up, and he'd have to thank Vincent somehow. "Okay," he whispered and cleared his throat. "But I think I'm going to need lots of help plundering all my depths."

"We have time. You've done fine whenever I plunder your booty," Vincent said dryly.

Jasper laughed, not even caring that it was a little shaky with the release of nerves. "You definitely jolly my Rodger, Sir."

"Oh my God," Vincent replied, sounding stuck somewhere between wanting to laugh or cry. "No more puns."

"Or what? You'll punish me?"

"Yes. With marshmallows."

Jasper grinned, relaxing against his pillow as the anxiety and worry melted out of him. "You drive a hard bargain, Sir."

"Oh good. Here I was worried I'd lost my touch," Vincent said. "Are you feeling better? Anything else we need to address?"

"No, I think I'm good now." Jasper bit his lip and shifted until he was stretched out on his back. "But if I'm not allowed any more puns, how about some phone sex?"

Vincent chuckled. "Good night, pet," he said, before hanging up.

Jasper scoffed and stared at his phone, not quite able to believe Vincent had *hung up on him*. And he'd even turned down *phone sex*.

"How rude."

Chapter Twenty-Four

Since Jasper had finals starting next week, Vincent dropped him off at home to study in peace before heading back to work.

When he returned in the void between late night and early morning, he found Jasper slumped over the dining table on top of his books. Vincent shook his head even as warmth curled its way through his chest. Coming home to Jasper waiting for him was something he could certainly get addicted to.

He moved up behind Jasper and leaned over him, kissing beneath his ear. "Time for bed, pet," he murmured.

Jasper moaned in protest and sat up with a sleepy pout. "I'm awake."

"Could have fooled me." Vincent tugged Jasper to his feet, brushing his thumb against the line on Jasper's cheek from a textbook. "Bed."

Jasper nodded and immediately leaned into Vincent, using him as support as they headed up the stairs. Somehow he managed to undress on his own before collapsing into bed.

Vincent watched for a few moments, then shook his head and changed. Once in bed, his fingers immediately found their way into messy blond hair, curling tight with a quiet sigh of contentment.

With Jasper's summer break around the corner, he planned to set aside ample time for them to figure out what they both wanted from this going forward. There'd be more issues to deal with, and more than a little exploring and experimenting, but that was half the fun.

Then there was Jasper's birthday coming up.

He wasn't sure what to get as a present. It was far too early to even be thinking of a permanent collar, and he wouldn't suggest moving in together until they had more than a weekend at a time together. Maybe a vacation was in order. One or two weeks for them to be alone without work or classes to see how well they worked without a break from each other.

He fell asleep thinking of all the different places they could go.

Morning came far too early, and Vincent was disappointed to find Jasper already out of bed by the time he woke up.

His disappointment faded when he reached the kitchen and Jasper offered him a cup of coffee, prepared exactly how he liked it. "Thank you, pet," he murmured, not missing the faint, almost serene smile on Jasper's lips.

"Breakfast is ready," Jasper said, offering Vincent a plate of scrambled eggs and toast.

"How's your studying coming?" he asked, taking the plate to the table. He stacked a few of Jasper's books and set them aside so they had room to eat.

"Okay, I think." Jasper settled next to him and dug in. "It's easier to study here. 'S quiet."

That was an understatement. A farm full of roosters would be quiet compared to a house with five other people. He sat back to sip his coffee as he studied Jasper. Despite not having any scenes planned for the weekend so Jasper could study, he still enjoyed having him here. Which made it all the easier to accept that he wanted to keep Jasper around longer.

"I've drawn up the new contract for you," he said, hiding his amusement behind his cup when Jasper turned wide eyes on him. "The only thing missing is discipline and punishments, if you're wanting to add them."

Jasper swallowed his mouthful of eggs. "Do you want to add them?"

Vincent opened his mouth to say he wanted whatever Jasper wanted but decided against it. While true, he knew he needed to start telling Jasper some of his own preferences so they both understood where their tastes aligned. "Yes," he said. "Punishments especially are something I enjoy, but discipline tends to make it easier to set and enforce boundaries."

"Oh."

"But it doesn't work if that's not something you want too. Your contract, your choice. The only nonnegotiable part I added is that we get tested. What we do with the results after is up to you."

Jasper bit his bottom lip and poked at the bite of eggs he had left. "I couldn't think of a suitable punishment for being a dick."

Vincent tilted his head. "Could you think of unsuitable ones?"

Jasper snorted. "You said spanking was a reward. And sex wasn't an option. Making me kneel in a corner seems pointless."

"Why's that?"

"You already scolded me, and I already apologized, so it's all good, isn't it?"

"Fair enough," Vincent replied, raising an eyebrow when Jasper stared at him in surprise. "You thought I'd insist on additional consequences?" Jasper's shrug wasn't exactly shocking, but he still hated whoever had made him expect the worst about everything. That was likely his father, but there couldn't have been many good examples in Jasper's life if he was still this wary.

"Discipline should be handled the same day of the incident, if not immediately after it. You made a mistake and realized it. We addressed the issue, and you fixed it. Nothing else is needed."

Jasper didn't bother to hide his suspicion. "Then why did you tell me to think of something?"

"I wanted to know how seriously you would consider your actions and the potential consequences. There's no sense in setting expectations or boundaries if you don't care about breaking them." Adam had thoroughly taught him that lesson.

"I hope you understand that discipline and punishments aren't there as traps for an excuse to hurt you," Vincent added after a moment, and the way Jasper flinched and stared at his plate let him know he'd finally found the problem. He sighed softly, but he wasn't sure what he could say to set Jasper at ease.

He picked up his coffee and drained the rest of it, then drummed his fingers against the side of the cup. "How about this," he finally said into the silence. "If you want to add punishments, we can do that, and we'll leave discipline off to revisit in six months." Jasper nodded while staring at his place, and Vincent eyed him, wondering what he'd missed. "Jas, if something's wrong, you need to tell me."

"I'm sorry," Jasper said in a rush, pushing his plate away and finally lifting his head. For some reason he looked guilty. "I said I trusted you, and I do, so there's no reason you shouldn't add—"

"Stop," Vincent ordered, shoving down the sudden burst of annoyance and anger to figure them out later. Neither of those emotions were helpful or needed right then. "The contract has nothing to do with trust. It's a guide, nothing more."

Jasper didn't seem convinced, but he didn't argue. Whatever was fueling this new misunderstanding, they'd need to get to the bottom of it soon, but studying for finals needed to take priority right now.

"I'll finish up the contract while you study. When you need a break, why don't we go get our tests taken care of?" When Jasper nodded,

Vincent stood and tipped Jasper's chin up, then leaned down for a quick kiss. "Still not angry, pet," he said, relieved when the tension eased out of Jasper's shoulders. He mentally added the phrase to his list and could only hope it wouldn't always be needed.

He refilled his coffee and settled on the sofa, leaving the dining table to Jasper and his mess of textbooks. He pulled up the contract on his laptop to put in the last few changes. While the previous contract remained, with Jasper's updated limits, the additions specifically included testing and that they be exclusive. His own request was for Jasper to be readily available outside of life responsibilities and previous obligations, and he'd provide the same in return. If they were going to move into a more explicit relationship, he'd likely start making more demands on Jasper's time.

Ideally, he'd prefer Jasper to move in with him. Which brought him back to birthday gifts. He didn't know Jasper's tastes well enough to choose, so he pulled up some travel packages online for overseas and some domestic locations he'd enjoyed or wanted to visit. He printed them all out with the contract and then turned to work.

For the next few hours, Jasper studied at the table, and Vincent set up a couple job openings for a general manager, another floor manager, and another chef for the club. He'd already had to shuffle some schedules around when he realized he really wasn't willing to give up all his weekends with Jasper, but he'd promised it wouldn't be a permanent change. The club was steadily growing, and he needed more staff anyway if he wanted to start scheduling events.

And if he was going to give Jasper the attention and support he needed, he couldn't sink eighty hours a week into the club anymore, even if he did enjoy the work.

He completely missed when Jasper brought him a fresh coffee an hour after they settled in. Between one absent sip and the next, it went from hot to lukewarm.

Jasper hadn't said anything, and he'd been quiet enough Vincent hadn't even noticed he'd moved from the table. Any doubts he had that Jasper might get overwhelmed with the lifestyle, or with adding service to his contract, faded almost completely. Sure there would be rough spots, but Jasper had proven several times now that he was a natural.

When Jasper finally joined him on the couch near noon, he curled into Vincent's side and nuzzled into his neck. "You should take me out to lunch."

"Should I?" Vincent replied, most of his attention on checking over the financial sheets his assistant had sent him.

"Definitely." Jasper pulled back when Vincent didn't respond immediately, glancing at the computer before settling next to him.

Vincent rewarded him with a hand on his thigh, squeezing lightly as he finished and sent back his approval. Then he closed his laptop and turned his attention to Jasper. "Break, then?" he asked, stealing a quick kiss when Jasper nodded.

It didn't take them long to dress, and he snagged the contract from his office and set it on the kitchen island for when they returned.

The trip to the clinic was quick and uneventful, and they were back in the car less than an hour after arriving. Somewhere between arriving and leaving, though, Jasper had gone quiet.

Once they were on the road again, Jasper cleared his throat, a flush creeping up his neck. "So when the results come back, you want to stop using condoms?"

"I would like to, if that's something you're comfortable with." When Jasper didn't say anything further, Vincent glanced at him. "Do you want to keep using them no matter what?"

Jasper didn't respond immediately, chewing on his bottom lip as he stared out the window.

The annoyance he'd felt earlier stirred, but he still hadn't worked out what exactly was bothering him. Obviously Jasper needed better communication skills, but he was receptive and responsive enough when the right questions were asked.

"Jasper," he said, keeping his tone neutral. He hadn't wanted to broach the topic of Jasper's father, but he needed to know exactly what he was dealing with, and he suspected Jasper's need to please him stemmed from his home life. "Have you been punished for disagreeing with someone?" He watched Jasper from the corner of his eye. Saw how Jasper went rigid and his knuckles whitened as he gripped his jeans.

It was all the answer he really needed.

Anger spiked in his chest, and he forced out a slow breath, turning his attention back to the road. "I'm not going to be angry if you say no.

Not using condoms can be a limit, same as anything else." He paused and glanced at Jasper again, but he was still stiff and staring out the window.

"I appreciate that you want to please me, but not if it comes at the price of self-sacrifice." After walking that path himself, even if it'd been for completely different reasons, he wasn't about to let Jasper start down it.

It took until Vincent parked at the sushi restaurant Jasper wanted to eat at for Jasper to respond. "Isn't all of this about self-sacrifice?" he asked softly.

Vincent stilled, dropping his hand from the key before he could shut off the ignition. "Not really," he answered slowly. So much for waiting to have these conversations until after Jasper finished his finals. "A sub chooses what they are willing to give up. But it's always an exchange. They receive something in return—pleasure, release, grounding, whatever."

He turned towards Jasper and lightly grasped his chin, coaxing him into meeting Vincent's eyes. "That is not the same as giving up your right to say no to something because you think it will please me. It won't," he added firmly. "And if you do, it will damage what trust I have in you to protect yourself."

"Okay," Jasper answered, too soft and far too quickly.

Vincent bit back his frustration, unsure how to get through to Jasper and make him understand. It wasn't just that Jasper didn't seem to know how a power exchange worked; it went beyond that.

Jasper didn't even seem to realize he had all the power in this relationship.

Maybe what he'd seen as *eagerness* had really been fear and desperation, and Vincent swallowed the disgust building in his throat. Surely he hadn't been so blinded by having a new sub that he'd misread everything?

No. Even if some of Jasper's actions were fueled by his fear of losing Vincent's interest, even a blind person could see that Jasper was a natural. There was no way he could have forced himself to submit like that for weeks without Vincent or Jasper's family noticing.

"Let's eat," he said, turning off the car and heading inside. The conversation was far from over, but they weren't continuing it on an empty stomach.

He requested the secluded booth at the back corner of the restaurant, and between the two of them, they ordered five of the specialty sushi rolls. Once they had their drinks, Vincent crossed his arms on the table and studied Jasper. "I want you to repeat after me, pet," he said, waiting until he had Jasper's full attention. "I, as the sub, have the power in this relationship."

Jasper frowned, clamping his mouth shut and keeping silent.

Well. That was interesting. He watched Jasper for several long seconds, to no avail. "Jasper."

"I don't want to."

"Why not?"

Jasper shifted in his seat, turning away and staring out the window. Another long minute passed, and then he said, "It feels wrong."

"Only if you're looking at it from the wrong perspective." At least they were getting somewhere. It was no wonder Jasper felt out of sorts if he had misconceptions that needed correcting.

"What other perspective is there?"

"Many." When Jasper shot him a disbelieving scowl, he sighed. "Would you prefer I have all the power?"

Jasper frowned. "That's how this is supposed to work."

"All right. So you would prefer a slave contract?"

Jasper hesitated. "What's that?"

"You sign over all rights to me. Everything, from how you dress, to what you eat, or what you do with your free time. All of it is decided by me. Slaves have no rights. Sometimes not even the right to say no." He paused, watching Jasper as he gave him a moment for that to sink in.

"If the Master wanted to piss in his slave's mouth and make him swallow, the slave would do it, regardless of any protests," he added, to ensure he drove the point home. He wasn't going to sugarcoat it, and he wasn't disappointed when Jasper's expression landed somewhere between disgusted and horrified.

"So is that the contract you want?"

He expected Jasper to say no; he'd as good as said so these past several weeks together. He didn't realize how much he needed Jasper to say no right then until Jasper didn't say anything. For the first time since taking Jasper on, he wondered if maybe this had been a mistake after all.

"Is that the contract you want, Sir?" Jasper finally asked, eyes focused on the center of the table.

Vincent could have said no. Maybe he should have. Instead he asked, "If I said yes, would you become my slave?" Because he had to know, right now, before this went any further, just how far Jasper really was willing to go to please him. If Jasper was willing to let Vincent control every aspect of his life because he thought that was what Vincent wanted….

A minute ticked by without Jasper answering, but his brow was pinched as he continued staring at the table like it had all the answers. Maybe it did.

Their food arrived, and Vincent waited until the server was gone. "Jas?"

With a shuddering breath, Jasper seemed to cave in on himself as he shook his head. "No," he whispered. "I'm sorry, Sir. I can't… I don't *want* to be a slave."

"Good," Vincent said, relief and pride leaving him momentarily breathless. "Good boy." That was something he could work with, at least.

He picked up his chopsticks, motioning to the food. "Eat." Jasper's incredulous expression fueled the quiet anger in the pit of his stomach, but he ignored it for now. "I'm proud of you, pet. I need you to continue making those decisions with your own well-being in mind. It's the only way you're going to find your real limits. Understand?"

Jasper carefully picked up his own chopsticks, poured some soy sauce into his dish, and mixed a bit of wasabi into it. "I think so, Sir."

"Good," he said again. That was good.

He let Jasper process that as they ate, then returned to the previous issue. "So if not a slave, then a sub. A sub has rights. They keep their autonomy. The *sub* chooses what they are willing to give, when to give it, and what they need in return."

"But you're the one in control," Jasper said, frowning as he picked up another piece of sushi.

Vincent tapped his chopsticks against his soy dish as he considered his response. "I'm the one in charge," he finally said. "There's a difference. It's my job to ensure we both get what we need, within the terms and limits that you set." He'd never been more grateful for his therapist than he was right then. Putting all this into words Jasper could understand would have been impossible without the past several years of digging into his own issues and relationship with kink.

"I might ask you for something you don't want to do, but it's your choice. Even if you agree, it's fluid, and you can stop it at any time."

"So can you," Jasper said, finally glancing up long enough to meet Vincent's eyes.

Vincent nodded. "All of this works exactly like your limits. It changes based on your needs."

"What about *your* needs?"

It took every ounce of control to keep from saying his needs didn't matter right now. That was only partly true. He was fine with taking what Jasper was willing to give while focusing on Jasper learning his limits for now. Instead, he waited for the server to refill their drinks before answering.

"You've been fulfilling my biggest need. It doesn't matter so much what you give up. I want your submission, and I want it given willingly."

They finished eating in silence as Jasper mulled that over. There was enough sushi leftover to fill a to-go box, and once Vincent paid, they headed back to the car.

Jasper settled in the passenger seat, his eyes on Vincent, which was much better than staring out the window. "You really mean all that," he said slowly. When Vincent shot him a questioning look, he flicked his fingers as if to indicate everything. "I have all the power, and you're not going to get mad if I say no to something."

"I meant every word."

"Even if I don't ever want to try something new?"

"You might not have noticed, pet, but I enjoy our time together," he said dryly. "So long as I have your submission, we can figure something out."

Jasper was quiet for a moment, before he reached over and lightly rested his hand on Vincent's thigh. "Thank you, Sir. You should teach a class or something," he said, grin evident in his voice.

There was an idea. He shifted his hand to grasp Jasper's fingers, rubbing his thumb along the backs of them. That really wasn't a bad idea at all. There'd been requests for demos and such, and there were enough members now to make it worth the effort. Small classes would certainly be easier to start with than theme events or tastings. "Would you attend them?"

"If you're teaching them?" Jasper asked with a soft laugh. "Yes, Sir. Definitely."

Vincent refrained from rolling his eyes. "No, I would find an experienced sub to do them." He might have the occasional desire to let his sub do all the work, but it wasn't a frame of mind he'd really explored. "They'd be able to answer your questions better."

"What if I don't like their answers?"

"Then you come to me and we find an answer that works."

Jasper rubbed his fingertips against Vincent's index finger. "Okay."

"Okay."

The rest of the drive was silent, but it was comfortable. He still didn't know if Jasper wanted to keep the condoms for the foreseeable future, but it didn't matter until the tests came back anyway.

He followed Jasper to the fridge and waited until he put the food away to press him back against it, claiming his lips.

Jasper wrapped his arms around Vincent's shoulders, his body unresisting and pliant. When Vincent finally broke the kiss, he licked his lips with a soft moan. "You could fuck me, Sir. Before I go back to studying."

"I could," Vincent murmured, moving his lips to Jasper's neck. He took his time leaving a mark there, finally lifting his head to study Jasper. "Can you tell me who has the power here?"

After a long beat of silence, Jasper whispered, "I do, Sir."

"And why is that?"

"Because I'm the sub." His voice still held doubt.

Vincent straightened and pulled his hands out from under Jasper's shirt to rest them on his hips instead. "Put your hands above your head." When Jasper obeyed without question, he left him like that a moment before asking, "Why did you do that?"

"Because you told me to," Jasper said, a frown settling between his eyebrows.

"And if Amber or Keith told you to do that? Would you obey them?"

The frown deepened as Jasper stared at Vincent's chest. "No."

Vincent hummed and found the warm skin above Jasper's jeans with his thumbs, rubbing small circles into it. "Strip naked, go outside, and run around the house."

Jasper scowled. "No way."

"Why not?" he asked, more amused than annoyed that Jasper needed such extreme examples to draw the line without hesitation.

"Because I don't want to."

"Okay. Why not?" Vincent waited as Jasper shifted against the fridge, dropping his arms as he clearly grew more frustrated.

"You can't make me," Jasper finally mumbled.

Vincent raised an eyebrow. It wasn't a reason, but he was surprised Jasper didn't seem to realize that was exactly the point. "You're right. I can't make you do anything."

Jasper stared at Vincent's chest, practically vibrating with tension, but he didn't try to pull away. "I know you said you wouldn't get mad," he said quietly. "But you could still take it out on me later. Punish me for not doing what you wanted. Make me think twice about refusing again."

Vincent almost flinched, gritting his teeth against the flood of memories of Adam doing exactly that. He'd lived that nightmare for years. He'd never inflict it on someone else. "I could," he said, letting out a slow breath. "And there are some Doms who do, and some subs who enjoy that kind of play. That's not something I'm interested in."

Jasper nodded faintly and glanced up, still obviously uncertain.

Vincent slid his palm up Jasper's chest, grasped his chin, and tipped his head back. "What if I told you to strip and lie on the table so I could tie you down?"

Jasper's eyes darted to the table, then focused on Vincent again. His tongue flicked out, wetting his lips as he nodded.

"Even without knowing what I want to do to you?"

Jasper frowned again, but he didn't hesitate. "Yes, Sir. I trust you."

"Trust me to do what, pet?"

"To not do anything I…." Jasper slumped against the fridge with a dumbfounded expression. "Oh."

"Oh," Vincent agreed.

Jasper fell silent and let out a few long shuddering breaths before speaking again. "I trust you to follow my limits. I… I'm giving you the power to use me how you want because I can trust you not to hurt me. Because you know where I draw the line. Even if that line isn't permanent."

Finally they were getting somewhere.

"Good boy." Jasper's hesitant smile was more than worth the frustration of the past few hours. He slid his fingers into Jasper's hair and curled them into a loose fist. "Once you're restrained, you're completely helpless. I could gag you and do whatever I wanted to you, regardless of your limits. But that's not the point, is it?"

"No, Sir," Jasper whispered.

"Do you understand why I need to be able to trust you to know your limits, then? To be able to safeword without worrying about being punished for it?"

Jasper's eyes widened, and he made a soft, desperate sound at the back of his throat. "Yes, Sir. I'm sorry I didn't—I thought I was supposed to let you take what you wanted and… hope you knew when it was too much."

Vincent pulled Jasper close, running fingers through his hair. "And now? You understand why the sub has the power?"

"Yes, Sir," Jasper said, voice muffled against Vincent's neck. "So you can take what you need without worrying about hurting me."

"Good boy. Very good, pet." He held Jasper like that for several long minutes, letting him soak in the praise. It was well-earned, considering where they'd started.

He pressed his lips to Jasper's temple and flexed his fingers in blond hair. "No matter how well we work together, I can't read your mind, pet. If you tell me green when you really mean red, you're hurting both of us."

"Yes, Sir," Jasper whispered. "I understand. I won't lie to you."

Vincent nodded, and when he finally pulled back, he tipped Jasper's face up for a quick kiss. "Good boy."

Jasper tightened his fingers in the back of Vincent's shirt, pressing close again and burying his face in Vincent's neck. "Thank you, Sir."

"You're welcome, pet."

CHAPTER TWENTY-FIVE

JASPER WAS still riding the high of his breakthroughs well into late Sunday morning. Once that fundamental piece of information finally clicked, everything else seemed to slowly follow.

He could trust Vincent because while Vincent might be interested in tormenting him, he had no desire to do any actual harm. They could explore whatever they wanted, because it wasn't about *what* they did so much as making sure they both enjoyed it.

But Vincent had to know where Jasper drew the lines so he wouldn't cross them.

The safewords were there to ensure they could stop if it didn't feel right anymore. If the reality of a scene didn't live up to the fantasy. He could use them because he trusted Vincent to listen and stop.

And once the fear and apprehension of having to commit to trying something new was gone, he found he had a *lot* of fantasies. They were still pretty tame, compared to things he'd seen people talking about online, but they were still new and exciting. At least for him.

And wanting to serve Vincent, to get his coffee and make sure he had breakfast waiting for him when he woke up…. That was only the start. He wanted to be needed and wanted outside of the bedroom and playroom. He wanted to make Vincent's life easier, despite the fact the dick was rich and already had it easy.

"What's so funny?" Vincent asked, coming up beside him.

Jasper tipped his head back with a grin. "Nothing, Sir. Just thinking about how much I like being yours."

The look Vincent gave him wasn't convinced in the least.

A soft sigh of content escaped him as Vincent ran fingers through his hair.

"How's the studying?"

Jasper whined. "Ugh. My head is going to explode." At least he felt like he understood most of it, though whether it was from actually understanding or overconfidence, he wasn't sure.

Vincent picked up the flash cards littering the table and sat beside him to flip through them. "How about a game?"

"What kind of game?" he asked, eyeing Vincent. Warmth flooded through him at that particular tone in Vincent's voice. He obviously wanted something out of it, but Jasper hadn't been disappointed with any of his suggestions yet. He doubted he'd ever be disappointed with Vincent when it came to sex.

"Every time you get an answer right, you can remove a piece of clothing."

Seriously? "You want to play strip quiz? Is that why you made me get dressed this morning?" Judging by the twitch of Vincent's lips, that was exactly why. He couldn't believe Vincent had *planned* this. Then again, he wasn't exactly surprised. "What do I get when I'm naked?"

"A reward." The heat in Vincent's eyes left no doubt what the nature of the reward would be.

Anticipation and arousal pulsed through his body. "Okay."

He moved his chair back when Vincent motioned him to do so, shifting in his seat when he was in full view. With Vincent's full attention on him.

The first question was easy enough, and Vincent allowed him to remove his right sock. He dropped it with a slight frown, realizing the rules were backwards, but it wasn't like it mattered.

His second correct answer only got him a single button of his shirt undone. "So not fair, Sir," he grumbled. "You said a piece of clothing for every right answer."

"A button is a piece of clothing. Next question."

Jasper huffed, refraining from rolling his eyes, but only barely.

Twenty minutes later, he was shirtless and had a sock on his left foot and right hand, since wrong answers required adding a piece of clothing, apparently. His pants were unbuttoned and unzipped, and it was getting harder to focus on the questions. Especially when Vincent kept absently rubbing himself between each one.

Two more right answers and he finally had both socks off.

And then Vincent casually pulled something metal out of his pocket and set it on the table. "Instead of your clothes, the next answer you get wrong, you'll put these on."

He stared at the little silver clamps, held together by a delicate chain. He bit his lower lip to stifle his moan at the spike of heat that went through him. Fuck. *Fuck.* This was so not fair. On the one hand, he remembered how good those had felt the last time. On the other, they'd hurt like a *bitch.* "Just those?" he asked. His voice came out strained.

"Just those."

Jasper licked his lips and forced his eyes away, glancing at Vincent instead. This was a scene. Nothing more. A game. He could say no. He could try to answer the rest of the questions correctly and not have to put them on at all. Or he could *deliberately* miss. Let Vincent attach them. Suffer the torment of clamps on his nipples until the game ended.

It was his choice. The thrill of exhilaration as that fact fully cemented in his head filled him with an entirely different kind of heat.

"Okay," he finally said, and the game continued.

He could have answered the next question correctly. Could have lost his pants and been one question away from his reward.

He chose not to.

When Vincent *tsk*ed and picked up the clamps, Jasper whimpered. Not that he could really complain. His dick was straining in his briefs even before Vincent rubbed his nipples into hard nubs.

And when the cold metal sank into the sensitive flesh, he hissed and arched in his seat. "*Fuck!*"

Vincent chuckled, running his thumb over Jasper's lips and stepping back. He sat and picked up the cards. "Only two questions away from your reward, pet. If you want it."

Jasper shivered, focusing on his breathing instead of his stinging nipples. He almost had to sit on his own hands to keep from ripping the clamps off. *Did* he want his reward now? Or did he want to drag this out?

In the end, he couldn't remember the answer to the next question anyway and shrugged his shirt back on.

Vincent was blatantly rubbing himself, and Jasper was completely sure it was meant as a distraction.

One that worked far too well. He couldn't even focus enough to understand the next question, much less answer it correctly. All he wanted right then was Vincent's hands on him. Pushing him down. Taking him. Making him come.

His breathing was unsteady as Vincent unzipped his own pants. That was so not fair. That was *cheating*. He shoved his hands under his thighs with a soft whine. "Please."

Vincent stood and crossed the short distance between them again. His fingers tangled in Jasper's hair, curling tight and forcing his head back. "Please what, pet?"

The moan that escaped him was low and needy even to his own ears. "Please fuck me, Sir."

"I plan on it," Vincent purred, leaning down to steal a kiss. "The only question is if you get off with me."

Jasper whined again, chasing after Vincent's lips, but he was already stepping back.

"Last question, pet. All or nothing." Vincent shuffled through the cards on the table and pulled one out, then eyed Jasper with a faint smirk. "What is the airspeed velocity of an unladen swallow?"

"What?" Jasper blinked and stared at him with a frown, confusion cutting through the arousal and distraction of his current situation. Why did that sound familiar? It sounded like… a quote? He grinned with relief as he remembered where it came from. Quick on its heels was the realization that Vincent was a giant geek. "African or European?"

Vincent laughed, tossing the card aside. "Very good, pet." He looked Jasper over with a soft hum, tracing a fingertip along his jaw. "On your feet."

Once up, Vincent pulled him into a kiss, the rough fingers in his hair making him gasp.

He clutched at Vincent's shirt, moaning into his mouth. Yes, yes, *yes*. Finally. He melted into the kiss, shuddering as Vincent took him apart with only tongue and teeth and fingers in Jasper's hair. A light tug on the small chain between the clamps sent a spark of intense heat straight to his dick.

His lips were tingling by the time Vincent pulled away.

"I'm going to bend you over the table, pet. We'll start nice and slow, just how you like, and then I'm going to hold you down while I fuck you," Vincent said, his voice low enough it sent shivers along Jasper's spine.

"Yes, Sir," he breathed, the heat that had been building since he'd lost his first sock pooling in his gut.

Vincent's fingers were warm against the back of his neck as those dark hazel eyes studied him. "You've said before that you like it rough."

Jasper's stomach flip-flopped. "Yeah."

"How rough?" he asked, fingers flexing to get a firm grip on Jasper's hair again.

Jasper whimpered and pulled against the hold, his knees threatening to go out on him when Vincent tightened his grip in response. "I don't know," he admitted with a shrug. "Never really...."

Vincent pressed another slow kiss to his lips. "You'll tell me if it's too much," he said. Ordered.

Jasper shivered, managing a nod despite the tight grip on his hair. "Yes, Sir."

It didn't take long to get him bent over the table, and then Vincent pulled Jasper's unbuttoned shirt from under him and slowly worked it down his arms and back. Hands and lips marked and claimed his flesh as each inch was bared.

Jasper shifted as he tried to find some relief, moaning and hissing by turns. The table forced the clamps to dig into his nipples, and the pain was exquisite. Vincent's erection grinding against his ass was a promise of things to come. By the time Vincent made his way down Jasper's back, Jasper could feel a dozen marks left in his skin. One on his shoulder still had a lingering ache from Vincent sinking his teeth in.

Once the shirt was off, Jasper pushed onto his elbows, breathing a soft sigh of relief as the pain on his nipples eased a bit.

Vincent pulled Jasper's pants down and let them drop to the floor, then kicked them aside when Jasper stepped out of them. The briefs followed, but only enough for cool air to caress his ass where Vincent's warmth had been, leaving his dick still trapped inside them.

With a hum, Vincent placed a kiss on Jasper's lower back, then each asscheek, before leaving bites on both. "Hands on your ass, pet."

"What?" Jasper blinked against the haze threatening to drown out the rest of the world and managed a glance over his shoulder at Vincent's amused expression.

"Spread yourself for me."

He blinked again, feeling the heat creeping into his neck and face. No way. No *way*. That was worse than touching himself while Vincent watched.

But that had also been really, *really* hot.

Jasper whimpered, pushing his elbow up for balance, then dropping his forehead to the table. He took two shaky breaths before reaching his other hand back and grabbing his own asscheek.

"Good boy," Vincent purred. "Now the other one."

Jasper squeezed his eyes shut with a soft whine of protest, but he did as he was told. He grabbed his ass with both hands, spreading his cheeks, his fingertips brushing against the briefs still partially in place. It should have been mortifying, and it was, but he couldn't ignore the way his dick twitched in approval. The position forced him onto his chest again, the clamps digging in hard enough to make him hiss.

"Good boy," Vincent said again. "Thank you, pet." He shifted behind Jasper, nudging his legs a bit farther apart. Following the snap of the lube-bottle cap, Vincent's fingers began pressing inside. They disappeared momentarily, and Jasper wiggled impatiently against the table, yelping as the sharp smack of a palm against his thigh made him jump. He managed a glare over his shoulder, but only for a second before he had to relieve the pressure on his nipples. He stilled as Vincent's hand settled against his lower back, anticipation curling through him, but the hard, blunt object pressing into him wasn't a finger or a cock, and he whined as it stretched him open.

It slid all the way in and nudged against his prostate, the other end tucked against his balls. And when it started vibrating, Vincent's hand was the only thing that kept him from arching right off the table. His voice caught on a strangled groan, his fingers digging into his ass as he pushed back, seeking more. "Fuck. Please."

Vincent's hand followed the path of Jasper's spine, leaving a warm ripple of shivery pleasure behind. "Soon," he murmured, pressing kisses across Jasper's shoulders and neck, his other hand adjusting the vibrator so it continuously bumped against his prostate, making him see stars. Maybe that was from the clamps digging relentlessly into his nipples, or the fact he couldn't steady his breathing.

He whined and tried to lift his chest off the table, gasping as Vincent immediately shoved him down with a hand on his back and a low sound of warning near his ear. It wasn't quite a growl, but the rough handling still sent a shock of surprise through him, and a tiny spark of fear and adrenaline that momentarily wiped the arousal from his mind. He panted for air as he went still, only then realizing he'd moved both arms to the table for leverage but hadn't tried to push himself up yet.

Vincent's hand slid into his hair, curling into a tight grip and forcing his head to the side. "Color," he demanded against Jasper's ear.

Jasper managed a deep, shaky breath, blinking at Vincent's hand where he'd grabbed Jasper's left wrist to pin it to the table. The vibrator was still buzzing away in his ass, and now that the initial shock was fading, he noticed he was even harder now; his briefs felt practically soaked where his erection was still trapped in them.

Vincent shifted, starting to pull away, and Jasper shoved his hips back, moaning at the feel of Vincent's cock grinding into him. "Yes," he gasped. "Green." He whimpered as Vincent's grip tightened, hesitantly fighting him when Vincent forced his hand farther up the table, past his head. The shock of apprehension as Vincent overpowered him made his stomach bottom out, and a soft whine escaped him.

He struggled a bit harder as his other arm was shoved up to join the first, his wrists held to the table with one hand. Vincent was stronger than he looked, or maybe Jasper was just weak or wasn't trying nearly as hard as he thought he was. He squirmed against the table as he was stretched out over it, chest heaving as exhilaration zinged through him. He expected to freak out any moment, and if it'd been anyone other than Vincent, he might have already been kicking and shouting for help.

He gasped as Vincent kicked his legs even farther apart, the vibrations suddenly vanishing as Vincent pulled the toy free. He didn't even have a chance to get a breath for a complaint before he was filled again, Vincent's thick cock pushing in without resistance and burying deep.

"Fuck," Jasper hissed, arching with a groan. Vincent's free hand braced against Jasper's back, forcing him down again, and he cried out from the painful pressure against the nipple clamps. He tried to lift up, to find any leverage to relieve the pressure, but he was well and truly trapped, pinned in place by Vincent's hands and his cock, fucking into him nice and slow as promised.

He flexed his wrists, seeking out that spark of exhilaration again, and was rewarded by Vincent slamming his hips forward and tightening his fingers to near bruising despite the awkward grip. "L-lemme go," he whispered.

Vincent's hand slid to the back of his neck as he leaned over Jasper, his breath hot and quick against Jasper's cheek. "Make me," he taunted.

Jasper shuddered, nearly coming from the hot spike of arousal. He struggled harder, more interested in sparking that helplessly trapped sensation again than actually getting free. At least until Vincent growled something and landed a solid smack to Jasper's ass before shoving his chest against the table again.

He gasped at the sharp bites of pain and pushed onto his toes, though they slid against the floor without giving him any purchase. "Please," he whimpered. "Please, ow, please let me up."

Vincent buried himself in Jasper's ass and stopped moving, yanking Jasper's arms down and then back to pin against his lower back. He held them there with one hand, Vincent's other arm sliding beneath Jasper's shoulders, lifting him up from the table enough to relieve the pressure on the clamps.

Jasper sobbed in relief and went limp, closing his eyes with a moan as Vincent started thrusting again.

"That's it," Vincent breathed, his teeth scraping against Jasper's earlobe. "Are you going to be a good little slut now?" he asked softly.

He'd never thought he'd like to be called a slut, but he couldn't help his deep groan from Vincent calling him one. His body clenched with pleasure, and they both moaned at the added friction.

"More," he begged, his eyes rolling back as Vincent immediately picked up the pace. The table legs skidded against the floor with every thrust, and Jasper was helpless to do more than tip his head back and take it.

Vincent released Jasper's wrists and slid his palm over Jasper's stomach. He hardly had time to process the sensation before Vincent ordered, "Time to come like a good little slut," and pulled the clamps off Jasper's nipples.

Jasper screamed as he came, his orgasm crashing through him on a white-hot wave of pain and pleasure. It left behind an intense, tingling warmth as he collapsed to the table, chest heaving between soft whines he couldn't stop for the life of him.

Vincent grunted against Jasper's neck, shuddering against him as he came, ragged breaths washing over Jasper's too-hot flesh.

A deep-seated curl of contentment threaded through his entire body, leaving him utterly satiated and floaty. The world went soft around the edges, and pleasure and exhaustion sank deep into every inch of him.

He was vaguely aware of Vincent cleaning him off, of being pulled upright and walking, but all he could really focus on was the warmth as he curled into Vincent's chest. Vincent smelled like his cologne, a nice sandalwood scent that wasn't too strong, and faintly like sweat and sex.

He didn't mean to fall asleep, but he was warm and comfortable despite the ache in his nipples. As he drifted off, he couldn't help hoping Vincent would want to explore pinning him down some more.

THEY WERE on the couch when Jasper woke up, with Vincent serving as a full-body pillow. It was nice, though he still felt floaty. Like he wasn't fully there. That should have worried him, but it wasn't like he didn't trust Vincent. He couldn't remember why it should worry him that he was more interested in sleep than getting up, but he couldn't bring himself to care.

He nuzzled into Vincent's chest and closed his eyes again, sighing in pleasure when Vincent stroked his hair.

"You awake, pet?" Vincent asked, his voice barely above a whisper. It was rough like he'd been asleep too, and that knowledge ignited a burst of contentment in his chest.

Jasper tried to answer, but his tongue refused to move, so he settled for nodding.

"Do you feel okay?"

He nuzzled into Vincent's chest as he wiggled his fingers and toes. His nipples still ached, and one of them stung a bit. His ass protested when he shifted his hips, but it wasn't too painful, so he nodded again.

Vincent continued stroking Jasper's hair. "Hungry?"

If his voice would have worked, he would have whined. As it was, he burrowed closer to Vincent and shook his head. The last thing he wanted was for either of them to move.

"All right." Vincent curled his fingers in a gentle tug. "We can stay like this."

Jasper relaxed with a long sigh and let himself drift off again.

AT SOME point, he was vaguely aware of Vincent moving and whispering something about dinner, but it wasn't important enough for him to get up.

IT WAS early in the evening when he finally woke up and felt more like himself again. He was still on the couch, covered by a blanket, but Vincent was gone. He could hear him nearby, though, which was good enough. There was a cold bottle of water on top of the blanket, and he pushed himself up to guzzle most of it.

Dinner smelled good. The scent of cooking garlic made his mouth water and his stomach growl. He pushed onto his knees and crossed his arms over the back of the couch to watch Vincent cook. The movement made him fully aware of the twinge in his ass, and he winced, unable to stop the groan, but the discomfort was totally worth it.

"Finally awake?" Vincent asked, glancing over his shoulder.

"Yes, Sir," he said, pushing up farther on his knees when Vincent set his skillet aside and moved around the kitchen island towards him.

Vincent obliged him when he tilted his head back for a kiss. "How do you feel?"

"Sore." Jasper couldn't help his grin as he added, "I think I know what ripping someone a new one means now." When Vincent flicked his nose, Jasper caught the finger between his teeth before nuzzling against Vincent's palm. "Can I stay the night, Sir?"

He peeked up at Vincent when he hummed, gently grazing his teeth over Vincent's thumb. "Please?"

Vincent sighed and pulled his hand away. "You're a menace."

"Mm, but I'm your menace," Jasper said, grinning when that earned a soft snort and a muttered "Lucky me."

Happy to take that as a yes, he propped against the back of the couch again, closing his eyes and trying to shake off the lingering hazy fog in his head until dinner was ready.

Sitting at the table wasn't the most pleasant experience of the day, but considering how he'd earned the ache, it was a miracle he wasn't hard again by the time they finished eating.

He went through his flashcards and notes one more time, then called it quits. Either he knew the information by now or he didn't, so he turned off the lights and went upstairs for a long, hot shower. Even after sleeping so long, he still felt exhausted enough to pass out again.

Vincent was propped up against the headboard and pillows with a book in his lap when Jasper stepped into the bedroom.

Jasper couldn't quite stop the happy sigh as he crawled into bed, unable to stop staring. Somehow, Vincent in an old T-shirt and glasses was even hotter than in a suit with his Dom face.

He inched closer, until he could rest his head in Vincent's lap, smiling against his stomach as Vincent stroked his hair. That was definitely becoming a fetish for him. Or maybe he was becoming a slut for Vincent's touch in general. Even the rougher ones. *Especially* the rougher ones.

His cock twitched at the memory of being held down and overpowered, but he was too tired to try to act on it. With a yawn, he wrapped himself around Vincent and drifted back to sleep. For the first time since he was a kid, being near someone stronger than him made him feel safe instead of terrified.

To Jasper's horror, he woke to his phone alarm and an empty bed. Throwing back the covers, he tumbled out of bed, cursing himself the entire way to the bathroom and through getting dressed. He should have set his alarm earlier so he'd be up with time to make breakfast, but it was too late now. He'd have to scarf a bowl of cereal and hope Vincent didn't hold it against him. Except when he reached the kitchen, Vincent was scraping eggs out of a pan onto two plates with toast.

"Sorry," he said, moving up behind Vincent and wrapping his arms around him. "I should have been up earlier."

"You needed the rest," Vincent replied, lightly squeezing Jasper's hands and offering him a plate. "Eat or you'll be late."

Jasper took his plate to the table and dug in. When Vincent joined him, he set a paper and a pen down next to Jasper, and he almost choked when he realized it was the new contract. He nearly pushed his plate away in favor of looking it over, but he needed to eat or he'd be starving all through his tests. He compromised by shoveling eggs into his mouth with one hand and picking up the top paper with the other.

This contract was even better than the last one, and he barely refrained from grinning like a maniac at the written confirmation they'd be exclusive. He shoved his toast in his mouth and held it there with his teeth as he snatched up the pen, adding punishments to the list of things he agreed to before signing.

He slid it across the table as he finished his toast, beaming as Vincent added his own signature below Jasper's.

"All yours, Sir."

Vincent's smile was somehow both pleased and smug. He'd already finished his own breakfast and leaned over for a quick, consuming kiss that left Jasper breathless. "All mine," he murmured, pulling back with a reluctant sigh. "Ready to go?"

Jasper nodded and glanced at the contract again as he stood, making sure it was real. With a grin, he landed a quick kiss to Vincent's lips and turned to grab his things.

A year. An entire year of having a guaranteed boyfriend and all the kinky sex he could ask for.

How could his life possibly get any better than that?

Continue Reading for an Excerpt from
Shadow's Wound,
Book #1 in the Elemental Thrones series,
By Saria Bryant.

Chapter 1

"You'll be stabbed and left for dead."

Cal stared out the window of the carriage as Julius' words echoed in his mind. Unfortunately, unraveling a Seer's vision to find who could possibly want him dead wasn't even the most pressing issue he needed to deal with.

His father's death had brought the court and general government processes to a grinding halt. Part of that was his own fault, as he refused to be crowned, but a month seemed like far too little time to pass before he accepted the throne.

He might have brushed Julius' vision aside as a nightmare, but his Sight was never wrong. Still, his experience with visions was that they were confusing at best, and Fate's way of fucking with everyone involved at worst.

The carriage jolted as the cobblestone road gave way to the dirt and gravel of the seedier part of the city. He'd been working on plans to restore the worst areas within the next few years, but even that would have to wait now.

"We're here," Julius said as the carriage rolled to a stop in front of the prison.

Dread and excitement burned hot in his gut as Cal stared at the large iron building. He glanced briefly at his left hand, at the shimmer of a red Fate string coiled around his little finger. It'd been there for as long as he could remember, stretching into the distance, so faint he'd been convinced it was just his imagination. Until several weeks ago, when it started growing brighter and he couldn't deny its existence anymore.

Whoever his fate was tied to, they'd finally arrived in his kingdom. And now the string was brighter and thicker than ever, pulled taut and leading directly into the prison.

He sighed and climbed out when Julius opened the door. He straightened his tunic and smoothed his hands over the fabric before striding inside. The threshold sparked along his senses, but the original function of the prison was so long forgotten, the lingering magic laid into its boundary was little more than an echo.

One of the guards took a single, imperious step towards them before shock settled on his face. He quickly bowed and fell into step behind Cal. "Your Highness."

Cal left the guard to Julius as he glanced at his hand, following the string deeper inside, past the iron-and-silver-wrought walls that still stood as testament to darker times, when they were needed to protect against the creatures and beasts that ruled the night. Creatures that hadn't been seen in Ages.

He ignored the oppressive weight of metal towering over him, his heart thrumming in his ears as the string brightened and seemed to pull tight enough to snap. He stopped in front of a solid iron door and found it locked. He flicked a glance to the guard. "Open it."

The guard hesitated. "Your Highn—" he started, but Julius didn't let him finish.

Julius stepped forward, grabbed the handle, and with a burst of condensed magic, wrenched the door open so hard the metal gave a sickening screech as it bent and twisted. He preceded Cal inside, but stopped two steps in.

Cal's heartbeat skipped at that hesitation, before the scent of blood, piss, and worse hit his nose. He grimaced and stepped inside, scanning the room. There were instruments strewn on iron tables and hung on the walls that wouldn't have been out of place in a torture chamber. Which, he realized, was exactly what this was. Most had signs of old blood, and all of them were iron or silver or sharp-edged metal.

His gaze landed on the table in the center of the room and the man bent over it, his back a bloody mess, his thin pants torn and soaked through. Two others stood near him. Not guards, they were dressed like human nobles. One held a whip, the other a single long strip of leather with jagged metal pieces woven through it, glinting with malicious spells.

His Fate string stretched out across the room, connecting him to the one strapped to the table.

"Release him," Cal snarled, taking another step into the room.

The man with the whip turned with a sneer that melted into horror. The other man ignored him completely and lifted his weapon for another strike.

Julius surged forward, but Cal was faster, lifting his hand as he gave his magic and rage an outlet. Coils of light wrapped around the man's wrists and throat, and he screamed as the magic burned him enough that he dropped his weapon, the stench of singed hair and skin mixing with the filth.

The other man hastily dropped his whip and scrambled back, hands lifted in surrender.

Cal stalked to the table, intending to release the man tied down, but Julius planted a hand against his chest.

"Don't you dare," Julius hissed, pushing him back a step and giving him a warning glare before going to the table himself.

Cal twitched at being denied, but he'd waited thirty-five years. He could wait a few more moments to get a look at the man Fate had decided belonged to him.

He ordered the new guards, arriving due to the commotion, to arrest the two men, as well as the first guard. Only then, as he turned back to Julius, did he notice his finger. The string was still there, glowing pure and bright and leading to the man now collapsed on the floor beside the table. Except it was thinner than before, because there was now another string, just as pure and bright and stretching to the other side of the room.

His breath stuttered as he moved to follow, faltering to a halt in front of what looked like an upright, rounded iron casket. He reached for the lock, but even when he strained with all his strength, it wouldn't budge.

"Juls," he said, his voice rough as his stomach twisted with a fresh wave of unease.

Julius appeared a moment later, pressing Cal back before studying the casket. He found the seam, gripped it, and heaved. Metal scraped against the floor with an ear-piercing screech. As soon as it was open, a slim form slumped forward.

Cal reached out instinctively, in time to keep the young man from being impaled on the spikes sprouting from the lid.

"Don't—" Julius started, but it was too late.

The magic inherent in the Fate bonds shimmered through him, and a heavy pulling sensation he'd never even realized was there eased away. It was almost enough to distract him from the very soft, furry ears brushing his chin.

"Don't fucking touch him." The words were slurred and rough with pain, but laden with a promise of violence.

Cal turned in time to see the other man he was bound to struggle to his feet, leaning heavily against the table to stay upright.

The man took an unsteady step forward and nearly collapsed again. "Give him back."

Cal ignored Julius' protests and slowly closed the distance to his other bonded. The man in his arms was barely coherent, but he was aware enough to keep his feet and seemed possessed of the same frantic need to be reunited with his partner. Once they were close enough, Cal released his hold and watched as the two clung to each other, like they'd never expected to survive this room.

He had a feeling they hadn't been meant to.

He turned to Julius. "Get a healer. And you," he said, pointing at one of the new guards. "Bring me whoever is in charge here."

SARIA BRYANT has been an avid reader since childhood and a fan fiction writer since middle school. They enjoy traveling and exploring and learning about other cultures and languages.

They are constantly dreaming up new ways to torment their characters, playing servant to their cat, or feeding a caffeine addiction.

Their favorite stories are M/M/+ relationships with a healthy dose of angst and drama with an HEA. When not reading or writing, they can usually be found watching anime or playing video games.

Saria can be found on Twitter/ Instagram / Tumblr / Bluesky @sariabryant.

SARIA BRYANT
SARCASM IS MY LOVE LANGUAGE
MAGE'S MARINES
UNDERWORLD MAGES
BOOK 1

Max Savino has spent his whole life refusing to conform to the expectations of his father, the head of the Denver mafia—until his defiance crosses the line and his father decides he'd rather have a dead son than a disobedient one. Instead of waking up dead, Max wakes up with a power he only dreamed he could possess.

When his father sells him to a pack of shifters, Max finds himself in a world he doesn't understand, claimed by three wolves and fighting for control over his new magical flames. He'll have to learn to trust these dangerous men and the devotion they're promising him, because now that Max's father knows he's a mage, he wants him back—and he doesn't care who he has to kill to get what he wants. It's time for Max to stop running if he has any hope of protecting his future… and the pack that's somehow become the family he's always wanted.

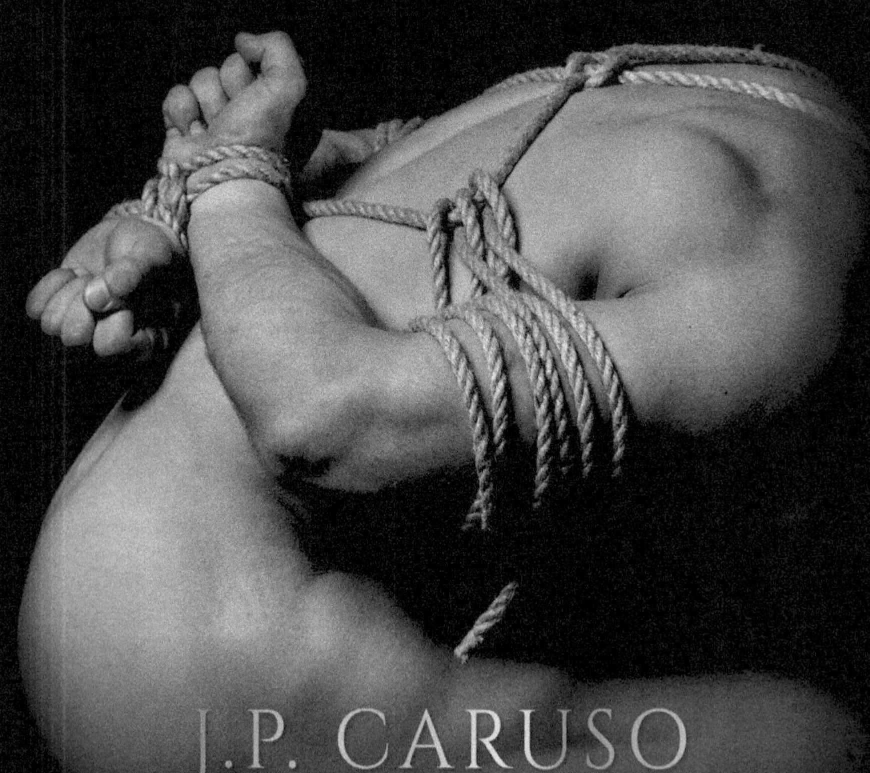

The Menagerie

No one comes to the Menagerie
looking for the love of their life

J.P. CARUSO

Rowan Campbell loves his life, finally. He's happy. He's happy, but… there's something missing. Some itch under his skin he can't quite scratch through his work as a paramedic or hobbies or family gatherings or casual hookups alone. Then one day he responds to a 9-1-1 call at an exclusive BDSM club, the Menagerie, and immediately splurges on a membership. He isn't expecting much… until he meets the notoriously hard-to-please club veteran, Malcolm Savaryn. Mal is a firecracker of a man: Sharp and witty with a take-no-shit attitude, he fascinates Rowan from the start.

Rowan has a big secret he's afraid to share, and Mal has walls that seem impenetrable. Both men have dark pasts, and mental health struggles have marred them, leaving them wary of relationships. Their chemistry is immediate and unmatched, though, and they quickly enter into a steamy Dom/sub relationship, meeting weekly at the club. It's just sex, right? But can they keep things strictly sexual, or will one or both of them develop feelings along the way? And if so will they find the courage to admit them and risk their hearts?

Hands of Power

T.J. MASTERS

Richard Doyle is a star on his semipro rugby team and a self-avowed ladies' man, but he knows something is missing. Caught up in his ultra-masculine world, he's resigned to making the best of his limited life—until an injury on the field brings him to the office of physiotherapist Alan Jennings and he feels the touch of a Master.

Alan Jennings isn't looking for love when Richard walks into his office, but something draws him in, and Alan senses that Richard's sexuality is coiled like a vibrating spring just under the surface.

The sex is amazing, but Alan will have an uphill battle if he means to convince Richard to trust him and to indulge fantasies that are taboo in his world. It will take all of Alan's patience and careful dominance—and a visit to friends in Cornwall—to convince Richard to embrace his new erotic identity as a submissive gay man and to trust the found family that comes with it.

BENT
NOT
BROKEN

Z. ALLORA

Stefano Rossi longs for the mystical—and so far unattainable—peace of reaching subspace. But can he accept that the person who can take him there is a man?

Riku Tao has given up on finding a sub who complements him. He'll stick with doing demonstrations at the BDSM club the Edge. He certainly doesn't have time for a closeted Catholic guy with internalized biphobia… and yet he cannot help but want to protect Stefano and give him what he needs. A history of physical and sexual abuse makes it impossible for Stefano to come out of the closet, and Riku certainly isn't going back in.

Perhaps an arrangement of six months to explore their desires will be enough to satisfy them both.

Or it might break their hearts.

To take hold of his future with the man he's coming to love, Stefano will need to move beyond the pain of his past, and he won't be able to do it alone.

OVERRIDE
SJD PETERSON

An Underground Club Tale

Don't judge a book by its cover….

At over six feet, with a body honed in the gym, auto worker Donavan Gregory is used to people assuming he's a dominant top. Unfortunately, they're wrong, and Donavan's desire to explore his submissive side goes unfulfilled.

Smaller and older than Donavan, Dr. Seth Manning might not look like a typical Dominant, but when the two men meet at Pride, Donavan realizes Seth might be his perfect counterpart. The trouble is, Donavan doesn't have as much experience with the BDSM world as he'd like. What could an educated, handsome, and confident man like Seth possibly see in someone like him? Seth must convince him that despite the differences on the surface, when it comes to kinky fun and discovery, they'll fit together just fine.

FOR MORE
OF THE
BEST
GAY
ROMANCE

DREAMSPINNER
PRESS
dreamspinnerpress.com

www.ingramcontent.com/pod-product-compliance
Lightning Source LLC
Chambersburg PA
CBHW070525100726
47907CB00004B/980